REACTION

THE EMERGENCE: BOOK 1

SETH M. BAKER

The Emergence Series
Reaction: The Emergence, Book 1
Redemption: The Emergence, Book 2
Reunion: The Emergence, Book 3

Copyright © 2012 by Seth M. Baker.
ISBN-13: 978-1-938830-06-8
ISBN: 1-938830-06-7
Cover design by Deranged Doctor Design
Published by Dark Hollow Press, 2012
www.sethmbaker.com

REACTION

1

Mansfield, Connecticut
Spring, Near Future

Amadeus Brunmeier vomited into the urinal. Acidic brown flecks splattered onto the index cards on which he had written his speech outline. He heard the bathroom door open. Someone grabbed a clump of Amadeus' loam brown hair and pushed him forward, smashing his forehead against a hard white wall. His body crumpled like a deflated balloon. On the cold tile, he vomited again, just as a kick went into his back, near his kidneys. He rolled over. Davy loomed above him, his eyes bulging from his fat pink face like a frog's.

"I told you I'd find you," Davy said.

"We both know you won. I already told you."

"Not what the judges said. This is grad school at Penn we're talking about. Penn State."

"I'm sorry, I'm sorry, it's not my fault they figured out you hired Pakistani freelancers to do your research."

"Somebody told them. I think it was you." Davy spit on Amadeus just before kicking him in the stomach. Amadeus wheezed. "You're lucky there are people out there, Brunmeier."

The bathroom door opened, and he saw a familiar figure step

in: his old friend, Grassal Delgado. Grassal stood a head taller than Davy, was just as wide, and carried himself like a bull.

"Especially me," Grassal said, grabbing Davy by the belt and tossing him against the wall. Davy cried out as his face slammed into the white tile. "Clean yourself up, you've got a speech to give ... valedictorian." Grassal had his hands on his hips. Davy started to stand. Grassal placed a foot on the small of his back and held him down.

"No. No way. I'm not doing it," Amadeus said. "I'm shaking, my stomach is sick, my face is bloody, and there are so many people, thousands of people. They'll be watching, looking at me, waiting for me to screw up."

"You worry too much," Grassal said. "Just do the speech. It's easy. We've practiced it a hundred times. You sound fine."

Amadeus remembered the crowd he saw only moments earlier, an echoing arena packed with well-dressed relatives. Amadeus sighed as Grassal helped him to his feet. He gave Amadeus a paper towel and put his arm around Amadeus' shoulder, guiding him out of the bathroom, leaving Davy on the floor. Amadeus tore a bit of the paper towel off, stuck it in his mouth, and started to chew.

"Yeah, maybe you're right," Amadeus said, dabbing at his nose, allowing himself to be led out the door. As soon as they stepped through the door to the concourse, however, Amadeus pushed Grassal's arm away. He ran through the fire exit doors and onto the sidewalk, leaving Grassal panting and bent over, hands on his knees. Amadeus found his motorcycle in the parking lot and roared away from the crowds, Gampel Pavilion, and the terror. His stuff was already moved back home, and he had had enough of UConn anyway. Amadeus decided someone else could give the valediction.

Two hours later, back in Stamford, Amadeus was sitting on a stone bench under the gnarled oak tree across from his mother's grave. When Amadeus heard the car he sat upright. Though his first instinct was to run, he stayed and watched, expressionless, as his father walked up. He smiled at Amadeus, his smile making his slight face appear full. Amadeus felt the shame all over again.

"I let you down," Amadeus said. "I let Mom down. I let everyone down."

"Maybe you did, maybe you didn't. It was just a speech. Scoot over." He sat down next to his son and put his arm around him. Amadeus' shoulders tensed, then relaxed.

"She'd be so proud of you. You're still valedictorian, even if you didn't give a speech."

"Now everyone knows I'm a failure."

"No, Amadeus. You failed at your speech, you've got blood on your face, you smell like puke, but you're not a failure. Every failure is an education, and you just graduated. Now you can fail even bigger." His father removed the band from his ponytail, letting his long, grey hair dangle over his shoulders. They sat in silence for a while. A spring breeze swept over the hill, making the plastic roses quiver. "But I still wish you were just a little more ambitious. I mean, geovisual analytics?"

"Geography is a great field, and I can continue my work on health mapping. Plus, I won't have to give speeches or present papers. I've got five job offers for this fall, and I intend to start working as soon as I've had a couple months to decompress."

"You'll either get bored or rusty, Amadeus, and I don't just mean this summer. Study quantum physics. You'll need a couple prerequisites, but it's not too late to get you into Cal Tech. This old man still has some friends at university."

"I'm not like you, Dad. I don't understand systems I can't see, can't handle and analyze. I struggled with Newtonian physics. Computers, systems, shaded blobs on maps, these things make sense. Calculus doesn't. Quantum physics makes my brain melt."

"It doesn't make your brain melt."

"You're disappointed. With me."

"Come on, kid," Tommy said, standing up. "Let's go home.

We've got relatives to entertain."

2

Amadeus followed his father back to their three-story house outside the city, parking his motorcycle in the garage. Inside the house, black and orange balloons covered the floor like a plastic fog. Jazz played on the stereo, something from the middle of the last century, cacophonous and frantic. The saxophone reminded Amadeus of a ball bouncing down a stairwell. His aunt and uncle, Mark and Annie, sang a processional as he walked in the door. *Dah duh dah duh* ... Amadeus' stomach grew queasy; the anxiety from earlier returned. He felt like he had forgotten to do something, but chalked it up to nerves.

Amadeus looked at his father, who sat at the big blond oak table beside his brother, and wondered how much time his father had spent locked in his room, studying and learning. He would've been a young man in the early days of the internet, so he never would've been short on access to research and people to contact. Amadeus would have to ask his father sometime. Amadeus' own childhood had been so quiet, just the three of them, then later just the two of them, though Grassal spent so much time at their house that Amadeus decided he should count him as well.

"Hey hey!" Amadeus heard Grassal yell in the hallway. "I'm glad everybody made it down here for our boy's graduation afterparty! Where's my weak-stomached friend?"

"You hacker trash," Amadeus yelled back. "I made a reasonable decision based on the circumstances." He heard Grassal plodding down the hall towards him. Amadeus gave Grassal his best defiant look.

"Bullshit on two counts. One, hackers aren't trash, we're respected information security professionals. And two, you gave up and let your anxiety get the best of you. Man, you should've seen the dean running around just before the ceremony. She looked like a little girl who'd just lost her puppy. But whatever," Grassal said, throwing a big arm around Amadeus' thin frame. "You're still my brother, even if you act like a terrified *conejito*."

"You're an asshole," Amadeus said. "What's a *conejito*?" Grassal just shook his head. Amadeus tried to slip from Grassal's grasp, but Grassal led Amadeus to the kitchen. Amadeus cringed when everyone turned toward him.

"Ah, there they are. Everyone," Annie said, "I believe Uncle Mark has an announcement." She held a half-eaten baby carrot in her hand. She motioned to her husband to start, then shot Amadeus an apologetic look. A boot-sized object covered in brown cloth sat upon the table. Mark placed one hand on the cloth.

"Now, in honor of our brilliant nephew Amadeus, I commissioned a work from our friend. He likes to capture people in transition, when they're at a big milestone or a turning point in their lives, ready to begin new adventures. His work is quite popular in ... some circles in New York. So, we told him about our little Amadeus, how he was valedictorian at UConn and getting ready to start his adult life. Our friend, his name is Twiggy, by the way, Twiggy said, 'Give me a picture of him, I can make something good.' So we did, Amadeus, and Twiggy ... made ... this!"

He removed the cloth to reveal a statue, about ten centimeters high, of a young man, sinewy and naked, one hand at his side, the other holding a sling draped over his back. The statue had Amadeus' face but, Amadeus thought, the rest was idealized and familiar.

"Oh god," Amadeus said. For the second time that day and the fourth time that week, he felt vomit escaping his stomach and racing towards his throat. No, he thought, they really, this is just a cruel joke. I have to pretend to like it. I can't puke. Have to lie, have to lie. "I mean, wow! It's, uh, wonderful. Wow!" He leaned in closer to examine the statue. The genitalia were larger than his own; maybe the artist was trying to do him a favor. A plaque at the bottom read "Amadeus Brunmeier: Onward and Upward." Who the hell, Amadeus wondered, was this artist? Surely his uncle had better taste than this. But maybe not.

"Watch this," Mark said. He pressed a button on the statue's back and said, "Record." He picked up the statue, panned it around the room, then set it on the table. The left nipple flickered and the scene Mark had just recorded projected itself onto the table, a bemused family and one embarrassed child.

"This would be great for a video journal," Mark said. "Think of it like talking to yourself. Sure, it hasn't got the fastest processor, but it's all off-cloud, non-Tivooki, just like your father likes, and can hold a ton of data. The sling extends into a USB plug." Mark pressed on the sling and a plug protruded from the small of the statue's back.

"Vintage," Grassal said. From his pocket, he pulled out a pink USB stick attached to a key ring. "Mine's more talisman than anything else, but it feels good to store my stuff on something tangible."

"Wow, thanks Mark," Amadeus said, looking over at Grassal. Grassal was trying not to laugh. Amadeus slunk back, almost out of the kitchen, covering his mouth, fighting his reflexes.

"Speech! Speech!" Mark said. Amadeus looked down at his feet, his face flushing. He started to back out of the room with its thin air and stifling heat, the five sets of occupying lungs taking all the oxygen from the room and replacing it with something noxious, definitely not carbon dioxide. Amadeus felt light-headed. All their eyes were upon him, waiting, expectant.

"Thank you, it's very nice. But ... excuse me," he said as he ran to the bathroom. His internal organs felt like wet nylon rope from which someone was trying to wring out the water. In the bathroom, he didn't puke but he locked the door, turned the lights out, and sat on the toilet, taking deep oxygen-rich breaths, enjoying the blurry, forgetful feeling that came along with so much oxygen. Between breaths, he tore off scraps of toilet paper and shoved them into his mouth, chewing them up and spitting them out. He expected some well-meaning knock at the door, but thankfully none came. After about fifteen minutes, his breathing slowed and he was ready to return to the kitchen. There, everyone was eating and talking as if nothing had happened. The statue sat in the center of the table, projecting a recording of Grassal contorting his face.

"There he is!" Mark said. "Annie, get this boy a plate of food."

"No. No." Amadeus put up his hands. "I'm fine. No, really." Annie got up from the table and started making him a plate. "You really don't have to do that, I can make my own food."

"You sit there, mister. Today's your big day, and maybe you can relax for at least one day of your life." A minute passed. She poured some sweet dip into a bowl and sliced up an apple. She lowered her voice. "I'm sorry about the statue," Annie said, her tone confiding. "That's all Mark, you know. The artist is his friend, and you know how he is, wanting to make everybody happy. I said to him, Mark, what's he going to do with a statue of himself ... and a naked one at that, just give him a little flex-screen, or some money, but he went on and on about Michelangelo's David as an ideal for any young man."

"I thought the torso looked familiar," Amadeus said, thinking back to his art appreciation class.

Annie set the plate of food down. "We're a lot alike. Mark likes to drag me to these society parties. So many people around, it looks like everyone is having fun, but I'd rather be in my office, alone, working on another piece."

"So everything still good at the *Times?*" Amadeus said.

"I love it," Annie said. "It really feels like I'm a part of something. Movers and shakers. Having an audience of millions."

"Sounds terrifying."

"It was, at first, but I worked my way up. It's not like one day I was forced to speak before all those people. But I'll leave you alone, Amadeus. Try to relax." Amadeus smiled for what felt like the first time in a week and said he would, but instead of joining everyone in the living room, he picked at the fruit plate, rolling a pale green grape around like a glass marble. After a few minutes, his father came into the room and piled several cubes of pungent, crumbly blue cheese on top of some roast beef slices.

"Amadeus, why don't you come in here and join us? It's not like you get to see your uncle Mark often. You seem so sad, just hiding away in the kitchen all day."

"I'm okay, it's just ... well, after today, I'm kind of ashamed of myself." His father frowned, then put his arm around his son.

"You've got nothing to be ashamed of. You're still the smartest boy in the class. Just because you freaked out, ran away, and let six thousand people down doesn't make you any less of a person," his father said, smiling like a salesman.

"Oh, thanks for that," Amadeus said, but he realized he was smiling, too. "Fine, I'll come be social. Are Mark and Annie staying here tonight, or are they staying at a hotel?"

"You think I want my drunken brother doing things to his lovely wife in the room next to me? You bet your ass they're staying at a hotel. Come on, kid." Tommy put his hand on Amadeus' elbow. Amadeus allowed himself to be led by his father and, together, they joined everyone in the living room. Amadeus eventually forgot himself and became caught up in the familiar rhythms of family banter. Hours later, when the roast beef trays sat nearly empty, rubbish was overflowing the bin, and Mark was staggering and slurring, the party was declared a success. Amadeus walked Annie and Mark to their car.

"Don't worry about the speech," Annie said. "The worst is over. Sorry about the statue. Keep in touch." She gave him a little kiss on the cheek. Amadeus blushed, thankful no one had bothered to replace the porch light that had burned out months ago. He went inside to find Grassal and his father finishing off a bottle of rum. Tommy grinned at his son.

"Guys, let's go to the basement," Tommy Brunmeier said. "I've got something cool to show you."

3

The basement was long and cavernous, divided into three parts: a storage area, a workshop, and the lab. The storage area held parts and components, neatly labeled in boxes and drawers. Long rows of shelving held a cornucopia of electronic components in various states of disrepair. In the workshop were fabrication tools: a lathe, drill press, and 3D printer.

The lab took up the most space and was a basement unto itself, complete with lead-lined walls, server racks, a separate control room for experiments, and a small cyclotron Tommy had installed several years ago. For as long as Amadeus could remember, a Union cavalry sword had hung over the interior lab door, right below the M4 carbine rifle his father had used in Afghanistan.

In the lab, Amadeus and Grassal watched as Tommy pried open a wooden crate. From it, he removed several black metal rods and a glass cylinder in a metal housing that glowed blue. He handed a couple of the rods to Amadeus. "A graduation gift from Jones. Amadeus, you remember Jones. We could use these to fabricate new pistons for your bike."

"That could be interesting," Amadeus said. He had considered selling the bike and using the money to take a trip to California.

"What's this other stuff?" Grassal said.

"Kipium. It has a negative mass but stays stable. Used to be called exotic matter. Some miners in West Virginia discovered their vacuum lasers were creating small amounts of it. Now the coal mines scrape the stuff off their ceilings."

"The same kipium you used for the teleportation research?" Amadeus said.

"I didn't ask him to send it. I told you I brought that work to an end."

"What work?" Grassal said.

"The work that I wasn't allowed to talk about," Amadeus said. Grassal raised an eyebrow. "Einstein-Rosen bridges, a.k.a. Lorentzian wormholes." Amadeus met his father's gaze and held it. Neither would look away.

"Awkward," Grassal said. Tommy cleared his throat then spoke.

"Einstein talked about 'spooky action at a distance.' The man was a master of understatement. I saw enough spooky action right here to last a lifetime. I'm done with that. I've returned to more 'respectable,' non-controversial research." He pulled his salt and pepper hair back into a ponytail and picked up a rod.

"But you wish you could've learned more," Amadeus said. "To keep going forward. Is that why you have this?" He grabbed the kipium from his father's hand. "You're going to risk everything you've worked so hard to build back up?"

"That's enough, Amadeus," Tommy said. "And that's not what this is. I told you I don't know why he sent it to me. Put it down. I'll, uh, send it back to him."

Amadeus' face flushed. He looked over at Grassal, who had busied himself with learning the operating system of the statue and was pretending not to hear any of this conversation.

Tommy took the kipium from Amadeus and set it on the shelf. "We used to need a whole building to keep stuff like that stable. Now, though ..." Tommy trailed off. "Hey boys, let's see how this metal likes the lathe. What do you say?" Amadeus remained silent.

"That's why we're down here," Grassal said, looking up from the display projected onto the workbench. "Think your lathe can handle it?"

"Jones said it should as long as we use a diamond-tipped cutting tool. Let's find out if he's wrong." He changed the parts, set the rod in the lathe, and put on a facemask. "I'll just cut down a couple millis and see how it works. You two turn around, don't want any bits of metal flying around. It's all fun and games ..." Amadeus threw up his hands and turned around. The machine spun to life.

"Way to change the subject, buddy," Amadeus said to Grassal. Grassal shrugged. *Ping!* A piece of metal ricocheted around the room. Everyone ducked.

"Damn," Tommy said. "That was the hardest bit I had. Maybe lower speed, or less pressure."

Amadeus' stomach growled. "I'm going upstairs for a sandwich. You guys want anything?" Both asked for beers but no food.

Upstairs, streamers hung from the ceiling like wires exposed in a partially demolished building. Amadeus felt hot despite the cool of the house. He made a roast beef sandwich. When he took a bite, the mayonnaise dripped out of the end onto a balloon by his feet. He picked up the balloon, popped it. Mayonnaise splattered onto his shirt. Cursing, he dabbed at the mayonnaise with another paper towel and stepped outside into the cool night to eat. Fog hung low over the field around the house. He finished his sandwich, went back inside, and stepped on another balloon. It squeaked under his shoe until it popped.

When it popped, the sound of crashing glass filled the house. Lights shone through the windows. Amadeus screamed in surprise and ran down the hall towards the basement. Another crash. Heavy footsteps tromped over wood floors. Lasers reflected off mirrors. At the foot of the stairs, Amadeus spun around. A man in a black helmet dusted glass from his clothes. He held a rifle and looked like death.

Amadeus slipped into the stairwell, closing and locking the door behind him. Three explosions tore up the door. Gunshots. Splinters landed in his hair. More shots. He stumbled downstairs through the workshop to the lab. His father held the door open and waved him in.

"Oh god, Amadeus, are you okay?" his father said. "Grassal, kill the lights."

Grassal ran out and hit the main switch on the breaker box. Darkness fell over the basement like a blanket. Tommy pulled out a flashlight, guided Grassal back into the lab, and pulled the door shut behind him.

"Bastards. Shot. At. Me," Amadeus said. He tried and failed to catch his breath. His heart wanted to jump out of his chest and run away. "Jesus, Dad, what is this?" Sound of footsteps running across the upper floors.

"I never thought it would happen," Tommy said, shining the flashlight from Amadeus to Grassal. "Amadeus, Grassal, I'm sorry. I brought this on us. It's my fault."

"What do you mean?" Amadeus said.

"I mean there are people who want to do some real nefarious shit with the work I've done," Tommy said. Through the window of the lab, towards the other end of the basement, Amadeus saw the first of the flashlight beams coming through the broken basement door. "Not much time." Flashlight in his teeth, Tommy Brunmeier grabbed the statue of Amadeus, pulled the plug out, and connected it to the server. Tommy entered a few commands into the server before Amadeus realized what he was doing: copying data.

A barrage of shots slammed into the lab. Instinctively, all three hunched down. The lead walls kept the bullets from coming through. He pulled two smooth black medallions from a drawer on the workbench and tossed them to Amadeus.

"Distortion field generators," Tommy said. "Fuzzers. They'll make you invisible to surveillance equipment."

"But we're not criminals."

"Not yet," Tommy said, grabbing the statue.

"Everything I've done is on here," Tommy said. "Journals. Videos. Notes. Schematics. I've made some mistakes. Now those mistakes are coming for me. Learn everything you can, Amadeus. You have to. Figure it out. My work, it could change everything." He put the statue in Amadeus' hand, closed his fingers around it. "Go to Colorado and find Jones." He scribbled down a phone number on a scrap of paper. "Don't look back. Don't come back for me. Grassal, I'm sorry, but you're a part of this now, too." Another round of gunfire. Tommy pulled the M4 from the wall and fired several rounds into the server.

"No! Dad, what is this?"

"All my work is destroyed except for what's on the statue. I had four partners. To open these files," he shook the statue, "you'll need fingerprints and blood samples from three of them. I don't have time to remove the security. Study my research to learn countermeasures. If someone with bad intentions replicates my research, the results ... it'd be brutal. Find out who did this."

"This is about the wormholes, isn't it? You know I can't understand any of that!" Amadeus said. Tommy touched his son's face, then stuffed the statue into Amadeus' pants pocket. Flashlight beams shined through the windows of the lab.

"You're a smart boy, son. You'll figure it out. I love you. Now get the hell out of here. Into the crawl space. Hide this underneath." He handed Grassal the kipium, then pointed with his rifle to the small grate. "Go, boys, go!" Tommy cracked the door open and fired a few rounds toward the flashlights.

"Amadeus, he's right," Grassal said, taking Amadeus by the shirt and pulling him to the floor. "In there." Grassal slipped into the crawlspace first.

"They're going to kill you."

"Go. Now!" Tommy fired a couple more rounds. "Before they gas the place."

Amadeus looked into the dark of the crawlspace, then took

one last look at his father, firing an assault rifle through a slit in the door. At that moment, he had no idea who his father was. He shut the door to the crawlspace. Amadeus started to open the door, but Grassal grabbed his arm.

"Come on, we've to go. You can't help him."

"Goddamnit, let go of me," Amadeus said.

"Don't make me drag you outside. You want to get us both killed?"

Amadeus started to cry and shake. He pulled a crumpled five-dollar bill from his pocket and stuffed it in his mouth. "This isn't happening. This is just another nightmare." His voice was muffled.

"Nightmare or not, Amadeus, we *are* getting out of here. You don't want to come? Fine. You stay and eat paper. And wait for them to put a bullet through your forehead." Grassal scrambled on through the crawl space, squeezing under the heating vents. He found a box of plumbing supplies and deposited the kipium inside. Gunshots came faster, louder, closer. Amadeus made his decision and started following his friend. "Garage," Grassal said. "Across the yard. Motorcycle inside. We got to run, buddy. You ready?" Grassal leaned back on his hands and kicked the main ventilation grate away. Amadeus started to run out, but Grassal stopped him. "Wait, got to check, make sure there's nobody out there." Amadeus leaned his head out. Nothing but an empty, fog-shrouded yard. They slipped out and hunched beside the house. When Amadeus stood, his knees and palms burned with pain. "Three, two, one ..."

They ran across the yard to the garage. Amadeus put his thumb on the doorknob, waited two seconds. The lock clicked and they stepped through the door into the cool garage. His bike sat inside. Beside it, a grey cloth covered his father's vintage, wheel-less Aston Martin.

"You start the bike," Grassal said, "and I'll throw the garage door open then hop on." Amadeus opened the key box on the wall. Grassal put on his usual helmet and handed one to

Amadeus. Amadeus put the key in and pressed the ignition button but got only a fast clicking sound. He looked down at the headlight switch. He'd left it on. More gunshots from inside, call and response.

"Battery's drained. Get the jumper cables," Amadeus said. He pulled the cloth off the Aston Martin, popped the hood, and started the engine.

"Too bad we can't take the car," Grassal said, grumbling to himself as he connected the cables from the car to the bike. "No wheels. What good is a hot rod on jack stands?"

Amadeus pushed the starter on the bike. Nothing happened. "Wait for it," Grassal said. Amadeus counted to ten, grinding the paper between his teeth as he did so. He tried again. The bike coughed to life, filling the garage with white smoke. Grassal lifted the garage door then hopped on the bike. Amadeus popped the clutch, took off with a squeal of tires, and drove through the damp grass behind the house. Over the roar of the bike's engine, more gunshots, this time louder, not muffled by the walls of a house. Coming from behind the house, making the turn, almost on the concrete of the driveway, the back end slipped out from under them. Amadeus put his foot down, righting the bike. Balanced, he drove on through the grass and onto the driveway. More gunshots. Both ducked and the bike swayed, but Amadeus kept it upright.

On the way down the long concrete driveway, Amadeus weaved an erratic pattern. Gunshots cracked behind them. He knew they had to escape, but he wanted to turn back and help his father, damn the risks. He couldn't let their last conversation be an argument. Amadeus had to go back and say more, but Grassal and the gunfire would lead him in only one direction: away. He turned on the helmet headset.

"You okay?" Amadeus said.

"I'm fine. You?"

"Oh, I'm great, just having a fabulous time. No, I'm not okay, you fucking moron. Of course I'm not okay." He turned from the driveway onto the main road, roaring away into the night. At first the road was dark, empty, the distance between them and the place they were leaving a black gulf growing wider and wider. But after only a couple minutes, headlights flashed in the rearview mirror. They grew closer, larger, expanding, looming. Amadeus opened the throttle on the bike, trying to go faster, but he was already pushing 120 km/hr and though Amadeus knew these roads, the curves made him nervous.

He had to get to the highway, take the bike as far away as fast as possible. The lights grew larger, brighter as the vehicle came closer. Amadeus thought they looked like lights from a full-sized van. The curves changed to suburbs. Only a few more kilometers to the highway. One hundred meters from an intersection, the light had just changed from green to yellow. On both sides of the intersection, cars sat, waiting to proceed. The lights from the van caught his mirrors, blinding him. He downshifted for more torque, pulled back on the throttle. The engine whined. The cars started to pull out, their drivers probably paying more attention to the GPS voices that told them where to drive than the traffic around them. Amadeus swerved to avoid the side of a truck, going into the other lane, then back with a meter to spare. Behind them, a crash. In the mirror, a green sedan spun around while the van pushed on through.

"What the hell is this?" Grassal said, craning his neck to watch the van behind them.

"I don't know, Grassal, I don't know. For all I know this is just an elaborate game, a learning scenario. It's got to be. God, I hope it is." Amadeus liked this idea. "We'll play along, but it's not real. Can't be. No way." Grassal said nothing.

After the intersection, the road became a four-lane highway. Red tail lights lined the way before him like runway lights. He rode the center line, honking as he passed befuddled drivers. He kept the bike in lower gears, redlining the engine. He had never driven like this. The handlebar grips were slick with perspiration. As he wiped one hand on his pants, the shooting started.

They both ducked. The bike swerved and Amadeus' shoulder grazed the side of a car. More shots. The left-side mirror exploded, leaving only the metal frame. The van was just behind them, closer, closer. Amadeus twisted the throttle, but the engine sputtered. A loud *thunk* and Amadeus' head lashed forward and banged against the speedometer. He had been shot. The bike started to veer right.

Grassal leaned forward and grabbed the handlebars. "Hey! Damn it, Amadeus, hey!" He smacked Amadeus' helmet. With a start, Amadeus jerked upright. His ears rang. He saw double. While Grassal steered the bike, Amadeus ran his fingers over the helmet, tracing the rough line the bullet had torn through the Kevlar-reinforced fiberglass. Close, so close. The ringing receded, replaced by the drone of traffic. Amadeus took back the controls.

"I'm okay," Amadeus said. Ahead, two tractor trailers were driving side-by-side in both lanes. Amadeus took a deep breath and squeezed the bike between them. He could've spread his arms and touched them both, like a giant in the Grand Canyon. He opened up the throttle. Hitting high RPMs, the v-twin roared like a bear. Amadeus made it through the trailer canyon and was back on open road. The van was stuck behind the trucks. It tried to pass on the left but couldn't get through. Amadeus took his chance and pushed the bike as hard as it could go. Behind them, the van grew smaller and smaller. Ahead, the elevated highway was plumb straight, like a spool of wire unrolled over the land. After several minutes of face-melting speed, Amadeus couldn't see the van in his rearview.

"Think we lost them," Amadeus said.

"Sure?"

"I'm not sure of anything." Amadeus looked at the sides of the highway, the high walls that projected the noise upwards, and thought if enough rain came, this could become an elevated canal or an aqueduct.

"We should get off the highway. Maybe they'll keep going," Grassal said. "Because I think this is real. Those were real bullets. Your dad, the expression on his face was real." Static crackled in their headsets. Amadeus realized this was an open channel. He slapped Grassal's knee, made a talking gesture with his hand, then a slashing motion across his throat. Grassal patted Amadeus' back, as if to say he understood.

"Yeah, we should definitely get off at the next exit. We need some gas. They're probably way back there," Amadeus said.

They continued past the exit and drove fifty kilometers farther before Amadeus drove onto a pull-off and parked in front of an abandoned semi, hopefully hidden from the highway. Amadeus got off the bike and examined his helmet, then handed it to Grassal.

"Still think this is a game?" Grassal said. "Do I need to say you're damn lucky?"

"No ... and no." His knees were weak. The world started to hum and spin. Something pulled on his insides, making breath scarce. He checked his pockets for paper, found none. Instead, he cried. Grassal held him and told him it would be okay.

"It's not okay, this isn't happening, this isn't happening." Cars passed by, unnoticed by Amadeus. Eventually, he was able to speak. "They were using a scanner or something to listen to us."

"Who keeps a scanner like that in their car?"

"Who smashes into a house and tries to kill everyone inside? No, they didn't kill everyone. They didn't kill anyone. We have to go back."

"No, man, no way. Your dad told us to go to Colorado. If they didn't ... if he can he'll contact us there. But you got to prepare yourself, man."

"What do you mean, prepare myself?"

"I'm just saying ..."

"What are you saying?"

"Nothing. I'm not saying anything except that we should

keep moving, stay hidden. Pretty soon we might need to ditch the bike, but right now we ride it for all it's worth. For all we know, they're tracking us right now. Which reminds me. Give me your phone."

Amadeus patted his pants pockets and came up empty. Sighing, Grassal pulled the phone from Amadeus' sweater pocket and threw it onto the ground. Amadeus tensed.

"You want to do the honors?" Grassal asked.

"Can I at least—"

"No."

Grassal placed his own phone beside Amadeus', grabbed a socket wrench from the bike's tool bag, and reduced their phones to glistening bits.

"Hope your backup daemon was running."

Amadeus looked at Grassal, debating whether to hug or hit him. He decided to decide later. Instead, he said, "I need more coffee."

They sped off down the highway into the red-tinted night.

4

They drove the dark highway for hours, away from the sprawling city, through cool night air rich with moisture. Neither spoke much. Amadeus thought about the journey and guessed they could reach Colorado in three days or less, depending on how long he could stay awake. He could ride I-80 all the way, or maybe pick up I-70 in Pittsburgh. But no matter what route they took, one thought loomed: his father was dead. Every few minutes, Amadeus had to force himself not to cry out and break down. Every few minutes, he returned his focus to driving. He couldn't escape gunfire only to die in a fiery motorcycle crash. His father was dead. He was alone, orphaned, not even twenty-three years old. This was too young, too young. His other friends had parents. This wasn't fair. Grassal's parents were both alive, even if they wanted nothing to do with him.

With one hand he patted his pants pocket and felt for the statue. Still there. His father's life's work. He needed to make a backup copy. This made him think of his father and his refusal to backup his data to the Tivooki Systems servers, the way he would say he didn't trust Tivooki, no matter what their adverts said about being safe and secure. No, he preferred to maintain his own databases. Had that been the reason they raided his house? What if they had only wanted the data? No, they would've sent a thief, not a paramilitary hit squad.

But, Amadeus thought, the one question he wasn't asking was the most important one: who were "they?" He had an idea of what "they" wanted, but that was almost secondary. For now, he had to assume that "they" were out there, that "they" wanted him dead, just like his father. No, not dead. He couldn't accept that.

For a moment he considered calling Annie, or even Mark, but decided that doing so would be risky for his aunt and uncle. He couldn't do that to them.

Realizing he was over the speed limit by about forty kilometers, he brought the bike back down to speed. A ticket or, even worse, an impound, wouldn't do him any good. The bike sputtered. Amadeus realized he needed fuel. Damn vintage bikes. He turned down the next off ramp and rolled into the well-lit filling station. The station had a red canopy and proudly advertised "all fuel and charge types here." Amadeus rolled past the electric charging stations and hydrogen dispensers to the petroleum pumps, far on the outside of the station. They both got off. Grassal grabbed one ankle and began to stretch his legs.

"You okay?" Grassal asked, flipping up the visor of his helmet.

"No."

Grassal put a hand on Amadeus' shoulder. Amadeus hugged him and began to sob. "He's dead," he said, their helmets clicking together. Amadeus stopped crying. He didn't say anything, just flipped the visor on his helmet down and held his wallet against the sensor. The LCD screen that had previously offered dried squid snacks now flashed an error message. He pulled his card out, the one linked to his main bank account, and tried again. Still, he received an error.

"Maybe it's the pump," Grassal said. "Here, I've got some cash." He pulled out some crinkled bills from his wallet and handed them to Amadeus.

Amadeus took the bills and selected the cash option.   A

clerk's face came on the screen and told him to pay inside.

He started towards the counter, but he realized he was hungry. Grassal probably was, too. He laid two bags of barbeque squid snacks and a big bottle of water on the counter then bought twenty dollars worth of gas. He took his change, returned to his bike, and pumped the gas.

"I'm getting dizzy off the fumes," Grassal said. "I'm surprised they haven't banned this shit yet." His helmet was off, sitting on the seat.

Amadeus topped off the tank. Some gasoline rolled down the side. He wiped it away with a paper towel.

"You ready?" Amadeus asked. With his clean hand, he shoved a handful of peanuts into his mouth, followed by a big gulp of water.

"Sure, of course I'll go to Colorado with you," Grassal said.

"I, uh, just meant, I assumed," Amadeus said. "They're after you, too."

"You assumed that I'd just go wherever you go? Of course you did. I always have. Right?" Amadeus started to speak, but Grassal smiled at him. "I'm mostly only fucking with you, brother. You know your father was like a father to me. More like a father than my own father, really. And, if they want to kill you, they probably want to kill me, too. I've practically lived at your house the past few years. I can imagine them crashing through the windows at my house—"

"Okay, okay." Amadeus put his hand up to stop him. "Thanks, Grass."

"Thank me once we get to Colorado. What is it, ten thousand kilometers?"

"Not quite. Might as well be. We'll need to find a place to sleep tonight."

"We could sleep at a rest area."

"Better than nothing." Amadeus put his helmet back on, tightened his shoelaces, and checked the air in the tires. Back on the highway with a full tank of gas, the minutes melted away into hours. Somewhere in Pennsylvania they stopped at a rest area. They got off the bike and stretched. Amadeus waved his wallet in front of the vending machine's card reader. The screen flashed an error message. Grassal tried his accounts. Same result.

"Shit," Grassal said. "Declined again. We've got to go, ditch the cards."

"I'm so tired. I want to rest."

"Then buy a coffee." Grassal handed Amadeus some money. "And use cash. Every time we try the cards, that's like sending up a flare and saying 'Hey, murdering assholes, we're right here, come find us.'"

"How much cash you have?" Amadeus asked.

"About fifteen dollars."

"Not enough to get to Colorado."

"That's not enough to get to Ohio."

Amadeus drank a coffee too hot to enjoy, then they set off, drove a couple more hours, and found another rest area. Amadeus stretched out on a bench and tried not to think, tried instead to get comfortable, but his bony body and protruding joints ground against the hard wood. When he finally fell asleep, he dreamed he was in a field, naked, watched by millions of unseen eyes. His father's voice spoke, but Amadeus couldn't make out the words, as if he were a man speaking a foreign tongue. Something rustled in a nearby patch of grass. Amadeus looked closer. A tiger sprang from the bush with a roar, swung at his face, and knocked him to the ground. He opened his mouth to scream, but no sound came out. The tiger began batting Amadeus' body like a house cat playing with a toy mouse.

5

A rest area attendant roused Amadeus from sleep by shaking his shoulder. "Wake up, son, you can't sleep here," he said. His skin was grey, his eyes sunken. "I let you sleep here a couple hours, only because I used to ride and I know how it is, but families going to start coming here soon and they'll be needing these picnic tables. You're going to need to leave. You understand."

"Yes, yes, fine," Amadeus said, still not sure where he was. Wisps of purple dawn streaked the sky like jellyfish tentacles. Everything came back to him in reverse order, the drive, the gunshots, the crawlspace, his father shooting his servers, the popped balloon. He tried to shake it all away, convince himself this was a dream within a dream, tried to wake up, but the man with the sunken eyes still stood over him. Amadeus grabbed Grassal's arm.

"Hey buddy, wake up, this man says we have to go."

"I didn't do it," Grassal said, opening unfocused, confused eyes. The attendant wandered off without saying another word. Amadeus went to examine the map nearby. "Where are we?"

"In Pennsylvania. The 78 changed to the 76. Next is the 70. We can ride that all the way to Colorado."

"I thought we didn't have enough money to make it all the way," Grassal said.

"I'm still working on that."

"You can start by checking coin returns." Amadeus walked off towards the facilities. Grassal called after him: "I'm not serious."

Amadeus washed his face in the bathroom. His face looked scruffy, but he wasn't going to spend money they didn't have on a razor. In the visitor's center, Amadeus sat on a wooden bench and picked up a flex-screen secured to the bench by a steel cable. He stretched the digital sheet to newspaper size and searched for news from the Northeast. The first headline turned his stomach. "Patricide in Providence! Police on the Hunt for Valedictorian Suspected of Murdering Father." Below the headline, Amadeus' senior yearbook picture, the one with his eyes half-closed. Amadeus set the tablet on the bench and took deep, deep breaths. He pulled a brochure for Amish country tours from the shelf, tore out a picture of a buggy, and stuck it in his mouth, feeling the calm spread over him as he ground the paper between his back teeth.

He returned his attention to the article.

Police are looking for two suspects, possibly armed and dangerous, after the controversial physicist Tommy Brunmeier was found dead at his home.

Amadeus fought back the tears. There it was, in ten-point Helvetica font. His father was dead. He read more.

Police suspect Brunmeier's son, Amadeus Brunmeier, 22, of the killing. Neighbors reported seeing him and a friend, Grassal Delgado, flee the scene on a motorcycle. An anonymous source told InterNews that, only the previous day, Brunmeier and Delgado had brutally assaulted a classmate before fleeing his own graduation, where, as class valedictorian, he was expected to give a commencement address. A representative for the family could not be reached for comment.

A small box showed video of a younger version of his father accepting an award.

"No," Amadeus said. "No, no, no, no." Blood filled his face, his heart tried to leap from his chest. Lights flashed on the periphery of his vision. He stood up, letting the screen fall to the floor. He stumbled back outside, trying to keep his walk steady and his posture confident. When Grassal saw him, he cocked his head like an inquisitive dog.

"What now?"

"He's dead, and they think we did it. I mean, the police, they think we killed my father. They're looking for us."

"Shit. Shit. No, that's not, no way. They can't. Why would they think that? No, that's fucking impossible, they should know better."

"Anonymous source," Amadeus said. Speaking was difficult, but he spit out the paper and it became easier. "They said we were armed and dangerous." He lowered his voice.

"You know what that means? The police will shoot us down if they get a chance," Grassal said.

"They won't shoot us if our hands are up."

"So, 'hands up, don't shoot?' Maybe that'll work for you."

"Good point. What about our lawyer?"

"Your dad's patent attorney?" Amadeus nodded then glanced over at the facilities building. The attendant was looking at them through the window. Amadeus looked back at Grassal, who said, "Our best chance is to find Jones like your father said and hope he doesn't believe this shit story."

"My father trusted him, but I'm not sure," Amadeus said. "What if we went to the police, told them what happened?"

"Do you really think that's a good idea?" Grassal said. He put his hands on his hips. "The police are nothing but attack dogs for the highest bidders. They don't care about what's right and wrong. They just do what they're told. When you're a little kid, maybe it's good to believe the police are your friends. But you're an adult now. An adult wanted for murder. You'll be lucky if they only beat you bloody and unconscious the second you walk into the station."

"It looks worse if we run," Amadeus said.

"Your father is dead, *we're* wanted for murder, and you're worried about how this looks? I'll tell you how this looks. It looks like shit all the way around. Maybe it looks like professional hit men were sent to kill everyone in that house. Maybe it looks like we shot up the house and killed your father because we're crazed psychopaths. It definitely looks like if we turn ourselves in, we're done for."

"I think you're paranoid."

"I think I'm pragmatic. And if we're locked up, what happens to the statue and your father's research? You think they won't find a way to get it? Especially if that's what they're after?"

"You're really certain about this."

"I am as certain as the sunrise. We have to do what your father said."

"I'm going to listen to you on this one, Grassal. I hope you're right."

"Would I tell you wrong?"

6

They ran out of money in Indianapolis, having bought fuel, scissors, hair dye, and instant noodles from a Food Carnival grocery store, then cut each other's hair at a rest area outside Columbus, Ohio. Now they both had short, bottle-black hair. While cutting Amadeus' hair, Grassal had suggested they sell the bike. Amadeus agreed.

In Indianapolis, they tried to sell the bike at three separate car dealerships. All turned them down because they had no title. On the outskirts of town, in a place with more vacant buildings than houses, they pulled into a dealership surrounded by a chain link fence topped with razor wire. A sign said, "We love to trade! We still buy gasoline vehicles! Come on in!" As they parked, a man in a suit came out and waved at them. He wore a plastic salesman smile. Amadeus greeted him.

"That's an eight fifty, right? Old V-twin? It's vintage but it looks good. Sounded good too, heard you coming. Awful big bike for a boy your size, no offense."

"None taken."

"Though with that big friend of yours, you might need all the extra power."

"Offense taken," Grassal said.

"I jest, I jest," the dealer said, putting up his hands.

"Yamaha always made a fine bike. Could outrun and outlast a

Harley any old day of the week."

"I'm glad you like this bike because I was hoping to get rid of it. It was my father's bike."

"Well, I don't normally deal in bikes, especially gasoline bikes, despite what the sign says. Most people don't want a dino-drinker anymore; everybody loves their electrics. Can't say I blame them."

Looking at the man's unlined face, Amadeus guessed the dealer wasn't much older than himself, maybe in his early-to-mid-twenties.

The dealer flashed them a big plastic grin, then dropped his voice as if he were preparing to drop a juicy secret in their lap. "Gentleman, I'll tell you what. I know a guy that's a huge fan of these bikes. He told me to keep my eyes peeled. Right now, my eyes are like a couple of oranges, because right here, in my lot, is exactly what he's looking for. Now, I can't promise that he won't part them out, but I can promise to give you a fair deal."

"But there's one thing," Amadeus said. "I don't have a title."

"If I touch it, will it burn my fingers?"

"Huh?" Amadeus said.

"He means, did we steal it," Grassal said.

"Oh. No, it belonged to my father, but he died." Amadeus' flat and emotionless voice surprised him. "And I need to sell this to pay for the funeral."

"Okay, okay, I'm really sorry for your loss. Look, I believe you, but without a title and out of state plates, I'm looking at a mountain of paperwork. Clean titles are expensive. I've got a lawyer, but you understand he's got a couple kids that absolutely have to attend Dartmouth."

"That's fine," Amadeus said. "Just give me enough to cover the funeral, I don't care." Amadeus didn't consider himself a liar; he had always thought the truth was easier, but this lie felt easy and natural. Maybe he should've started lying sooner.

The dealer leaned over to examine the bike. "Any problems? Ever been wrecked?" His tone became flat, precise, a little cold.

He ran his hand over the spark plug wires. "You mind if I take it for a ride?" Amadeus said that was fine. The dealer put on the helmet and drove the bike off the lot. Amadeus and Grassal stood, watching the traffic blow by. After ten minutes, the dealer returned, more steady on the bike than when he left.

"Runs great. I'll give you seventy-six fifty for it."

"What? It books for almost fifteen," Amadeus said. He imagined his hands around the dealer's neck. He reached in his pocket for a scrap of paper, found none. He balled his hands up into fists. Grassal grabbed his arm and pulled him to the side.

"Amadeus, just take it. That's as good as it gets. It's only money. It's only worth that under the best circumstances, and these are far from the best circumstances. In fact, these are the opposite of the best circumstances. And once we get everything straightened out, you're not exactly going to be wallowing in poverty."

"You really believe we'll get this straightened out?"

"I do."

"Fine. I see your point." They returned to the dealer. "Eight thousand two hundred," Amadeus said.

"Seventy eight fifty," the dealer said, the plastic smile returning to his face.

"Seventy nine hundred ... and a ride to the train station," Amadeus said. The dealer considered this, looked at his watch, and nodded.

"You've got yourself a ride."

7

The dealer dropped them at the train station, a sparkling new hub on the just-opened New Empire Builder line. Indianapolis had the second-largest station in the revitalized Midwest high-speed network. If a train was headed anywhere besides Chicago or Texas, it ran through Indianapolis. The glass-and-steel building towered above the old brick buildings of downtown like a metallic spider with its legs sprawled straight out. Outside the main entrance, people pulled little black suitcases. Through the silver doors and inside, more people hummed across polished marble floors. The station reached up ten floors to the sky, a tower of travelers with walkways crisscrossing the open space, connecting one side to the other. Above the concourse hung a restored steam-powered clock. Below it, a four-sided digital display showed destinations, train numbers, and departure times.

"Well, valedictorian, we need to figure out which line goes to Colorado. Easy enough, right? Maybe San Francisco via Denver, something like that. Denver won't be the final destination."

"What are there, like four lines going west? Let's ask somebody." Amadeus took off across the room, past a coffee shop where men in suits were working on their computers. Nearby, a man in a blue uniform was lifting a bag of trash into a bin. When Amadeus saw the uniform he started to turn around and walk away, but he forced himself forward. A janitor wasn't going to give him any trouble.

"Excuse me, do you know which train goes to Denver?" Amadeus asked him. The man looked up from the trash can.

"Do I look like a computer?" he said, not removing the headphones from his ears. He pointed to a cluster of machines across the concourse. "Over there, over there."

On their way, Amadeus asked Grassal, "You see any cameras on those things?"

"Not on the machines, but they're everywhere else. It don't matter too much. The fuzzers should screw up the recognition software's confidence levels."

"I hope so. But even if they don't, the million other people here are pretty good cover."

Using the money from the sale of the bike, Amadeus keyed in instructions on the touch-screen terminal to purchase two seats in a sleeper car on the next train, departing in twenty minutes, estimated time to Denver, twelve hours, with stops in St. Louis and Kansas City.

Tickets in hand, Amadeus went to an internet terminal and searched for news on the Brunmeier murder. Nothing new, only that police were still searching for the suspects. The police spokeswoman had said they believed they were headed to Mexico on a stolen motorcycle and that the FBI was now involved in the search.

Amadeus felt relief, but only a little, and in the open of the station, he also felt exposed and vulnerable. As people passed him by, Amadeus thought their eyes lingered on him just a moment too long, as if they knew him, his face, his crimes, and were scrutinizing, judging, and remembering his every move. Near the gates, a security guard spoke into a radio, looking directly at Amadeus as he did do.

"I've got to get out of here."

"Don't worry, it's only a few more minutes."

"You don't understand. They're all staring at me. I'm freaking out. Look at my hand." Amadeus held up his hand. It shook like a frightened sparrow. "They know, man, they know."

"Amadeus, calm down. Relax."

A buzzer went off. Amadeus hopped out of his seat and ran towards the bathrooms, bumping into people in his haste. In the bathroom, he locked himself in a stall, sat on the toilet, and gasped for breath. From the toilet paper roll, he pulled several sheets and tore them into little strips, balling them up in between his fingers. Some he let fall to the floor, some he put in his mouth. Toilet paper was his favorite paper, and this was good for a public restroom.

A familiar voice rose from the stall next to his, resonating off the bathroom's tile. "It's okay, buddy, it's okay. We're going to get on that train, and we're going to go to Denver, and there everything will be fine," Grassal said.

"It will never be fine. If I'd just—"

"Get a room you two," a man's voice said from nearby. Amadeus hated his voice.

"Do you know what it feels like to have a knife stuck into your scrotum?" Amadeus said. A gasp, then hurried footsteps shuffling out the door. Grassal brayed with laughter.

"Jesus, where did that come from?" Grassal said. "You should've heard yourself. You sound like a mad man."

"Maybe I am," Amadeus said.

They left the bathroom and found their train at platform seven. The platform stretched ahead almost five hundred meters. At the end, the station opened up into the grey of the city. Amadeus looked up and down the train, a long, sleek metal and steel contraption. They stood in line and, with some help from a disinterested porter, found their plastic-walled cabin. When Amadeus sat down he felt he was sinking, becoming one with the comfortable faux-leather chair. For the first time since the night everything started, the tension in his shoulders eased. He didn't have to drive, run, or hide; he could just sink into the seat and enjoy the ride. He hoped their cabin remained empty. As he closed his eyes, the train began its smooth crawl forward, rolling out of Indianapolis and onto the prairie, leaving the east behind.

8

Amadeus awoke to see two women sleeping in the seat across from him. They wore white dresses. One had her head on the other's shoulder. He checked his pockets and confirmed he still had both his wallet and that ridiculous statue. Grassal slept with his head against the window, his mouth hanging open. Outside, the dark landscape stretched for miles, a great black void. Time passed, and though he was tired, he could only grind his teeth. He got up and walked down the dim train, past the sleeping compartments full of sleeping passengers, and down the hall to the dining car. The lights were a little brighter, but still dark enough to allow a good view of the night sky through the windows. He grabbed a paper from the rack, bought a cup of tea from the vending machine, and took a seat facing the window. He sipped the lukewarm tea and tried to read but couldn't focus.

The first night, he thought, life divided into the time before and the time after. Every round of thought made his muscles tense a little, and after a few minutes of this his muscles felt like coiled pressed springs. He put his head in his hands, thought he might cry. Then he felt a shift around him, a presence in the room.

When he looked up, he saw a taut man in a grey suit sitting in the chair beside him. He had close-cut grey hair and deep age lines on his face, lines that could've been cut with a scalpel. His shoulders were broad, his eyes brown and energetic. "What do you want?"

The man smiled, flashing a mouth full of white teeth. "You look like a troubled boy. I thought you could use some company. My name is Claudius, but people call me Gravity." Gravity stuck out a thick hand. Amadeus shook it without enthusiasm. His hand was smooth, dry, and warm, a rock smoothed and worn by the desert sun. His face was the shade of mahogany.

"Charlie Mankowski," Amadeus said. Gravity smiled a little at this. "Why do people call you Gravity?"

"Because I keep things down-to-earth. Sometimes, Charlie Mankowski," Gravity said after a deep breath, "things don't make sense. It's like the world tilts on its axis and begins to shake, and everything turns upside down. You've got to fight just to hang on, to keep from falling away." Gravity patted the table for emphasis. "You either learn to hang on ... or you don't. I've seen men survive against unimaginable odds, and I've seen ones that had it much easier fall away. You know what the difference is? The ones who fall away, they give up just a little too early."

Amadeus looked at him, wondered if he was drunk or insane. He didn't seem drunk. In fact, something about him, or maybe his speech, seemed familiar. "So they fall away because they gave up. And why are you telling me this?"

"Because you look like a man who's about to fall away." His voice was slow, deliberate, but he seemed on the edge of chuckling. "The nature of your troubles I don't pretend to know. But I promise you other people have survived worse."

"I hope you're right."

The man wished Amadeus luck and left as quietly as he arrived, melting into the darkness of the sleeping train. Except for a young couple at the end, following the train's route on a dimmed flexscreen, Amadeus was alone in the dining car. He gazed out at a city that reminded him of chemical crystals growing on a rock, the way the buildings just rose out of the dark, jagged and almost random while still adhering to some predetermined, underlying structure. Spotlights darted across the cloudy night sky.

A man dressed in porter garb, vest and hat, passed through the lounge pushing a little cart. As he rolled through, he stared at Amadeus through narrowed eyes. Amadeus felt his face flush. He looked at the floor. The porter rolled on by, but out of the corner of his eye Amadeus could see his head turning as he walked by. The porter left the car, and Amadeus decided it was time that he, too, return to his car and try for sleep.

When Amadeus opened the door to his compartment, he was greeted by three simultaneous, hushed "hellos." Grassal sat between the two women, now awake and smiling. They had set up the table between the seats and were playing cards. A green bottle of liquor sat on the table. Amadeus greeted the women and plopped onto the seat across from them.

"Girls, this is Amadeus, my best friend. He's the one I told you was going to work for Stanford, just after we visit his uncle in Colorado," Grassal said. Amadeus scowled at Grassal. He thought he should shout him down for using their real names, for making friends when they should be keeping their heads down. Amadeus nodded to the girls.

"Hello, Amadeus. I'm Zella." She had a thin face with high cheekbones and violet eyes.

"And I'm Lucretia," the other girl said. Lucretia had the same cheekbones but she wore tinted glasses and dreadlocks. "We're on our way to San Francisco to sing at Mephisto." Amadeus asked about Mephisto.

"Just the nicest hashish bar in the city," Zella said. "You're a cute one, even if you look like a boy who just lost his puppy. Amadeus, my new friend, have a drink, see if that doesn't warm you."

"It's absinthe," Lucretia said, holding up the green bottle. Amadeus looked from the bottle to Grassal and back. Grassal inclined his head slightly, as if giving Amadeus permission to drink.

"Um."

"It's okay, it won't turn you into a green monster, unless you're freakishly jealous," Zella said. Amadeus shrugged and took a drink from the bottle. The drink burned from his throat to his stomach, as if he had swallowed a mouthful of boiling water. The aftertaste reminded him of the smell of rubbing alcohol. He coughed. The girls both smiled. Amadeus returned the smile but he knew it looked forced.

"You boys like to play cards? Rummy?" Lucretia asked. Amadeus and Grassal nodded. She pulled a beat-up pack from her purse and started dealing. After four rounds and one seat change—Grassal had accused Amadeus of peeking—Zella was in first, Amadeus second, Grassal last. The bottle was half empty. Amadeus, feeling warm and almost happy, accidentally burped.

"So rude," Zella said, "belching in the company of ladies. That's fine when you're with your buddy here."

"Sorry," Amadeus said, feeling redness rise in his face. Zella grinned.

"You're so easy to pick on," Zella said. "You just roll over and take it. Do you always do what people tell you?"

"Not always."

"Then let's find out. Kiss me, young Amadeus," Zella said.

"Um," Amadeus said. He looked at her, then across at Grassal and Lucretia. They were waiting, watching. Amadeus shrugged and kissed her. She put her hand on his cheek and leaned against him, her soft lips tasting like licorice and alcohol, all heat but no burn. Amadeus heard a catcall from Grassal. His face was red but he didn't care. They stopped kissing and pressed their foreheads together.

"Mmm, that was nice," Zella said.

"You're not so bad yourself."

"You haven't kissed many girls."

"Why do you say that?"

"Because I had to tell you to kiss me. Either you're really dim or woefully inexperienced. I'm going to guess the latter. The college boy who learned about everything but girls."

"A toast, then," Lucretia said, filling their shot glasses. "To the end of innocence."

"To the end of innocence," Amadeus said. "But I think my innocence ended a long time ago." Grassal raised one eyebrow. Amadeus pointed his finger at Grassal. "You know what I mean." They played a few more rounds of cards, laughing and drinking as the flat dark land rolled by. Between hands, Amadeus leaned on Zella, eventually falling asleep on her shoulder.

9

He woke to a slowing train and a throbbing headache. Beyond the windows lay a city awash in a thousand colors, each shade promising a different variety of excitement. Grassal was already awake.

"Where are we?" Amadeus said. "St. Louis? Kansas City? What time is it?"

"Late in the night, early in the morning," Grassal said. "It's got to be Kansas City. We've been on this train for what, four hours? Five? I have no idea. If a train leaves Indianapolis at seven p.m. and travels west at ..."

"Grassal, buddy, stop. It's too early for math problems. Or is it late?"

The train pulled into the station, brakes hissing and whooshing as it came to a stop. A reflective green sign read "Kansas City, City of Fountains." Like the new Indianapolis station, this one was all glass and steel, but unlike that station, this one sprawled across the plain, taking advantage of the great horizontal spaces. On the platform flanking their train, families waited on loved ones, businesspeople waited on regional trains, and young people on holiday sat on backpacks. A crowd of people bottlenecked around a door from the waiting area, trying to reach the arriving train. The crowd writhed, tensed, then scurried apart, making way for six police officers.

Dressed in body armor, holding assault weapons at the ready, the officers looked like a paramilitary attack squad intent on assassinating some third-world kleptocrat.

"We've got a problem," Amadeus said. The sickness in his stomach grew worse, and he thought he might vomit on Zella. He struggled to keep it down. Grassal threw the blanket off and stood up.

"That's a hell of a welcoming committee." He closed the curtains over the window.

"Think they're here for us?" Amadeus asked. Grassal shrugged.

"How many wanted men you think are on this train? Apply Occam's razor to this situation."

"Um."

"Amadeus, you think we can slip away from them?"

"Don't have much choice, do we?"

"Oh, you don't have to leave," Zella said. "We're not in Denver yet. Besides, we're just getting to know each other." She spoke with a voice still raspy from sleep and recycled air. "But if you really got to go, then look us up in San Francisco. We'll be performing under the name The Interstellar Sisters."

"Easy to remember, 'cause you ladies are out of this world," Grassal said.

"That's awful," Lucretia said. "So obvious."

"At least he tries," Zella said.

Amadeus stood, then staggered and stumbled. He felt like someone had pummeled his neck and back with a mace. Grassal helped him regain his balance, then pulled open the door. Amadeus leaned his head out, peered up and down the hallway, and ducked back inside the compartment.

"No good," Amadeus said. "They're maybe two cars down."

"You two seem too innocent for this shit," Zella said. "What's going on?"

"Later," Amadeus said. "What do we do?"

"No place to hide, not on the train," Grassal said.

"What about the bathroom?" Amadeus said.

"They always check the bathrooms first," Zella said.

"We could just make a run for it," Amadeus said.

"Why?" Lucretia said. "You guys are obviously not criminals. I've known a few in my time."

"No we're not, but the police think we are. It's a long, sad story," Amadeus said.

"Aren't they all," Lucretia said.

"Come on, Grassal, think, man, think," Amadeus said.

Lucretia went into the hallway. A moment later, she reported back. "They're checking IDs."

"The overhead beds!" Zella said. "You guys lie in them. We'll fold them up and let you out after they pass. It'll be tight but you can fit. Lucretia, take your shirt off." Zella motioned for Grassal and Amadeus to climb onto the upper beds. Grassal and Amadeus looked at each other, shrugged, and climbed onto the upper beds.

"What?" Lucretia said. Grassal raised one eyebrow, smiling as he leaned over the bed. Amadeus, already on the upper bed, blushed. Zella stripped her shirt off. After a moment's hesitation, Lucretia did the same. Both wore matching black bras covered in red orchids.

"A distraction, girl. We'll act like we're still sleeping. Help me with this big fucker first," Zella said. They stood on the lower seat and, with both hands, strained to push Grassal's bunk up. They pushed until the latch snapped closed. From inside the bunk came some muffled words from Grassal. "He's a heavy one."

"Too many cheeseburgers," Lucretia said. "Now for the little one."

"Hey," Amadeus said. They pushed. The bed under him tilted upwards and the compartment grew dark. The latch finally snapped closed, and Amadeus was squished between the soft bed and the hard plastic wall. He couldn't move his arms or his legs, only his feet, as if his body had been bound with duct tape and thrown into a soft, cottony ditch. Some time passed, and outside the car he heard a hydraulic hiss. A moment later, the compartment door slid open.

"Oh, excuse me," a man's voice said. "Do you mind putting some clothes on? We need to talk to you." The door closed. Zella said she didn't mind at all. After a moment the door opened again and the man's voice asked for identification. His voice had a flat accent. Some shuffling, then beeps as the cops scanned the girls' IDs. "Have you seen these two men? We think they're somewhere on this train." Amadeus' face warmed, and he felt like an animal in a trap. He took deep breaths and thought about the ocean.

"Yeah, I saw them out on the platform," Zella said. "The hispanic guy is the big one and the white boy is kind of small, right?" The cop gave his assent. "They perverts or something? They both had a definite creeper vibe. I only noticed them cause they walked right past our compartment and kind of stared inside."

"More of a leer, really," Lucretia said.

"Did they have bags with them?" the cop asked.

"I dunno, just that they were getting off," Zella said.

"They were getting off alright. Weirdos," Lucretia said.

"Miss, this is very serious. These two are dangerous, suspected of murder. We believe one of them killed his father while the other tried to set the house on fire. Now, you say you saw them getting off the train. Were they getting on another train, or were they setting off on foot?"

"Shit, I dunno," Zella said, her voice sounding less confident. "I told you what I saw."

"That's enough for now," the man said. "Have a great day." The door closed with a *whoosh*. Minutes passed. Amadeus heard a knock on his bed, then Zella speaking in a stage whisper. "What. The. Fuck? You are not coming down from there, no way, not until you explain to me why I might have just covered up for a murderer and an arsonist-in-training."

"God, no," Amadeus said, followed by a harsh cough. "It's not like that. Please believe me. Men came into my house and killed my father. They tried to kill us too, but we got away. I loved my father. This is a nightmare. They tried to make it look like we did it."

"Ladies, does he look like someone who killed his father? If his father were his mother he'd be a mamma's boy. He was a mamma's boy, but his mother's dead too."

"Mmm," Zella said. "Lu, what you think?"

"They're rich kids, but I think they're telling the truth."

"Listen to your friend, Zella, she's right. Except I'm not rich," Grassal said.

"I think you're right," Zella said. "But for now, it's best they stay up there. Lu, good work. You know, maybe we could keep them for ourselves, our very own cabana boys."

"Mmm hmm," Lucretia said.

The train started up thirty miserable minutes later. The girls said they saw some police get off, but they couldn't be sure it was all of them. The police, they decided, were federal, so they could have very well stayed on the train. Zella said she'd take a look around. A few more minutes passed, then Zella returned and said everything seemed cool.

The girls unlatched the beds and helped first Amadeus then Grassal down to the floor. Amadeus shook and stretched, working the kinks out of his arms.

"We owe you both, seriously," Amadeus said. "You saved our asses."

"I'm sure we can think of something," Zella said.

Fifteen minutes later, Amadeus sat on the carpet, working his fingers into the rough skin of Zella's feet. Grassal did the same for Lucretia. For the next six hours, they acted as personal masseurs to the Interstellar Sisters as the sun rose high in the sky and they drew ever closer to the mile-high city of Denver, Colorado.

10

Just before they arrived, rain began to fall, streaking the windows. Lucretia wrote down an address and told Grassal to look her up if he was ever in San Francisco. Amadeus shook hands with both women and said awkward goodbyes. The doors opened and they stepped onto the platform. Lucretia watched them through the window and waved, mostly at Grassal, as the train departed.

Amadeus took deep breaths, but the air was thin and wet. He remembered reading about elevation sickness and decided that, combined with the alcohol, would mean he was in for a hell of a headache. Standing beside the train, watching it leave, he felt exposed and naked. They'd made it to Denver, but that didn't mean they still wouldn't be hunted, both by the hit squad that had started this horror, and every police department south of the forty-fifth parallel with resources to spare.

Crossing the concourse, Amadeus said, "We need to buy some aspirin or something and go someplace less ... public." He thought he might start coughing and was afraid of the attention that would draw to himself. Grassal pointed out a little convenience store beside a Japanese restaurant. Amadeus bought a jar of aspirin and two umbrellas. After he paid, he asked the guy behind the counter if he knew of any payphones.

"There's an internet cafe a couple blocks south, by the

campus," he said before returning his attention to his phone. Amadeus swallowed three aspirin without water.

Outside, taxis lurked around the station, waiting on fares. Steel, brick, and solar-panel-covered buildings towered above, some reaching over a hundred floors, as if being a mile high wasn't enough for Denver. Glass-covered walkways hundreds of meters off the ground connected the buildings. Heading south, they passed stores selling cheap phones and computers, train tickets, and a place with two barber poles advertising "sensual massage for the weary traveler, best prices in town." On a nearby sidewalk, a man was selling roasted chestnuts from a cart. The city smelled cleaner than Indianapolis, but the air was cooler. Even with their umbrellas, the rain soaked through their clothes, and they both began to shiver.

Ten minutes of walking through rain-swept streets found them in a neighborhood with Spanish signage and restaurants selling roasted chicken smelling of cumin. A poster read *"llamar Guatemala, muy barato!"* Amadeus and Grassal ducked inside.

A clerk with slick-backed hair stood behind the counter. Grassal nodded to Amadeus.

"Buenos días. Quiere usar un teléfono," Grassal said, pointing to Amadeus. *"Cifrado, por favor."* The clerk smiled and waved Amadeus over to a row of phone booths. Grassal continued to converse with the clerk in Spanish. Inside the phone booth, Amadeus fished the crumpled scrap of paper from his wallet and dialed.

The phone rang a few times. No answer. He tried again. A girl's voice came on the line.

"Um," Amadeus said. "I'm trying to reach Jones."

"He can't talk right now," the girl said, the opposite of friendly. "He's quite busy."

"Who is this?" Amadeus asked.

"I'm his daughter. Who is this?" Amadeus smacked his forehead. Of course! How could he forget Lilly? But the last time he had encountered her, she was a squeaky–voiced girl who played with magical plastic ponies.

"Lilly, this is Amadeus Brunmeier. I need help."

"Wait a second, little Amadeus? The weird kid with the map collection? The boy who used to hit me? I guess you want to talk to my father. Hold on." A click as she dropped the phone. Amadeus heard her yelling, "Daddy, it's Tommy's boy." Amadeus heard more clattering and wondered why she didn't bother to put him on hold.

"Amadeus Brunmeier, this is Holden Jones. I'm deeply sorry about your father. The world is a lesser place after this tragedy. I've read horrible rumors about you, but I know they're not true. Right?"

"Jones," Amadeus said, giving Grassal a thumbs-up through the glass, "you know right. They aren't true. But right now, we're in trouble. People are looking for us."

"Your father told me a few months ago that something bad was brewing, a disagreement with some powerful people. Now, though, we'll need to get you out of there and down here to the estate. Let me see." He tut-tutted into the phone. "Light rail doesn't run out here, but three times a day there's a bus to Leadville, the nearest town. No self-drivers out this way due to a damnable county ordinance I can't quite get repealed."

"You don't drive?"

"Ah, your father never told you. My condition, right now I, eh, can't really leave my place. I'm hooked up to some rather complex medical equipment, and I'm sure you don't want to hear about it. The contractors are off for some well-earned recreational time, and Lilly certainly isn't driving to the city in this weather. The bus will get you here, no problem. Let's see, I'm guessing you're near the station. My boy, go to the main entrance, there's a bus stop. Take the fifty two and get off at the post office. Lilly can pick you up from there. Less than a dozen people know we're out here, and most of them don't know the way up. And thanks for using an encrypted line."

"I did?" Amadeus asked, before repeating the directions back to Jones, who confirmed them. Amadeus suddenly remembered playing with Lilly a couple times when he was younger; he had hit her, but only after she punched him in the kidneys, surprisingly hard for a little girl. He hadn't seen her since then. He resolved to apologize for hitting her, even if she had struck first, Han in the cantina. Amadeus supposed that made him Greedo. Then he thought of his father and mother, of the happier times, all gone.

"Also, Amadeus," Jones said, "there's a bakery called Ramona's near there, on Center Street, two blocks from the station. A big shopping area, you can't miss it. I need you to do me a favor and pick me up a custard pie with hushberries. Can you do that? Won't take but a minute."

"I suppose," Amadeus said, though he had never heard of that kind of pie. "What exactly are hushberries?"

"They're a regional thing, like rocky mountain oysters." Amadeus hadn't heard of those either.

They walked back to the train station, dodging puddles as they went, and found Center Street. A clear plastic roof covered the five-block pedestrian-only strip. Restaurants and novelty shops filled the store fronts. Couples strolled arm in arm, wandering from shop to shop. The smell of chili and baking bread filled the street. Some children carried balloons they'd bought from a man selling them nearby. Amadeus imagined popping their balloons, one by one.

"This place is making me hungry," Grassal said.

"Come on, let's just get that pie and get out there. You'll survive until then."

Grassal shrugged, looking not a little surly. Amadeus studied his friend. After only three days on the road, he looked like someone else, his hair mussed and his clothing disheveled, so different from his normally neat and fastidious appearance. Amadeus guessed he himself didn't look much better. His face itched, and he could smell himself. Grassal didn't seem to care, and Amadeus realized how lucky he was to have his friend along.

"You know what, Grassal? Maybe you're right. We've made it this far. I think we could have a meal. Why not? You see anything that looks good?" Grassal stretched, looked over the crowd, and scanned the street.

"There's a cool-looking vintage diner down that way, neon sign and all. I could probably get a malt, that sounds pretty swank. Hey, even better, Ramona's is right beside it."

"Perfect." Amadeus peered through the wide glass window of Ramona's Bakery as they walked by. A woman wearing a floppy white hat and matching apron was pounding out dough. He guessed that was Ramona.

The diner had movable white letters on a black felt menu board. On the wall, a red and blue hand-drawn sign advertised steak burgers, shakes, malts, and rocky mountain oysters. A group of teenagers sat in a red booth in in the corner of the otherwise empty restaurant.

"Hey," Amadeus said, pointing to the sign. "Jones mentioned those oysters, they must be good. I think I'll try them." Grassal shrugged and said he was getting a burger. When their food came, hot and greasy, they ate without speaking. The oysters didn't taste like oysters, but Amadeus ate them anyway. Through the window, a group of people dressed as elves and forest nymphs passed by. Neither commented, they simply watched. One rode a unicycle and juggled bowling pins. Amadeus liked seeing this spectacle; it made Grassal and himself inconspicuous by comparison. After their meal, they went next door to Ramona's Bakery.

"Hi," Amadeus said, "are you Ramona?"

"Nobody else works here," she said, not unfriendly. She wore gold hoop earrings and a small diamond stud on the side of her nose. Her skin was the color of honey. "What can I do for you?"

"Umm, this might seem a little strange. I'm supposed to pick something up for someone, a, uh, hushberry pie. He said you'd know what I'm talking about."

Ramona smiled and said, "No problem, hold on just a minute." She went to the back and returned with a small package wrapped in blue paper. "You take this to old Jumpin' Jones, he's been pestering me about it for a week now."

"It doesn't look like a pie," Amadeus said.

"You'll have to excuse my friend," Grassal said. "He's a little slow sometimes."

Ramona smiled at them, a faint twinkle in her dark eyes.

"That's okay, boys, you just tell him—" *Bang!* A gunshot. Ramona's face went slack. Glass shattered. A small red hole grew in the center of her forehead. More gunshots crackled. Ramona backed against the wall and collapsed to the floor. Amadeus felt Grassal pushing him down. The broken glass threatened to tear through the soft skin of his hands. They scampered behind the counter. Ramona's body was sprawled on the floor. Blood oozed from her forehead and dripped onto her clean white apron. Amadeus' stomach turned.

"Out back," Grassal said, crawling over her body. More gunshots, screams from outside. The floor was covered in flour. The flour mixed with Ramona's blood and made a red pasty batter that stuck to Amadeus' hands. They crawled through the door to the back of the bakery, the store room. Bags of flour, the smell of yeast and strawberries.

"Okay?" Grassal said, catching his breath.

"Not more gunshots. It's awful, it's like a demon is after us." Amadeus scanned the room and saw an exit sign. "There's the back door."

"What the hell kind of pie is that?" Grassal asked. Amadeus looked down at the solid, heavy package in his hand, surprised he still held it. "Think the alley's safe?"

"I don't think any place is safe."

Amadeus threw the package into the air. A gun fired twice, a round hitting a bag of flour just over Amadeus' head. The flour poured out and dusted his hair.

"Damn it," Grassal said. "Back door, let's go."

Still crouched, package in hand, Amadeus followed Grassal as he pushed a metal bar and flung the back door open. A klaxon siren screamed. More gunshots and crashing glass. They scuttled into the alley. A dumpster overflowed with bags of trash.

They ran.

As they approached the end of the alley, a door opened, and they nearly smashed into a man in a grey suit. He held a rifle. Amadeus let out a little cry and started to backpedal.

"I'm a friend," the man said. "Get behind me." After he spoke, Amadeus recognized him: the man from the dining car who called himself Gravity. His wrinkles didn't look so deep in the rain. The man raised his rifle, his motions fluid and practiced, and fired three shots toward the bakery's back door.

"Cover there." He pointed to the corner. Just before they rounded the corner came another barrage of shots.

"Ahh!" Grassal cried and fell to the asphalt, clutching his left calf. Amadeus and the man dragged Grassal to cover. Blood seeped through his jeans and from between his fingers.

"Stay put," the man said. "Amadeus, get pressure on it."

Amadeus knelt and used his wallet to staunch the wound.

Gravity leaned around the corner and fired off several more shots.

In response, a half-dozen rounds exploded chunks from the concrete sidewalk a meter away. This was followed by several silent seconds, each as long as an hour. Amadeus' ears rang. In the distance, a police siren screamed.

"Be ready to get your buddy on his feet," Gravity said. From the inside pocket of his jacket, he pulled something that looked like a pack of cigarettes. He pressed down on the object with his thumb, tossed it, and crouched down. "Cover your ears," he said. They did. *Boom!* Gravity stood up, ejected the magazine from the rifle, and tossed the rifle into the dumpster.

"Seizure grenade. He's down for now. Can you walk?" Gravity asked Grassal, who rocked back and forth, holding his leg, tears streaming down his cheeks. Grassal shook his head.

"We'll help you," Amadeus said. "Grassal, buddy, come on now. On your feet."

"He shot me. He shot me," Grassal said.

"It'll be okay, I promise," Gravity said, kneeling and putting his hand on Grassal's shoulder. Amadeus was surprised by this sudden show of tenderness. "But right now, you need to get your shit together. Can you do that for me?"

"Okay," Grassal said, looking at Gravity with soggy red eyes.

"Wait, hold on there, Gravity. On the train, I told you my name was Mankowski. How do you know my real name?"

"Later," Gravity said. "We go that way. I have a car waiting for us." He pointed in the direction they had come from. They helped Grassal up and carried him, one arm over each of their shoulders, back into the alley. The man Gravity shot lay on the ground. His leg twitched a little. Blood was splattered inside the clear plastic mask. His eyes were open, and through the mask they seemed to be entirely black.

"My god," Amadeus said. He recognized the mask, the gear, the build. The same as the men who came to his house and killed his father. Amadeus cried out then and kicked the man in the ribs. He enjoyed that. "I'm going to kill him!" He kicked again. Gravity pulled him back by his shirt.

"No, Amadeus, don't. Back off. It's done."

"But this is one of them."

"It won't do you any good."

"You were shooting at him."

"I didn't kill him. I don't like to kill, not anymore, not if I can help it. I know you're angry, but right now we have another objective."

"Fuck it, fine."

Carrying Grassal between them, they dashed through the pedestrian area before reaching the car. The streets had emptied. Two people lay sprawled by the Center Street fountain, bleeding. One was the balloon man. Amadeus looked up and saw a rainbow bundle of balloons floating up into the rainy Colorado sky.

11

A long black sedan with tinted windows pulled to the curb beside them. Amadeus cast a worried look toward Gravity, who opened the back door. Together, they laid Grassal across the back seat. Gravity knelt in the floorboard, pulling medical supplies from a duffel bag. Amadeus took the passenger seat and told the navigation system to choose the shortest path to Leadville. The navigation system's feminine voice flatly informed them manual control would be required in approximately one hour. The sedan pulled away from the curb. Grassal was pale but conscious, muttering curses in a mix of Spanish and English.

By the time the car found its way to the highway and merged into the automation lane, Gravity had stripped the denim from Grassal's leg and cleaned the wound with water. His movements were fluid and practiced, as if he'd done this a hundred times before. Presently, he removed a large, syringe-like object filled with tiny white balls from the bag.

Grassal's eyes grew wide, tracking the object as Gravity plunged it into the wound, first to the entry point, then to the exit wound. The former was the size of a dime; the latter, a quarter.

"Anti-hemorrhagic. Filled with hundreds of tiny sponges," Gravity said. "Seeing as how we can't go to a hospital, it's the thing that's going to save your life."

"I've been fucking shot in the fucking leg, man. I want to go to a fucking hospital," Grassal said, his words clipped. He tried to sit up a little. His arms shook.

"In a case like this, it's not the gunshot that kills you, it's the henchman watching hospital admissions for trauma wounds. Amadeus, turn up the heat. You, hold still." Gravity pushed Grassal back down in the seat. "We may have removed one pawn from the field of play, but I expect others are waiting in the wings."

Amadeus felt heat rising in him, and it had nothing to do with the air from the vents. If only he'd pressed to leave sooner, made a stronger case to stay out of public places ...

"All patched up," Gravity said. "I won't lie to you, it'll be just about the worst pain you've ever experienced. You're going to be on crutches, and you might end up with a limp. But the sponges will break down and help the tissue heal, and you'll have a great story for the grandkids."

The car was now uncomfortably hot. Gravity stripped the latex gloves from his hands, retrieved two bottles of pills from his duffel bag, and dumped some into his palm.

"Pain killers and antibiotics," Gravity said, handing the pills, along with a bottle of water, to Grassal, who swallowed them.

"Thanks," Grassal said. "But why are you carrying this shit around with you?"

"Old habits from another life. Amadeus, time to switch. I need you to keep pressure on the wound, keep his leg elevated, and make sure he doesn't fall asleep."

Gravity climbed into the driver's seat. Amadeus took his place in the rear floorboard. Grassal grabbed Amadeus' shoulder, covering his mouth, and spoke to Amadeus in a wavering voice just over a whisper.

"Don't fucking trust him, man," Grassal said. "He could be one of them."

Amadeus just blinked in response. He couldn't process the

thought. So, he spoke.

"Let's get this out of the way: why are you helping us?" Amadeus said. "Don't get me wrong, I appreciate it, but—"

"Your father contacted me last year, told me there was trouble brewing, said if anything were to happen to him, I was to make sure you were safe. Paid me a handsome retainer, too. But that's not important right now. What is important is keeping your friend calm."

"I am calm as I can be, given that I'm bleeding out."

"You're not bleeding out," Gravity said.

"How did you know my father?" Amadeus asked.

"We were in the same unit in Afghanistan."

Amadeus nodded. On the rare occasions when his father had mentioned his time in the service, he'd only talked about the food, never about the fighting. "He's never told me much about that."

"I doubt he would. There was some ... heavy stuff. I was glad for him when he got out."

In the back, Grassal moaned as he held his leg. "Hospital," he said between breaths. "I want to go to a hospital."

"Do you want to go to a hospital?" the navigation system's voice asked.

Gravity and Amadeus responded with a simultaneous, "No."

A moment passed, then Amadeus continued with his questions. "So, meeting you on the train was no coincidence?"

"Your father had a heartbeat system set up on his research server. When the heartbeat stopped, it emitted a signal with the system's location. I was in Washington when I picked up your signal. I caught up with you in PA, followed to Indianapolis, and bought myself a train ticket. I'm guessing he transferred the system onto some kind of network-connected storage device for you."

"Um, something like that." He touched his pocket, felt the statue's outline.

"Ditching your phones and selling the bike, that was clever.

You and Grassal didn't mean to, but you did a pretty good job of not being predictable. I'm still not sure how the police guessed you were on the train, or how you managed not to get dragged off in handcuffs, but good work."

"Thanks. We had help."

Grassal muttered something and shut his eyes. Amadeus grasped his friend's hand and held it tight.

"If the signal went out over a public network, how was it that only you could pick it up?"

"The signal coming off the transmitter uses public key encryption, just like a million others floating through the ether. If you don't have the correct key, they all just look like gibberish. And I'm the man with the key." Out the window, the terrain had changed from flat suburban tracts to rolling, pine-covered mountains. The houses grew smaller, more squat, most covered with late-model solar panels. "Your father, he was researching something with huge potential, but there were ... complications."

"What complications?" Amadeus asked. Grassal's breathing was shallow, and his palm felt clammy. Amadeus squeezed, just enough to hurt, and Grassal managed a slightly pissed-off grunt.

"Internal strife. Disagreements with his partners-slash-investors."

Amadeus' stomach tightened. Tommy hadn't given it up.

"I need details. Who were the partners? What was the research?"

"Unfortunately, I wasn't privy to all of the information. Your father tried to keep his work as quiet as possible. Something to do with kipium-based quantum teleportation."

"Jesus. What else do you know?" Amadeus said. The heat in the car was stifling.

"Manual control required in two minutes," the navigation system said. Gravity took the wheel.

"I'm a soldier, not a scientist," Gravity said. "I always knew he would do something amazing, possibly profound, and that I wouldn't understand a tenth of it. But the implications, on the other hand ..."

Amadeus felt Grassal's hand relax. He pushed down panic, and used a finger to open one of Grassal's eyelids. It stared off into nothing.

"He's out."

"Pass me the bag," Gravity said. Amadeus did so, and after a moment Gravity handed him a smelling salt.

"You know how to use that?" Gravity asked. Amadeus said nothing, only focused on snapping the capsule and getting it under his friend's nose. The effect was immediate. Grassal sucked in a lungful of air and opened his eyes.

"What the ..."

"You're okay, Grassal. You're okay. Stay with me."

"You have Jones' phone number?" Gravity asked. Amadeus handed the slip of paper to Gravity, who then dialed the number on his phone.

"Yeah, this is Gravity. I'm a friend of Tommy's. Amadeus and his friend are with me. His friend was shot. No, no, he'll be fine. Okay. Right. We're almost in Leadville. Yeah. Yeah. I guess you heard about Denver. Rattled, understandably. The Greely Mine? Fine. We'll meet you there."

They drove through the tiny town of Leadville, Colorado, past a school, a post office, and a small hospital. Here the rain had stopped. Somehow every traffic light turned green for them. Grassal had given up on speaking and just hummed a steady tone.

"Is this normal?" Amadeus said.

"If you were low on blood and high on opioids, you'd be humming, too."

Past the town, Gravity turned off the paved road onto a dirt track that wound up the mountain. They came into a clearing littered with rusting machinery. Gravity pulled off the road and killed the engine. "What do you know about Jones?"

"That he's some kind of aeronautical engineer and that he

has some health problems. I met him a few times when I was a kid. What about you?"

"A few things. I looked him up because your father mentioned him as a possible ally in case things went pear-shaped. First, he and your father had some overlapping research interests, mostly dealing with kipium. Second, he's good at what he does: a few years ago he developed technology that made Predator drones obsolete. Third, he's also filthy rich, both by accomplishment and inheritance. Apparently, one of his great-great-something grandfathers once controlled a large minority of the American steel industry, and he was smart enough to set up a trust that his descendants couldn't fuck up. Finally, his condition is degenerative—he's presently confined to a wheelchair, and he'll be lucky to see the end of the decade."

"Ramona called him 'Jumpin' Jones' before she gave me the package. Seems a cruel nickname for a man in a wheelchair."

"He used to be a hell of a basketball player, did the college thing, could've gone pro, but he decided to pursue an engineering career."

After twenty minutes, an old Jeep bounced down a path hidden by trees. The Jeep had come from a part of the mountain with no visible road, only rough, brushy terrain. The Jeep came closer and finally pulled up beside their car. A young woman with a thin face and wide nose hopped out. Bright red hair stuck out from beneath the blue-and-green plaid scarf she had wrapped around her head. Amadeus recognized the grownup version of the girl from his childhood: Lilly Jones. Gravity rolled down his window, but Amadeus stepped out of the car. He held his arms out to hug her. She narrowed her bright green eyes. Amadeus let them drop.

"Ramona's really dead?" Lilly said.

"I'm sorry, it's, I mean, we were there, we had no idea. It's awful. This is my fault. They were after me; she had nothing to do with this."

"This *is* your fault," Lilly said. "Ramona never hurt anyone.

She didn't deserve this. Amadeus, let me make myself clear. This isn't a good time for us. My father and I, we had other plans. But I ... I guess I'm glad you're okay. And look at you, you're all grown up."

"I'm not the only one," he said, giving her an awkward half-smile. Amadeus realized he was undressing her with his eyes and stopped. Lilly either ignored or pretended not to notice.

"I wanted to tell you I'm sorry about your father. I can't imagine how you feel."

"Angry, mostly. I'd trade, god, I'd trade almost anything to have things go back the way they were."

"Hey," Gravity said, "this reunion is sweet, but we need to get our boy here some basic medical attention."

"Can your car handle a Jeep trail?" Lilly asked. Gravity smiled.

"I guess we'll find out."

12

They tried to follow, but Gravity turned back after half a kilometer, muttering something about destroying his suspension and the rental car company being a racket of cutthroats. They all piled in the Jeep. Amadeus sat in the back with Grassal's legs across his lap. The storm threatened another deluge with lightning and thunder, but nothing came of it. Up the bumpy, pine-covered mountain, over the rough, muddy road they drove. The engine whined like a wounded animal. Amadeus lost sight of the abandoned mine after the first rise. After two more, he realized if he were dropped off at that very moment, he would probably end up wandering around lost. Death would come from dehydration or a hungry grizzly. He wasn't sure which he would prefer. Then he imagined the Jeep tipping over, tumbling again and again down the slope ... but, after watching Lilly intently for about a minute, he came to understand she was a competent driver. He guessed she was familiar with the Jeep; it smelled like her, after all.

The road leveled off and they arrived on a plateau above the tree line. They drove over bare dirt and gravel. A few scrub pines dotted the landscape. Near the middle of the plateau, a single mound rose up another few hundred feet. Snow covered the top. A house-sized chunk was gone from the east side, apparently blown out by dynamite, leaving a sheer rock face.

Lilly drove directly towards it. Amadeus watched her and tried to remain silent, but when the Jeep was less than a hundred meters away and she hadn't slowed down, he couldn't stop himself.

"Lilly, what are you doing? You do see that we're headed right for a huge rock, right?" Lilly nodded, said she saw it, but that was all. Gravity looked back at Amadeus and raised one eyebrow. The Jeep lurched as she downshifted then slapped a white button on the ceiling Amadeus hadn't noticed before.

The rocky side of the mountain drew open like a garage door, revealing a tunnel cut into the earth. When they entered the tunnel, the engine noise washed over Amadeus, muting his thoughts. Fluorescent tubes connected by thick grey wires lit the way. After about two hundred meters, they turned a corner and the tunnel opened up into a cavernous steel hangar.

The hangar reminded Amadeus of the train stations he had recently passed through; only here there were no tracks, no trains, only a few contraptions in various states of dismantlement: a wingless Cessna, a news helicopter, and a large engine Amadeus couldn't identify. Beside all these sat a bright orange hearse, circa 1988. A fake arm hung from beneath the back door. Just behind the hearse, Amadeus noticed a visual distortion as large as a car, an object covered by some kind of cloaking material. Along the back wall, a large window opened to another control room, a door with a round metal handle, and a hallway leading presumably to more rooms.

"There's a stretcher here somewhere, if we need it," Lilly said.

"Grassal, buddy, we're going to move now," Amadeus said. Grassal moaned but refused to move. Amadeus slipped his arm under him. With Gravity's help, he pulled him from the Jeep and carried him across the hangar. Lilly threw open the door to the hallway and led them to a small room, inside of which was a cabinet overflowing with medical supplies, a bookshelf stocked with canned food, and a brown leather couch. She pushed a pile of clothes from the couch and they laid him down on it. Gravity unwrapped the wound and examined it. Grassal whined and writhed but never opened his eyes.

"Amadeus, Lilly, watch and learn," Gravity said, pointing to Grassal's leg. "The bullet went into his calf here, went through to the other side. Here, hold this light." He pulled a flashlight from his pocket and shined it on the wound. Amadeus' stomach turned.

"That's awful," Lilly said.

"It was just tissue damage. There's no bone trauma. Could've shattered his tibia or fibula." He applied clean bandages. "But he lost a lot of blood. He'll need sleep. And a better course of antibiotics than what I've got. Lilly, an IV would be nice ..."

"This isn't a hospital. What you're looking at is what we've got. We don't exactly get many bullet wounds here. Most of the heavy medical artillery is for Dad."

"Where is he?" Amadeus asked.

"He fell asleep, this medication he's on, got him sleeping half the day. You'll see him tomorrow or maybe late tonight, rolling aimlessly through the hangar. That reminds me, you have the package he asked for?"

Amadeus looked down at his hands, as if he were still holding the package. He'd left it in the sedan. "Um ... yes? Just, not with me."

"But you've got it?"

"Yes, it's back in the rental car. So what are hushberries, anyway?"

Lilly smiled. Amadeus liked her smile.

"Medicine. For my father. Besides being a baker, Ramona is, was, a biochemical engineer. Made compounds the FDA couldn't even dream of. Dad uses them to treat his tumor. The side effects aren't as bad as the legal stuff. We'll go down and pick it up tomorrow," Lilly said, then pointed to Grassal. "What about him?"

"We'll keep him dosed up on painkillers for a couple days.

Keep him relaxed and immobilized. For tonight, we should check in on him every fifteen minutes. Amadeus can cover him until two, then I can take over. Maybe in a couple days, we'll put him in a wheelchair if he's ready. Seems to be enough of them here." Gravity looked around. "So, it's just you and your dad living out here?"

"Gravity, that's a borderline creeper question. But yeah, it's just us, unless you count the contractors. They're here during the day most days."

"Contractors?" Amadeus said.

"That's right, they're helping with the Pachyderm."

"You have a pet elephant?" Amadeus said.

"It's an experimental aircraft," Lilly said.

Gravity whistled. "Amadeus, that's why I love scientists. Never a dull moment. Now, Lilly, how about a bed fit for an old man?"

"I've got cots set up for you in the hangar. Anything else?"

"Is there a secure computer here?" Amadeus asked.

"We've got running water, electricity, and air scrubbers. What more do you want?" Lilly put her hands on her hips.

"Oh," Amadeus said. Gravity shook his head at Amadeus and leaned against a stack of boxes.

"I'm joking. We've actually got a data center, mostly to run simulations and the modeling AI. Come on, I'll show it to you. Gravity, want to join us?"

"No, I'd rather sleep. I feel like a crate of potatoes that fell off the spud truck. And I don't really like computers anyway." Amadeus and Lilly looked at each other and shrugged. "I probably don't have to tell you, but don't log in to any of your usual accounts."

"I hadn't planned on it," Amadeus said. Gravity left for the hangar, and they walked to a room at the end of the hall. Lilly pulled open the door.

"There's the data center, everything you should need," Lilly said, sweeping her hand in front of her. A flexscreen covered one wall, illuminated with menus, applications, and news feeds, one of which was dedicated to reports regarding the various crimes of Amadeus Brunmeier. A leather dentist's chair faced the flexscreen. Beside the chair, a bar supported a transparent touch interface, as well as an old-style qwerty keyboard. A legless table hung from adjustable poles bolted to the ceiling. A short server rack stood guard in the back, bolted to the floor. On a table beside the server rack sat a selection of legacy equipment: a stack of old laptops, each labeled with its respective operating system, along with card readers, floppy drives, a CD-ROM drive, and a scanner. "You know how to use all this?"

"I think I can manage," Amadeus said. Lilly stood with her arms crossed, feet apart, and her eyebrows furrowed. He knew Lilly didn't want him here. "Lilly, I ..."

Lilly interrupted him. "Amadeus, I want you to understand something. I'm sorry for what happened to your father, but you couldn't have come at a worse time. I'm going to help you so that, hopefully, we can send you on your way as soon as possible."

"Um. I'm sorry. That you don't want me here. I don't know what I did to you. If this is about when we were kids ..."

"For Tommy Brunmeier's son, you're kind of slow on the uptake. No, it's not because of when we were kids, though that doesn't help."

"What is it?"

"What is it?" Lilly shook her head. "God, you're thick as a brick. My dad said you were supposed to be valedictorian at your school."

Amadeus' face flushed. He decided to change the subject. "I need to review these files, to try to learn what my dad was doing."

"I'm going to watch."

"I don't mind."

"I wasn't asking," Lilly said as she rolled a chair across the concrete floor and sat down beside Amadeus.

13

Amadeus pulled the statue from his pocket. Lilly grabbed it from his hand, smirking as she examined it.

"It's not funny," Amadeus said. "My uncle has poor taste."

"Are you really that ..." She smiled and pinched the statue's cock. "Endowed?"

Amadeus blushed. Lilly didn't seem to notice. Instead, she plugged the statue into the server and, using an old keyboard, entered a couple commands. A window containing a list of directories appeared on the flexscreen. She handed the keyboard to Amadeus. He opened a directory entitled "journal," which contained an index.html file that listed links to journal entries, research, schematics, software, image backups, reference materials, and videos.

"I've seen pages like this. It looks like something from the nineties. From the old web?" Lilly said. "Why wouldn't he use a modern content manager? I mean, this shit is *ancient*."

"Dad used whatever was easiest for him. He was a quantum physicist, not a programmer, putting his project together using the HTML he learned in school." Amadeus clicked the folder named "research," but a popup window told him this file was restricted. "Schematics," "operational procedures," and "software," gave the same result. The only files he could open were the journals, videos, logs, and a few text files.

He opened a file entitled "readme.txt." It read:

Journals and logs are not encrypted. Unfortunately, due to a previous security incident, I am contractually bound to encrypt sensitive intellectual property using the Rettinger-Hashiyada two-factor DNA-based encryption algorithm. Decryption requires fingerprints and blood samples from 3/4 of the project investors.

Filing this information away, he opened one of the videos, choosing randomly from a list of about thirty files. He pressed play. The video showed the basement lab at his house. A contraption consisting of a pair of metal pillars two meters high spaced two meters apart appeared on the screen. Blue-tinted glass spheres sat on top of each pillar. Loops of copper wire formed concentric circles on the floor. Unbundled rainbows of coated colored wires tumbled down each pillar. Amadeus thought the contraption looked like the feral twin offspring of a Tesla coil and a jet engine.

His father's voice came on. "Trial seventeen of the Lorentzian Generator. Like others in this series, there is no corresponding exit node. Minor adjustments to amplitude, journal ref ten seventeen forty-four. Let's see if this works." The camera then panned, tracing the path of the wires to what Amadeus guessed was a control unit on the workbench. Connected to the control unit was a laptop, its screen displaying a frequency analyzer and two windows full of numerical outputs. Leaning against the workbench was the same rifle his father had used on the night of the attack.

Seeing his father at home in his lab, Amadeus quaked in his chair and fought to hold back tears. He paused the video and looked around the room, as if examining the walls. Lilly saw this, put her hand on his shoulder, and told him it was okay. He shook his head and started to reply, but instead pressed play.

"Here goes nothing," Tommy Brunmeier said. Amadeus

watched as his dead father's hand turned a black plastic dial on the control unit. The glass spheres glowed vacuum-tube blue. Kipium.

His father said a little countdown: five four three two one. White, blue, and purple electric arcs licked from one pillar to the other then began to coalesce about a meter off the ground into what looked like a satellite image of a dwarf star.

"So far no change," his father said. A sound started on the video that reminded Amadeus of a rabbit breathing. His father made some adjustments. "Reducing middle spectrum frequency by ten percent, down to four hertz." The dwarf star remained the same, but the crackling grew louder. "Speaking into the microphone now." He raised his voice. "Hello? Can anyone hear me? Is anyone there?" The light flickered and the rabbit-breathing sound stopped. Silence filled the room, followed by a scream like a thousand animals large and small, trapped in a cage surrounded by fire, tortured, agonized, terrified. The speakers on their computer distorted and the dwarf star began to pulsate then split into two orbs stacked vertically, reminding Amadeus of a model of the probability density of the hydrogen atom, only much, much larger. The hairs on the nape of Amadeus' neck stood up. He looked over at Lilly. She had crossed her arms in front of her like she was hugging herself.

"God, that still gives me the heebie-jeebies," Tommy's voice said. "No difference. Damn. Shutting down." A keyboard clicked, the two orbs became one, as if returning to their original state, then the orb faded out like an old picture tube television shutting down. "Same results as previous five trials. Amplitude and frequency adjustments made no significant changes." His voice sounded flat, clinical. Anyone besides Amadeus probably wouldn't have heard the thin sliver of fear trembling within it.

"Besides being the creepiest sound I've ever heard, what was that?" Lilly said. She was shaking, as was Amadeus.

"I have no idea."

They viewed three earlier videos. All were similar. Amadeus felt strange, sad, and more than a little uneasy as he watched his father conduct these secret experiments in the basement of Amadeus' childhood home. Watching them felt like a violation of the old man's privacy. Yet, Tommy had entrusted these files to Amadeus, and Amadeus had a responsibility to figure it all out, to learn about his father's secret life. Even if it meant learning things he didn't want to learn.

"Maybe you can find some explanations in his journals," Lilly said. "I mean, I understand if you don't want me helping you go through all this. I know it's kind of private."

"No, no, that's fine. I would like your help. What privacy do the dead have, anyway? But I almost forgot something. You have an external drive?" Lilly handed him a small storage device. "I need to make a backup." With that, Amadeus copied the files and gave the backup drive to Lilly. "Don't tell anyone about this."

"Amadeus, you know that was the first thing I was going to do."

"Not funny."

Lilly made coffee, sticky, sweet, and rich, and they read long into the night, pausing only to check on Grassal. At first, the entries seemed normal enough, scientific data, records of standard experiments with kipium, how it interacted with other elements old and new. Lilly said she found an entry entitled "practical application." She summarized for him.

"Your father made a discovery a couple years ago. He was, and I quote, 'playing with kipium.' That's when he figured out he could use the negative mass of the kipium to create a stable Einstein-Rosen bridge."

"I thought negative mass created a huge energy deficit."

"It does ... or at least it's supposed to. But according to your father, charged kipium creates its own equilibrium."

"That shouldn't work."

"Hey, I'm not the quantum physicist here, I'm just reading

what he wrote."

They returned to their reading, sharing whatever they found interesting. The earlier entries mostly tracked variations on the experiment that they had watched. Every time Amadeus looked up, the hands on the wall clock had crept forward. Reading and learning kept him from thinking about all that he had lost, and he liked it that way. But when his head hit the desk, he knew it was time for sleep.

"I'm done, spent," Amadeus said, rubbing his eyes.

"I'll keep watch on Grassal," Lilly said. Amadeus acknowledged this kindness with a sleepy half-smile. He glanced at the clock but looked away before his mind could register the time. He didn't want to know. Lilly still seemed wide awake, and he left her to read into the tiny hours of the night.

14

Lilly woke Amadeus early the next morning by shaking his shoulder. When he opened his eyes, he thought he was looking at her through a tunnel of autumn leaves, but it was her hair hanging down. "Amadeus, you have got to see this. Hurry." Groggy, he yawned, then rolled off the cot. Gravity was still snoring on the cot beside his.

"I want to check on Grassal first." He stepped into Grassal's room and turned on the light. Grassal groaned and covered his face with his arm but didn't wake. His face had more color. When Amadeus felt his forehead, he felt warm but not feverish. Satisfied, Amadeus followed Lilly to the data center. He stretched out on the dentist's chair.

"Watch this," Lilly said. She typed rapid-fire commands on the keyboard. A video began. It looked like the other ones, his father conducting an experiment, recording the dial settings, only this time the orb of light grew larger.

"What happens?"

"Just watch." Amadeus watched.

The animal screams started, just as before, but this time the sound combined with a murmur of a thousand voices. The light changed from white to blue to red, its center deep orange and pulsating, like the glowing ember of a coal fire. The shape changed as well, having one then two then four orbs around a center point, like a flower with constantly changing petals.

"This is strange," Tommy Brunmeier's voice said. The light collapsed in on itself, like poking a half-filled balloon, then something happened: a creature emerged from the orb and landed on the floor. "What the ...?" Tommy said, his voice more intrigued than baffled. The creature had four legs, was shaped and sized almost like a dog, but had more mouth than head. Columns of eyes covered the thighs of its forelegs, and where the head should've been, a million needle-like teeth sat in a lipless mouth. The skin was mottled grey. It walked, shaky on its legs, as if it had just been born, and its claws, three on each leg, clicked on the concrete floor. The creature turned to face the control room and shrieked, distorting the sound from the video.

The light started to collapse in on itself. Another leg began to emerge. Tommy shut off the power. The light faded away. When it did, the leg that had been sticking through fell to the ground. Immediately the first creature started gnawing on it.

"What have I done?" his father's voice said.   Amadeus watched as his father left the screen. He entered the control room with his rifle. The creature looked up from his meal, turned to his father, and growled just before Tommy started firing at it. The creature shrieked and started for him, but the bullets knocked it back. When it fell to the floor with its legs splayed, Tommy kept shooting at it, shooting until he emptied the magazine. Then he lowered his rifle and leaned over to examine it, putting his hand over his heart in some gesture Amadeus didn't understand.

He kicked it. The creature twitched. Tommy jumped back, raising his rifle. A moment passed, then he turned it over with the rifle barrel. He got the camera and zoomed in on the creature. Its blood was greenish-black. His father stepped on its paw and the claws extended out even farther. The skin was cracked like dried leather, covered with tiny scars. The eyes, they weren't quite on the knees but just above them. Using the rifle, Tommy peeled back a fold of skin that covered a column of eyes going up the leg to the creature's shoulder.

"I have no idea what I'm looking at," Amadeus' father said, "but it's the ugliest damn thing I've ever seen." The video ended with his father looking at the camera and shaking his head. Amadeus grabbed a scrap of paper sitting by the keyboard. He started to put it in his mouth but Lilly put her hand on his and stopped him. Amadeus let the paper drop to the table.

"What's the date on the video?" Lilly asked.

Amadeus checked and found it was after his official censure. So his father had continued his work.

"This isn't the last video, is it?" Amadeus said.

"No, there are more, but as far as I can tell, that's the only, um, thing besides the sounds to come through." Amadeus shook his head and went to make a pot of coffee. When he came back, they set to work, reading and reviewing the remaining videos. It was early, just after five in the morning. Outside, the sun was beginning to break over the mountains and stream through the skylights. At seven o'clock, a man in an electric wheelchair rolled through the door. Jones. The pupil of his right eye was swollen; it glinted like polished onyx. Wires ran from his neck and back into a box attached to the rear of the chair. Amadeus stood up and went to shake his hand.

"Good to see you, my boy," Jones said. "I guess I didn't look this bad last time I saw you, what, fifteen years ago?" Amadeus nodded, said that was right. "Time and disease do awful things to a man, but at least I've still got my mind." He tapped the side of his head with a curled finger. "Right, Lilly darling?"

"Daddy, you lost that a long time ago," Lilly said, smiling at him but not getting up.

"She's great, isn't she?" Jones said. Amadeus nodded. The silence lasted just a beat too long. "And Amadeus, I'm terribly sorry about what happened to your father. I warned him, I said 'Brunmeier, you're playing with fire.' And you know what he said? He said, 'If I get burned, at least I'll have the scars to show what I've done.' And now you see what he was working on?"

Amadeus nodded and told him about the portal.

"Do you understand why he was interested in this kind of research?" Jones asked.

"He was a theoretical physicist. This was his passion. Figuring out ways to exploit the properties of kipium to create a teleportation device," Amadeus said. Jones smiled a sad little smile.

"Maybe that's how it started, but along the way he changed his focus. Have you ever asked yourself what drove your father, what made him abandon his academic career and all his previous research interests for the last, what, eight years? Understand that the man wasn't some mad scientist. He was grieving. This work ... was his way of dealing with your mother's death. Her death almost killed him. And if it weren't for you, I doubt he would've even bothered living."

"I'm not sure I understand."

"Amadeus, some theoretical physicists have postulated that *all* time exists at *one* time in an infinite number of universes. Rather than our standard linear understanding of time, imagine everything that's ever happened happening at once. This theory was impossible to test ... until your father figured out how to use the negative mass of the kipium to stabilize an Einstein-Rosen bridge. You see, my boy, your father had practically abandoned point-to-point teleportation. He thought that if he could find the right quantum-level wave frequencies, he could use the connection for communications with the past, to hear, maybe even speak with, your mother one more time. In short, he wanted to talk to the dead."

15

Amadeus, Lilly, and Jones sat at a stainless steel table in the bunker's kitchen, a coffee cup before each of them. Over the last half hour, Jones had explained how Tommy had called him years ago, excited after his first successful trial at using kipium to create a stable bridge a micrometer in diameter. Jones had been intrigued, and had followed Tommy's work closely. Time passed, research continued, and photons were teleported. Soon, though, technical progress slowed. Amadeus' mother died. Tommy went off the rails with the spooky communication stuff. Finally, the grant money dried up, and Tommy went looking for investors.

"I couldn't provide any funding," Jones continued, "but I connected him with a high-rolling venture capitalist in New York I knew through an acquaintance. Esther Elgers. Tommy told me she practically frothed at the mouth when he told her about the practical applications. Think about it: reliable, low-energy teleportation of digital information, possibly even physical objects. Of course the kinks had to be ironed out, and that would take at least another decade."

"One kink being horror-show monsters manifesting in the basement," Amadeus said. "Yet, he continued."

"He never mentioned the ... things on the video. Not to me, or anyone else, as far as I know. Maybe at the time he didn't know. But even if he did, the desire to continue, to carry on regardless, is understandable. Imagine you've built a hyper-efficient engine capable of a million horsepower ... but didn't have a vehicle to put it in. He needed partners and funding to turn his research into something practical, to help build a vehicle for his engine."

Amadeus felt something twist and pinch in his gut. Had things gone differently, his father could have remade the world.

"Who else would know the technical details?" Amadeus said.

"As far as I know, only Esther, the other partners, and myself."

"You, uh, don't look like the killing type," Amadeus said.

"Thanks for that, my boy," Jones said. "But someone betrayed him. I can vouch for Esther, but not the others."

"Betrayal is one possibility. Simple theft is another," Amadeus said. He described the note about the reason for the biometric encryption on the research files.

"Looks like you're going to be playing detective," a gravelly voice said. Gravity. He was leaning against the door frame, two days worth of stubble making his face look like weathered, unpainted wood.

"Why?"

"Besides the fact that it's your best chance at clearing your own name, do you understand the damage you could do with a piece of tech like that? You could destabilize an entire continent. Forget about quantum computing or talking to dead people. That's peanuts. Think about what you could do if you could, and let's call a crow a crow, summon *demons* from another world. Demons, Amadeus. Think of all the theocrats, dictators, and military contractors that would love to get their finger on the trigger of this tech. You're playing detective because if we seek external assistance, it's almost guaranteed they'll hear about it"

"Gravity, what did you know about this?" Amadeus asked.

"Not much. Your father told me he was up to something

really big, that's it. And, as I said, that he might need my help. Looking back, I wouldn't have told me either. Who can you trust in a situation like this? It was a simple matter of operational security."

"Well, his security was apparently shit," Amadeus said.

"Then we have to assume two things," Gravity said. "One, the demon gate tech could already be in the wild. He's probably had bad actors sniffing around his filesystems for years. Chances are somebody saw something interesting before he added the extra security. And two, we won't be able to do a damn thing about said tech unless we understand it."

"So let me get this straight. Evil henchmen killed my father because they wanted to keep the research for themselves. Then they framed me for murder, but only because we managed to get away. Now I get to go figure out what my father was doing. If I manage to make sense of it, I'm supposed to, what, turn what I learn into evidence? Use that to establish a motive? To build my own defense that this wasn't just some psychotic suburban kid killing his dad, but instead an elaborate cover-up for what could be military-industrial espionage?"

"More or less," Jones said.

"I'm qualified because ..." Amadeus said.

"You're not, not alone, but you won't be alone," Gravity said.

"You forgot about the demons," Lilly said. "The little side effect."

"Of course," Amadeus said, "How could I forget about the existence of inter-dimensional demons? You know what? Four days ago, you know what I was worried about? That I had to give a commencement address at my university graduation. I thought that speech was the worst, most terrifying thing I had ever done. And you know what?"

"Congratulations, by the way," Jones said.

"I freaked out and ran away. I'd trade those problems for these any day. But I'll be damned if I run away again. I am going to find whoever did this and murder them. In a painful way. I'm going to—"

"Easy now," Gravity said. "You can't just run around killing people willy nilly ... You need a plan first. Trust me on that. Right now, our ignorance is a serious problem. Recklessness will only make matters worse."

"Lilly, honey," Jones said, "can you start a deep search on Tommy's digital life, especially anything related to his schedule and his contacts?"

"Dad, you know that I can't ..."

"You'll be fine."

Lilly nodded. Her brow had furrowed, and she'd crossed her arms over her chest.

"Even if we determine who the investors are," Gravity said, "there's going to be some field work. Two-factor biometric encryption ... that's blood samples and fingerprints, right?"

"That's right. For three of the four partners. But as I'm wanted for murder, I can't exactly hop on an airplane," Amadeus said.

Jones laughed. Everyone looked at him. He beamed like a proud father. "I have the perfect solution to this conundrum. Follow me." He turned his wheelchair and rolled out of the room towards the hangar, the motor's whine reverberating through the hall.

16

Jones rolled out to the big visual distortion in the middle of the hangar. Amadeus had seen cloaking tarps before, but he wanted to see what was beneath this one. He looked over at Gravity to see if he had any idea what Jones was going to show them. Gravity shrugged and followed Jones over. Jones grabbed one side of the tarp and told Gravity to pull the other. Together, they pulled the tarp away to reveal what looked like the body of a plastic and steel insect, all grey, dome-shaped like a beetle, only instead of legs, three cylinders the size of 55-gallon drums stuck out from arms on either side; two smaller ones were mounted on the tail. Amadeus pointed to one of the cylinders and said, "Variable–pitch turbofans?"

"Nailed it," Jones said, smiling, proud.

"But ... what *is* it?" Amadeus said, gesturing at the machine.

"What is it?" Jones repeated, feigning insult. "Why, it's only the future of personal transportation you're looking at, that's what it is. Using the latest in solar-powered hydrogen generation, this machine can transport two hundred kilograms almost six thousand kilometers on a single charge. Gentleman and lady, may I present the Pachyderm." No one said anything for a moment. Finally, Gravity broke the silence.

"Isn't a pachyderm an elephant?"

"Well, yes."

"But that doesn't look like an elephant," Amadeus said. "It doesn't have a trunk."

"Okay, look. I build things, but I don't do marketing. I couldn't sell food to the famished. So I hired a branding consultant. She told me an elephant with wings would be a great logo. What was that old movie with the flying elephant?" No one answered. "And before anyone says anything about elephants being heavy, let me ask you this: what do you know about nanosteel?"

"It's lighter than lithium and stronger than any other modern alloy or carbon fiber," Amadeus said. "It's nearly bulletproof. You sent me some, but it's a bitch on a lathe."

"Sorry you never got to use it. Anyway, this material is perfect for avionics. Most people can't get it yet, but I've got a guy who knows a girl who knows a guy that can get me all that I want."

"Have you actually flown this thing?" Gravity said.

"I've developed simulations and built models that operated in wind tunnels under unfavorable conditions."

"But you've never actually flown it," Amadeus said. He crossed his arms.

"You thick, insensitive ableist bastard. Look at me! Look at my body," Jones said, smacking the armrest of his wheelchair. "Do I have the physique of a test pilot? Do you really think I could safely fly this? Look, Amadeus, I am extending this as an offer to you, as a favor to the son of my old friend. You'll be the first person who will successfully fly the machine that will cause a paradigm shift in personal transportation. In fact, I would be *honored* if you would use my machine ... but if you mock it, I will retract the offer as one takes a toy from a petulant child." As Jones spoke, he craned his neck forward, holding onto the edges of his chair. After he finished, he leaned back and seemed to relax. "I assure you, the research is sound. I've worked on this for almost five years now."

"Still looks dangerous," Gravity said.

"Thank you for your astute observation," Jones said. "Of course it's dangerous, it's an experimental aircraft. But our young friend being wanted for murder and pursued by paramilitary hit men is pretty dangerous as well. In fact, I think he's damn lucky to have gotten here." He looked around the room. Amadeus nodded and took a deep breath.

"So how do you fly this thing?"

Under optimal conditions, the Pachyderm was fully autonomous, thanks to a proprietary navigation system Jones had hired a company to develop. However, Jones insisted that Amadeus learn to fly the Pachyderm using entirely manual controls. Amadeus, more aware than anyone that optimal conditions could turn to nightmares within minutes, was more than happy to oblige.

The first four times Amadeus crashed the Pachyderm, he hadn't even gotten off the mountain. The fifth time, the simulator informed him he was safely in the air.

On a smaller computer nearby, Gravity was also learning to operate the Pachyderm but was having less luck. He said the craft handled like a floating barge. Most of his crashes occurred when he changed directions too fast. The Pachyderm would tip over; upside down, with the automation disabled, the turbofans would make the ship rocket towards the ground.

"I need at least seven days to get her flight worthy," Jones had said. "We'll need to have you both do a couple of test flights. A simulator's one thing, but it's just that, a simulation. I'll call in the crew."

Early the next morning the contractors arrived, a group of three men and a woman. The men went right to work on the Pachyderm. "They're Koreans," Jones said, nodding to them, "but they're shy about speaking English. Terrified, in fact. Su Min, that's the girl, she's the team lead. I flew them in from Seoul a few months ago. I've never seen a harder-working team." As if hearing him talking about her, Su Min walked over to Jones, said something in Korean, gave everyone in the room a little nod, and hurried off to work on the Pachyderm. Jones rolled out of the room behind them, talking to them in Korean.

Amadeus spent the rest of the morning on the simulator. Eventually, he could remain stationary in the air, take off, and turn around. He still crashed on almost every landing. Banking still baffled him. When the Pachyderm crashed, a little cartoon angel floated up from the wreckage, playing a harp on its way to the sky. "That was me," Lilly said. "I had the programmers put that in there. Just a reminder that every action has consequences."

That afternoon, Amadeus returned to his father's journals, starting with the last entry.

July 16: I have decided to suspend this project. Results not consistent with hypothesis. Potential for harm is too great.

July 12: Same result, different creature. Like the others, it has mammalian, reptilian, and arachnid features. Yet, there's also something familiar about them, but I can't say what. Anyway, today I saw a claw; just the tip came through but it was the size of my head. I shut the machine down, severing the claw. Had to use the engine hoist to move it. I buried it in the backyard with the other ones.

Most days had a short entry, usually no more than two hundred words. Amadeus scanned through the entries; most talked about having the same results as the day before. One entry, however, caught his eye:

June 7: I've made a terrible mistake. I forgot to password-protect the server, and I'm pretty sure someone has gained access and downloaded the schematics and research. Not sure who, but the IP address was associated with a Mexican VPN provider. My first thought is the fourth partner, but maybe I'm blaming him because I already don't trust him. Need to implement tighter security measures.

Amadeus looked up from the computer. "Who is the fourth partner? Lilly, have you found anything else out about the other partners?"

"Only that your father did an excellent job of keeping them anonymous," Lilly said. "We've got Esther, that's it."

"Someone downloaded the schematics," Amadeus said. "I thought he was paranoid, but Gravity is right. Somebody out there knows how to make a demon gate."

17

In the evening, Gravity told Amadeus that, while they were waiting on the Pachyderm to be finished, he would teach him some basic self-defense. "Just in case this shit storm turns into a turd typhoon. Kung fu, karate, though, most of that's not really going to help you. It's not really practical. You need to know some judo and hapkido moves, get a guy in a position you can either punch his throat or kick him in the balls."

"Isn't that fighting dirty?"

"Sorry, Amadeus, but you're a scrawny bastard. Would you rather fight fair and die or fight dirty and win? If someone is attacking you, are you really concerned about fighting clean or dirty?"

"Guess not."

They rolled out an old carpet in the hangar. Gravity showed Amadeus how to throw a punch, break a hold, and the best way to fall. Nearby, the contractors drilled and welded as they disassembled and reassembled various parts of the Pachyderm. Occasionally showers of sparks would light up the room. When caught in freeze frame as they rained to the ground, they looked like the glowing branches of a weeping willow.

After only an hour of lessons, sitting on the mat after his last fall, Amadeus' lungs burned, his sides hurt, and his legs quivered like custard. "Enough, enough," Amadeus said.

Gravity smiled, helped him up, and slapped him on the back.

"Not bad for a coddled suburbanite," Grassal said. Gravity smirked. Grassal had quietly rolled himself into the hangar to watch them train. He was in a manual wheelchair, his foot wrapped and elevated on a stirrup. He still looked spaced out, but he had just awakened from two days of sleep.

"Hey Grassal," Amadeus said, kneeling next to his friend. "I am so sorry for what happened to you. This is my fault. You never should have been involved in this."

"Damn it, Amadeus, stop saying that. You're like a brother to me, and your father was like my father, okay? Of course I'm involved. We're entangled. And did you shoot me?" Amadeus shook his head. "Then relax."

"Still, it feels like it's my fault."

"Okay, fine, it's your fault. You shouldn't have shot me, you trigger-happy bastard."

"Grassal, I really am sorry—" Amadeus began, but Grassal interrupted him.

"No worries. Okay?" Amadeus looked at Grassal's elevated leg and furrowed his brow. Grassal arched his eyebrows. "Okay?"

Amadeus nodded as he stood up.

"How's the pain?" Gravity asked.

"Lilly's a good nurse. She gives me all the pills I want, said she's going to help me forget about the gaping hole in my calf."

"That's great news," Amadeus said. "About the pills. Not about the gaping hole. Just don't enjoy them too much."

"Grassal is a trooper," Gravity said. "And we're all entitled to a little vice now and then."

"That's right, listen to the big guy there," Grassal said, rolling his chair around in a tight circle. "I'm getting a little better on this thing. Next I'll be entering races."

"You'll be able to walk without a cane in a couple months," Gravity said. "You've just got to give it time to heal."

"Don't remind me," Grassal said.

"Were you a medic?" Amadeus asked.
Gravity nodded.
"Among other things."

18

After a shower, Amadeus settled into the data center with Grassal and Lilly. They ran a split screen on the wall, each of them sorting through different parts of the files. Grassal downloaded some scripts and cracks, trying to unlock the encryption. After a couple hours, he pushed the keyboard away in frustration.

"Damn it, you just can't crack these biometrics. Impossible," Grassal said.

"It's all good," Amadeus said. "We'll get what we need. I've got to track down all these people anyway; I'll get their fingerprints while I'm there."

"Or their fingers," Gravity said, leaning against the doorframe.

"God, Gravity. Really?" Amadeus said. Lilly giggled. Amadeus wasn't sure if she was giggling with him or at him.

"You do what you have to do," Gravity said, "and sometimes that includes partial dismemberment." Gravity winked at Amadeus.

"Um," Amadeus said. He imagined cutting off the fingers of the people who'd come into his house and found the thought not entirely unsatisfying.

"Amadeus, I think you should read this," Lilly said. She passed him a tablet. Running her hand across the top, she moved all the layers and files aside except for one, his father's journal. "This is an older entry, one of the longest, and, well, it's kind of personal. I stopped reading about halfway through."

Amadeus peered down and read words his father had written almost a year and a half ago. This, Amadeus realized, would've been after the one and only time he tried his hand at deviance and was caught shoplifting some electric wire from the local Uber Mart.

November 22nd: Amadeus is a resilient kid and I'm proud of him, but he's so scared of everything. This paper eating habit, it can't be good for his intestines. Maybe he's like me when I was his age, only he shows it in a very different way. One shoplifting charge? That's nothing. Uber Mart is a shithead company anyway.

Hell, I was a lot worse, drugs, fights, vandalism. I had my own crises, sure, my parents had divorced and I had to live with my dad, except the difference was my dad was a bastard drunk. Is it any wonder I did what I did? But one day, I think my son's going to be a better man than I could ever hope to be. He'll be strong, stronger than me I think. God, if it weren't for him ... after Celia died, I would've given up. I just hope he can find his focus. UConn's a great place, but he'd get so much more out of it if he really knew what he wanted. Maybe I've been too easy on him. I really should tell him all this.

Amadeus felt the tears start. He tried and failed to hold them back. Too much had happened. The world had changed. He didn't even care if anyone saw him cry. Seeing his father's words laid out like this, he felt like he had lost the world. Yet, he hadn't even given his father a funeral. He owed his dad that much. Closing the file, Amadeus addressed the room.

"We're having a funeral for my dad in two hours," he said, his voice a little too loud. "Grassal, I'd like you to say a few words. Gravity, you too, and maybe Jones can speak as well. Lilly, can you print off a picture of my dad? You should be able to find one online."

Two hours later, they had gathered at the edge of a rocky cliff near the bunker. Gravity had picked some wildflowers. Lilly had arranged the flowers around a picture of Tommy Brunmeier, adding a row of short candles in the front. The Koreans stood back at a respectful distance, silent, their hands crossed behind them. The wind tried to extinguish the candles, but they kept burning. Jones and Grassal had made it up the hill without any trouble; the path was smooth enough for wheelchairs. Grassal spoke first.

"Tommy Brunmeier was like a father to me. No, not like a father, he was a father, at least as close as I ever had to one. He was also a man who couldn't let go, and I think we could all learn something from his persistence," Grassal said, tearing up. He sniffled and gazed down into the valley. Lilly placed her hand on Grassal's shoulder. Jones spoke next.

"Once, back in the old days, when I was at MIT with your father, when we were just a little older than you kids," he nodded at Lilly, Amadeus, and Grassal, "and mastodons roamed the earth—Gravity, you probably remember those days —we were up on the roof of our apartment drinking beer, the old kind that came in cans, I forget the brand. After a few, your father, Amadeus, stood up and began making a speech to the woman who would become your mother, only at that time she was just a girl, a couple years older than Lilly is now. He said, and I remember this clearly enough to quote it, 'One day, you mark my words, I will change the world.' Well, now, here we are, Tommy. Your words have been duly noted and marked in the unwritten book of the world. You have indeed changed the world ... only the world doesn't know it yet."

After Jones' eulogy, Gravity began to sing "Amazing Grace" *a cappella*. His rich, battered baritone sounded like honey on sandpaper, with a vibrato that wavered like a flag in the breeze. The wind picked up even more and Amadeus began to sing.

Lilly joined him, taking his hand in hers. Grassal, Jones, and the Koreans joined in as well, their voices blending in harmony. The candles flickered and danced as the wind carried their song out over the cliff and across the rocky valley into the approaching night.

19

In the following days, when he wasn't learning to fly the Pachyderm, Amadeus learned the arts of war from Gravity: judo, hapkido, and shooting, as much of each as Amadeus could handle. "Maybe you'll never use these skills," Gravity had said, "but just knowing them will make you stronger." To teach him to shoot, Gravity took Amadeus into the woods, setting up targets first at ten, then thirty, then at one hundred meters. At first, Amadeus had been gun shy, jumping like popcorn at every shot, timid as a politician at an anarchist rally. This fear soon passed. Five days and four hundred rounds later, Gravity said he was impressed with his progress and thought Amadeus would have made a good sniper.

After the first week, Jones reported that the Pachyderm wouldn't be ready for at least another three weeks, that the new stabilizers were taking longer than they had expected, and that he was still waiting for a new batch of nanosteel to arrive. Amadeus shrugged and said that was fine; he still had a lot to learn. He didn't say that he rarely reached for paper.

In the evenings, after hours of flight and fight training, Amadeus spent his time with Lilly and Grassal, his personal CIA, working to assemble together a comprehensible narrative. So far they'd had little luck. Too many things remained hidden. Most nights they worked late, tweaking and refining the story, not unlike the contractors perfecting the Pachyderm: piece by piece. So far they had a pretty clear idea of what his father had made, and why, but not the how, the whos, or the whens. The identities and actions of the partners remained hidden. Amadeus had to assume that at least one of them was connected, involved, or holding information that could help him.

One evening, two weeks after they had arrived, Grassal had retired to bed early, grumbling about his leg, leaving Lilly and Amadeus alone in the lab. Lilly had loaded The Band's *The Last Waltz* on the music player. Amadeus was studying a journal entry. He called Lilly over and asked her to look at it. He watched her lips as she read the entry, mouthing the words. He wanted to pull her close, to feel her lips against his. Stretching his neck like a turtle, he tried to kiss her. As soon as his lips brushed her cheek, she grabbed his wrist, twisted it behind his back, and leaned him back in his chair.

"Just what do you think you're doing?" Lilly said, looking down at him and digging her fingernails into his forearm. "Do I look like your fuck puppet?"

"Oh my god, I'm sorry, I just thought that ..."

"You thought I was being nice to you because I was in love with you? Is that it?"

"Um. Not love, but—" Lilly let the chair fall backwards. Amadeus broke his fall with his hands.

"Let me tell you something, Amadeus Brunmeier. We knew each other when we were kids, but that doesn't mean we have some automatic relationship. I'm not helping you because of that. You make me nervous. I get tense around you. You're not unattractive, but ... you're kind of weird. And you smell like cheese." Amadeus looked away.

"Then why are you helping me?"

"Besides the morbid curiosity factor? Because the sooner we get your shit straightened out, the sooner I can get out of here."

"You want to leave?"

"You're as dumb as a dumpster, aren't you? Before you showed up, I was going out of my mind. My father and I were weeks away from leaving. We had just submitted a bid on a huge house near Seattle. The movers were ready to go."

"Why do you want to leave?"

"Why do I want to leave? Look around you, Amadeus. We live in the goddamn middle of nowhere. In a *semi-secret underground bunker*. My father has to import expensive contractors to work here. And look at my situation. I want to live, to go to concerts, to be able to walk outside and see something besides scrub pine. All my school friends have moved away, and even if that weren't the case, my current situation isn't particularly conducive to an active social life."

"Why not just leave by yourself?"

"It's not that simple. My father, he depends on me. You've seen him. You know he's very ill. And nurses, he scares them off. We've gone through three LPNs and an RN just in the past year. But then you come along, and poof!" She made a gesture of a celebrant throwing confetti into the air. "All our plans are gone. Now I'm stuck. With you. A weird skinny kid with the social skills of a tree stump."

"Lilly, I'm sorry, I just misread the situation."

"Misread? You're not even using the same *language*. You don't know a damn thing about the world."

"You're right. I am a nerdy kid. I don't have any social skills. And I'm sorry for trying to kiss you. It seemed like the right thing to do. But don't think I'm not grateful. For your help, your company, it really makes things easier, right now is ... with everything. You make things less awful." Amadeus began to cry. He put his hands over his eyes and turned away from Lilly. She couldn't see him like this.

"Oh, shit, Amadeus." She placed a hand on his shoulder. Amadeus felt the heat of her hand conducting through his shirt. "Amadeus?" Amadeus said nothing. "Amadeus? Look at me." He turned to face her. The anger had drained from her face.

"I'm sorry, too. I didn't mean to be that way. It's okay. I didn't think ... let's be a team, okay? As equals? I'll help you, and that will help me. Okay?"

"Okay," Amadeus said. "As long as you don't hit me too hard."

"I won't hit you if you don't try to make out with me."

20

Five weeks after Amadeus and Grassal had arrived at the Jones compound, wounded and terrified, after Grassal had moved from wheelchair to crutches, after Amadeus had learned what his father was really working on, after Amadeus had grown stronger than he had ever been, and after he'd realized he was falling in love with Lilly, Jones announced over a static-shrouded PA system that the Pachyderm was ready for its first test flight.

The tall Korean pulled the hangar door open. Another taxied the Pachyderm through the open door and outside with a forklift. Everyone in the hangar followed the Pachyderm, a little parade. Jones spoke with the contractors, first in English then in Korean, asking questions about the condition of this or that part, double-checking that they had double-checked everything.

"Lilly, your dad's as nervous as Amadeus before a graduation speech," Grassal said, leaning forward on his aluminum crutches.

"No," Amadeus said, "he handles it much better." Amadeus felt ready, confident. He had logged over a hundred hours on the simulator, hadn't crashed for a week, and, just to see if he could, even managed to land the Pachyderm on the head of the Statue of Liberty. Yes, it was only a simulation, but it was a good simulation. Amadeus called it his crowning achievement. Lilly had smacked his arm for that.

Su Min said, "*Urineun Pachyderm Two hyuenjae imnnida.* I present Pachyderm Two!" When she finished speaking, her face was bright red.

"Um," Amadeus said, pivoting on his heels to face Jones, "what does she mean, two? You never said there was another Pachyderm. What happened to the last one?" Jones looked at the contractors. They all examined their feet. Finally, Lilly broke the silence.

"It crashed and the pilot died," Lilly said. "Engine failure." Jones shot a laser look at his daughter, but she shrugged. "You said not to tell him, but you didn't say what to do if he asked."

"Jesus, Lilly," Amadeus said, putting his hands on his hips.

"Wow. This is awkward," Grassal said.

"There's nothing to worry about. This one has six vertical turbofans and two horizontals. Even if four verticals fail, you'll still be able to land." Jones said. "And on the first Pachyderm, I'm ashamed to admit, I was too cheap to use the best. I used second-hand turbofans and scrounged helicopter parts. It was only supposed to be a prototype anyway, used in a wind tunnel. The pilot insisted he take it out. This one has all new parts, the best of the best: Lockheed turbofans, Boeing avionics, electrically-charged cloaking paint, top-of-the-line solar-hydro fuel generation, and the body itself, it's entirely my design but it checks out one hundred and ten percent."

"How do we know your design is sound?" Gravity said. A mischievous grin spread over Jones' face before he spoke.

"Because I designed it." After waiting a beat, Jones continued: "But seriously, I sent schematics, nondisclosure agreements, and bottles of twenty-year-old single malt to some aeronautical engineer friends of mine; these guys are serious rocket scientists. They returned my designs with only slight suggestions for improvement. I followed their recommendations, sent them back, and they gave me the all clear."

Amadeus and Gravity looked at each other, shrugged their shoulders, and climbed up into the Pachyderm. Amadeus had sat in the cockpit before but only in the hangar. Out here, on the top of a mountain, with the grey and green land spread out below him, it seemed more real. This was no simulation. More than one or two mistakes, and he would die. But not today, he thought, not today. He wouldn't make any mistakes. A sudden *cheucrash* made Amadeus jump. He looked over. Jones held the neck of a broken champagne bottle he had smashed against the Pachyderm.

Gravity sat in the copilot's chair, hands folded in his lap, as Amadeus ran his preflight checks. Battery level full. Wind speed low. The control panel was flat black with silver switches, one switch for each of the horizontal and vertical engines, a level for thrust control, a yoke, and, Jones' idea of a joke, a pair of fuzzy dice hanging down from the ceiling. On a sturdy stand, a large tablet computer functioned as the interface for the communications and navigation system. Besides the fuzzy dice, the interior was unadorned, nanosteel walls and frame covered with spray-on sound dampening. The floor under them was grated, all the wires and interfaces for the avionics exposed. The door sealed out the outside air, allowing cabin pressurization. The features were intentionally limited; according to Jones, every extra gadget and feature was a potential point of failure.

On the computer, Amadeus opened the navigation system and entered a short course around the ridge, a round trip of two hundred kilometers, all manual navigation, no autopilot. He would stay low, just in case. No matter what Jones said, he wouldn't trust this machine until he had some actual time learning to fly it.

A low vibration filled the cockpit. "Sound okay? Can you hear me?" Amadeus said into his headset. Gravity nodded, tested his, and came through loud and clear. Through the window, Amadeus could see everyone backing away from the

Pachyderm.

Before he started, he remembered the first time he rode a motorcycle. It was a small bike, a 50cc Honda. He and his parents had gone to a resort in Maine. Near the resort, a dirt bike track offered rentals. After making a flurry of soon-forgotten promises, he persuaded his mother to rent the bike for him. At first he was unsteady, keeping his feet down, driving slow. Within fifteen minutes, he had crashed. The proprietor of the rental shop came over and helped him up. Amadeus was twelve at the time, the proprietor in his twenties. Amadeus did everything he could to be strong and hold back his tears. The proprietor told him riding a bike was like riding an orca: if it smelled fear, if you weren't confident, it would throw you into the water and eat you up. If you show it who's boss, though, you'll totally own it. Amadeus didn't think to ask how many orcas the proprietor had ridden.

He increased the speed of the verticals and the Pachyderm lifted from the ground. Confident, like an orca rider, Amadeus made the craft rise higher and higher, the altimeter creeping steadily upward toward 3,330 meters. Below, his friends grew smaller and smaller. Amadeus flipped the switch to run a current through the cloaking paint. Looking through the window, the engines faded away, replaced by a slightly blurred view of the ground below. If anyone were looking up, they wouldn't see anything more than a breeze.

They flew north, dry mountains passing underneath them. As Amadeus flew, he thought of Lilly. He was angry she hadn't told him about the dead pilot, but he still wished she could join him; he'd rather have her with him than Gravity. Though, he supposed that if things went bad, this strange war dog might be a good man to have by his side.

Beneath them, farmland, its irrigation circles in the middle like chips on a bingo card, gave way to suburban houses, five-bedroom single-family homes that had been converted into four-family apartments, each development serviced by autonomous buses bound for Denver. According to his map, Denver lay over a hundred kilometers to the west.

"Want to see Denver?" Gravity asked him. Amadeus thought about it for a moment, wondered how many laws he would be breaking by flying over a major city, and decided not to.

"That can't be legal."

"You're still worried about the law?"

"A little. Maybe."

"Maybe you ought to get over that. Think of it this way, the law is like inertia. It works for you until it starts working against you. Right now, it's definitely working against you, and if you want to get it working for you again, you're going to have to get comfortable in grey areas." As he spoke, Gravity gazed out the window. His brow seemed to have some extra wrinkles in it.

"I don't understand," Amadeus said, achingly baffled.

"All I'm saying is don't worry until you're actually in trouble."

"That doesn't mean I should go around and flagrantly smash every law like a drunken monkey," Amadeus said. "And I'm kind of already in trouble."

"Hmm. You've got a point. If you hadn't guessed, I'm more a direct-approach kind of guy."

A little tone dinged in his headphones. They had reached one of the way points he had programmed onto the map. Amadeus turned the craft west, making a forty-degree banking turn away from the suburbs and towards the Pacific Ocean. Waves of the Pacific crashed far away, but Amadeus would forever associate west with the Pacific, east with Atlantic. Canada was north, Mexico south. His perspective on geography was decidedly American.

"Let's take this thing up and see what it can do," Amadeus said. Gravity mumbled something into the headset. When Amadeus asked him to repeat it, he wouldn't. In fact, Amadeus noticed Gravity was gripping the armrests of his chair as if he might fall out should he let go. "Are you okay?" Amadeus asked him.

The clouds were lower in this direction, puffy and bubbly like clusters of white grapes. At first, they flew just beneath them, then Amadeus began to vary their altitude, flying into, then out of, the clouds. The altimeter read 4,300 meters. Snow covered the mountain peaks below.

"No, I'm fine, just fine."

"If you're fine than you won't mind when I do this," Amadeus said, pushing the yoke forward. The Pachyderm dropped. Amadeus felt his stomach lift, just like on a rollercoaster. The phone Jones had given Amadeus rose from the console. For just a moment, they were weightless. Amadeus leveled things out and came to a floating stop.

"Please, don't do that again."

"Airsick some?" Amadeus asked. "Sorry about that. I had no idea."

"Take me back. I can't do this," Gravity said.

For the last leg of the trip, Amadeus kept things steady and level. They followed a river for awhile, and passed over a couple of abandoned strip mines. The areas left behind looked like an artist's imagining of earth after a nuclear holocaust. The slopes were gone, the rich wrinkles of the earth's crust replaced by blasted, stripped, flattened, bulldozed, and grated fields. By the time they reached the third waypoint of their loop, Gravity was pale, silent, and still visibly nervous. Amadeus wondered how anyone could find flying so disagreeable; he felt focused, exhilarated, and sharp as a needle. Such freedom; he could go anywhere in the world. Sure, the Pachyderm wasn't as fast as a jet, but he didn't have to deal with other passengers or go through airport security. The best part, he was in control of his craft and his trip and his life, not in the hands of some nameless, faceless pilot. For the first time since before his graduation, he felt his sense of independence returning.

With ease, he brought the Pachyderm around for the last leg of the test flight and landed without any trouble, dust spinning and swirling around the craft. Jones and the contractors had monitored the entire flight on handheld computers. Amadeus hopped out, energized by and satisfied with the flight. Gravity, however, staggered out, looking like he'd had too much to drink, leaned against the craft's hull, and gagged.

"No problems?" Jones asked. Since they had left, he had donned an old leather pilot's cap, making Amadeus think of children who, in the early days of television, would dress up in costumes to watch their favorite show. But Jones wasn't that old.

"I was about to ask you the same question," Amadeus said. "We were going to fly over Denver, but I was worried about showing up on radar."

"Nanosteel is not only light, but it's also radar absorbent. Combine that with the cloaking paint, and the Pachyderm is damn near invisible."

"Gravity and the Pachyderm don't seem to play well together," Amadeus said.

"I'm sure he has his reasons. This is an experimental craft we're talking about, not exactly like hopping on a 767, now is it?" Amadeus shrugged. Jones yelled something to the contractors in Korean. Su Min gave him a thumbs up. "The first flight of the Pachyderm Two is a success. Bonuses for everyone!"

21

After a celebratory cookout, catered by the Koreans, Amadeus was re–reading some of his father's log entries when Jones rolled into the room. "I've contacted Esther. She'll be expecting you. But she's a very busy girl and doesn't have much time to spare. Here are the coordinates, address, and phone number." He handed Amadeus a scrap of paper with neat, handwritten numbers. "Esther lives in Midtown. Happily, her building happens to have a helicopter pad. Once you get into the city, you'll need a disguise. Just in case anyone might recognize you." He pulled out a little brown satchel. "Esther said she's seen your picture in the paper, but I explained things to her and she's, um, sympathetic to your situation. She's a friend; she'll help us. As for the other partners, she might be able to help you find at least one, maybe even two of them. If we could crack this ridiculous security that your father used, then maybe you wouldn't have to run all over the world, but right now ... you've got to run all over the world."

"I don't mind," Amadeus said. "I kind of like flying, and it feels better than sitting around."

Amadeus spent the remainder of the evening studying an aeronautical chart of North America with a ruler, pencil, and notebook, manually plotting out his flight to New York. The computer navigation system would work fine, but having a backup never hurt. Besides that, maps, with their implicit promise of adventure, excited him and gave him something to do while the contractors made final tweaks to the Pachyderm.

Later in the evening, after Gravity and Jones had gone to bed, Amadeus, Lilly, and Grassal were in the data center together, but instead of working on the files they were playing rummy, enjoying each other's company and some well-earned downtime. They were playing to one thousand points. So far, Lilly was two hundred points ahead of either of them. Grassal laid down four aces, leaving Amadeus with a handful of unplayed royals.

"Why?" Amadeus said, smacking the table. "I thought we had a truce."

"All's fair in love and torture," Grassal said.

"Which one is this?" Lilly asked.

Lilly ended up winning the match, with Grassal in second. Amadeus couldn't regain his momentum after the betrayal. Grassal said something about basking in sweet defeat then crutched off to bed.

"Why didn't you tell me about the other pilot?" Amadeus said. "And don't say I didn't ask. How was I supposed to know?"

"You weren't supposed to know," Lilly said. "I'm sorry, maybe I should have told you. But my father needed a test pilot. I thought it would complicate things. It's not a big deal. This design is much better."

"That is a big deal. How am I supposed to trust you?" Amadeus said.

"Maybe you're not," Lilly said. She spread the cards across the table in a practiced flourish then scooped them up. With her thumb, she flicked the top card from the deck into Amadeus' lap. "Good night," she said. Amadeus watched her stride off, out the door and into the hallway. He picked the card up from his lap. The king of hearts. The suicide king.

22

Morning came. Everyone at the Jones compound rose early. Outside, quarrelsome streaks of saffron-colored clouds hung overhead, but satellite images of the continent showed nothing but clear skies. Amadeus loaded his limited supplies into the Pachyderm.

"I'm trusting you to take good care of this craft," Jones said. "We've put years of work into it. Flying it, I know, is not without risk, but you've shown yourself to be a capable pilot. Keep it safe."

"I will. And, thanks, Jones, for everything." Amadeus bent down and gave Jones a hug, as much as he could. "I wish I could take you for a ride in the Pachyderm."

"I wish it, too, my boy," Jones said, "but nature hasn't been kind to my body. Lilly always said what I lack in the body I make up for in the brain. Isn't that right, honey?"

"That's right, Daddy," Lilly said. "Amadeus, do be careful ... out there." Amadeus noticed she said this the same way her father did, giving "out there" the same tone someone would use to describe a lecherous waiter.

"I know you'll have Gravity with you, but still." She gave him a chaste hug. Amadeus felt his face warm. Neither had mentioned what had passed between them last night.

Grassal came up and leaned on his crutches. "My man, you

fly safe. I know you, you will. Here's the phone, finished right on time, just like we talked about." Grassal handed him a black phone a little larger than a business card with a small white attachment. "It's got all the data from the statue, a thumb scanner built in to the touch screen and a glucometer, like the kind diabetics use, on its side, for the blood samples. It was a super-simple mod. The phone is pretty old, Jones gave it to me, but it'll work. It has GPS and all that, but you shouldn't need it. Ten years ago it would've been a super computer, but you know how it goes, Moore's Law and all that. But for what you need, it's first-class." Grassal had a faraway look in his eyes, still on a prodigious amount of pain pills. Amadeus wanted to say something to him, but decided this too would work itself out. His friend was no fool. Amadeus thanked him for modding the phone.

Finally, there was nothing left to do except leave. All the goodbyes had been said. Without another word, Amadeus climbed up into the craft and started his preflight checks. Gravity climbed up on the side after him, but instead of sitting in the copilot's chair, he just shook Amadeus' hand. Amadeus felt a slip of paper against his palm. Gravity mouthed the words, "Read this later." Amadeus stuffed the note into his pocket with as much discretion as he could muster.

"I'm sorry, I can't go," Gravity said, his voice at full volume. "You saw what happened to me on the flight. Besides, I'm an old man. I would just slow you down."

"Old man? What do you mean?" Amadeus asked, but when he looked at Gravity's face he did seem older, as if he had aged ten years overnight.

"I'm glad you say that, but I have," his eyes darted to Amadeus' hand and back, "other concerns to address." Amadeus wanted to open the note right there, to find out why Gravity was backing out, but Gravity had made sure to give it to him out of sight of everyone else. Amadeus decided it was better to wait.

"Suit yourself. I would love to have you along, but if you can't go, you can't go," Amadeus said. The Pachyderm rattled. He adjusted then equalized the speed of the turbofans and smoothed things out.

"Good boy, that's the spirit," Gravity said. He reached into his pocket, pulled out a white envelope, and handed it to Amadeus. "Five grand in unmarked, untraceable greenbacks. A tiny part of the retainer paid me by your father." Amadeus furrowed his brow. He wanted to refuse, but he needed the money.

"Thanks," Amadeus said as he took the envelope and put it in his pocket. "For everything." Gravity hopped down from the Pachyderm, surprisingly agile for a man with such a haggard look. As Gravity walked away, Amadeus heard Jones asking him why he wasn't going.

Amadeus fired up the verticals, running the RPMs up until he felt the craft begin to lift. All around, dust flew up in little tunnels, making everyone squint as he lifted off. Out the window, he watched the ground fall farther away, and his friends, the closest thing he had to a family, grow smaller and smaller until they were only small, round points of life on the earth below.

He hovered, stationary, as he double-checked his heading and waypoints on the flight computer. A hissing sound filled the cabin as the automatic pressurization system started up. He rose and applied forward thrust. He leaned his chair back and prepared for the long flight over the mountains, across the prairie, and off to the great green East.

Curious about the note from Gravity, he pulled it out and read it.

Jones isn't what he seems. I'm going to try a different approach to this situation. And I don't get airsick. Good luck.
—Gravity

Amadeus wondered what he meant. Jones had helped Amadeus, had given him the ability to get the answers he needed, and now Gravity was saying Jones wasn't what he seemed? What was he, then? Amadeus decided he would have to wait to find out. This note didn't change anything.

After two hours, somewhere over Kansas, at around 4,500 meters, once he had finally settled into what he expected to be a ten-hour flight, a dust storm started, the brown earth swirling around him, the view outside as clear as static on an old television. He flew entirely with his instruments, keeping an eye on the turbofan function monitors. Needing reassurance, he called Jones. Jones' face came on the screen.

"Hey, I'm in a dust storm. Is there anything to worry about? Dust in the engines, anything like that?"

"Shouldn't be. How bad is it?"

"I can't see a thing," Amadeus said, "except brown. I'm flying through the Sahara Desert here." Amadeus turned the camera outside to face the storm.

"Just in case," Jones said. "You better take it down. Where are you, Kansas?" Amadeus said that was right. "Mostly farms and fields. Take it down, cover the Pachyderm with the tarp, wait it out. We never really got to test it in the dust."

Just then, a red light began flashing on the turbofan monitor. Amadeus said, "I'm having engine trouble. The Pachyderm doesn't like the dust."

"Then stop talking to me and land the damn thing," Jones said.

Amadeus began his descent. At 800 meters, he still couldn't see the ground. Trying to keep the Pachyderm level with what he hoped was flat ground, he went lower and lower, his rate of descent as slow as he could make it. The wind whipped around the craft, occasionally rocking it back and forth, but he kept a tight grip on the yoke.

Thirty meters from the ground, an alarm began beeping. Diagnostics reported the troublesome turbofan had shut itself down. As he examined the error log, the craft lurched, and he heard the creaking and groaning of metal on metal. The Pachyderm tilted as its skids touched down on what Amadeus realized was a sloped metal roof. He had landed on a building that, given the nearby fencing, he suspected was a barn.

Before he could get back into the air, the barn collapsed underneath him, tilting sideways under the weight of the Pachyderm. After it came down, the craft sat askew atop the rubble. Amadeus still held the yoke, as if to prevent the craft from floating away. Seeing no one in the fields around him, he called Jones to report what had happened.

"You'll need to take it apart. Best bet is probably to clean the motor with compressed air, degreaser or, if you're in a pinch, gasoline. Don't use water."

"Gasoline," Amadeus said, as if he had never heard anything more unsavory. He didn't mention the collapsed barn. "How far can I fly with a broken turbofan?"

"You could theoretically keep going, but you'll have to stop more often to recharge and, if another one fails, you'll be grounded for a while. Best to take care of it now. It shouldn't take you more than a couple hours. Use the tarp. With the power off, the cloaking paint won't work as well."

So Amadeus waited for the dust to pass and the turbofan to cool. Within an hour, the dust had died down, but the air was still hazy. He put on a pair of goggles, donned leather gloves and, holding the small toolbox, jumped out onto the metal wreckage below him. He unscrewed the housing to the turbofan, put the screws in his pocket, then lifted the unit from the pitch control arm. It was bulky but lighter than he expected. Back in the small cargo area, he sat on his duffel bag and disassembled the unit, removing first the duct fan then the compressor, which was as big as his head but as light as a basketball. When he turned it in his hands, sand poured out, and he found a length of bailing wire had become entangled with the compressor.

As he unwrapped the last of the bailing wire, the cabin door opened. When he turned, he was staring at a sun-bleached man with big sideburns and a straw hat. In his hand he held a tire iron.

"Shit," Amadeus said.

"Shit indeed. Son, you smashed my barn," the man said. At first Amadeus couldn't understand his accent. "Well, what say you? And what in creation is this thing?"

"I'm sorry, I didn't mean to, it was a dust storm and I had to land somewhere. The air was so bad I couldn't even see where I was landing."

"You're lucky weren't no cattle in there, I had them out grazing when the storm came. But now, where they going to stay? I can't exactly put them up in the living room." The farmer adjusted his hat. "Son, when I saw your machine come down here, I had no idea what in the hell I was going to see. I say, half a my mind thought I was going to see a spaceman sitting in this here craft. Now, though, I see this was an honest mistake, an accident. So tell me, son, who are you?"

Amadeus gave the farmer his good-student smile before he spoke.

"My uncle is an inventor.   I'm his test pilot. My name's George Lawson," Amadeus said, the lie rolling off his tongue like honey.

"Well, George Lawson, you done a heap of damage to my cattle barn. Now, what do you propose to do about it?"

"How about two thousand dollars cash, right now?" The farmer arched an eyebrow and whistled through his teeth.

"That's a whole bunch of money for a test pilot to be carrying, but I'd need twice that to rebuild."

"Sir, I'm really sorry. It was an accident. I can give you thirty-five hundred." Amadeus thought fifteen hundred would last him at least until after New York. The farmer nodded his head and gave him a non-committal grunt.

"A flying machine," the farmer said. "I never seen such a

thing. Sure, I've been around Cessnas and Pipers and things like that, but this ... hmm ... how much weight can you carry?"

"For short trips at a low altitude, I can strip it down and carry just over four hundred kilograms," Amadeus said. The farmer thought about this, seemed to be doing some calculations in his head.

"I tell you what. I'll make you a deal. What you offered won't cover me, but I need a job done, and if you do it I think it'd be worth the remainder. Right now, see, the spider mites are swarming our soybeans, they're having a regular bonanza out there. Me and a couple other fellows, we hire the same old boy to dust them with insecticide, but unfortunately he's lost his license for flying on the bottle," the farmer said. Amadeus raised one eyebrow, confused at this last expression. He imagined someone riding a bottle of champagne across the sky, using the fizz as a propellant. Seeing Amadeus' expression, the farmer made the international sign for drinking. "The boy was drunk, you see, on corn whiskey or some thing or another, and he lost his wings."

"I see. Okay, how would this work?"

"I started working on that the second I saw your plane, or whatever you call that thing."

23

The farmer set to work. He placed a plastic drum inside the Pachyderm and attached a wide bar with several nozzles to the bottom back of the craft using nylon straps. The Pachyderm, though not designed for cargo, did have latch points on the inside floor. While the farmer worked, Amadeus contacted Jones. When he told Jones about his situation, Jones laughed and said, "Do what the farmer asks, just don't let him call the cops, drill holes, or do any welding; any of these things could fuck up my craft and/or your precarious legal situation."

By late afternoon Amadeus was flying low, dumping pesticide over straight green rows of soybeans. The rows reminded him of the wires of an old IDE hard drive cable. Between runs, he would land and hop out. He and the farmer, wearing dust masks, would load more pesticide onto the Pachyderm. During his final trip, the sun began to set, and he flew the last trip in the dark using instruments, memory, and landing lights. When he finished, the farmer shook his hand. His hands were surprisingly soft.

"Boy, you did good work, a lot faster than that old drunk of a pilot who used to do it. I see you're a man on your way somewhere else, but if you ever needed an honest occupation, you could keep yourself busy with that thing for years. Why, you could work all spring and summer here then spend your winters down on some Mexican beach."

Amadeus smiled. "I guess I could, but I'm just so busy with these test flights. Maybe in the future."

"The future's a long way away. For now, why don't you stick around for dinner? The wife's made up a roast with fixins: potatoes, carrots, corn. Put some meat on you, you are a skinny little guy." Amadeus was pretty hungry, and he certainly hadn't eaten any home cooked food since, well … maybe since his mother was alive. At the Jones compound, at university, and back east with his father, he'd eaten too much prepackaged and carry-out food. His father had done well to boil eggs, and within two years of his mother's death, Amadeus had learned the menus of most of the local franchise restaurants by heart.

"Okay, I'll eat with you," he said. The farmer slapped him on the shoulder and told him to follow him inside. On the wooden porch of the farmhouse, under a moth-swarmed light, they sat across from each other at a glass-topped wicker table. The farmer called out to his wife in Spanish.

"You speak Spanish," Amadeus half-asked, half-stated.

"Kind of have to when your wife is Guatemalan," the farmer said. "I never did properly introduce myself to you. Name's Clifton McComas. My wife's name is Zora."

His wife came out the screen door. She reminded Amadeus of a black–haired bowling pin. She was smiling when she came out, but when she saw Amadeus she narrowed her eyes. As she scrutinized him, a current ran up his legs to his stomach. She knows, he thought, and she knows that I know that she knows.

"It is nice to meet you," she said in English, her voice flat, a little accented. She set a glass pitcher of lemonade on the table. The ice cubes clinked against the sides. "The roast is almost finished. Ten minutes." She went back inside.

"How did the two of you meet?" Amadeus asked.

"I was in the military, stationed near Tuxtla Gutierrez, Mexico during the Narco War. The *traficantes* had pretty much taken over Guatemala, demanding tribute from the villages. I'd say a quarter of the country was coerced into working for them in some way or another. Ugly, bloody stuff. My job was to help refugees. You see, I'm not a fighting man; I was actually in the military as a conscientious objector.

"Well, my job was in relocation and re-settlement. And poor Zora, she came into my office. All the damn NGOs had given her what we call the Yankee Shuffle, going from one place, one camp to another. Even after all she'd been through, I had never seen a more beautiful girl, and she was a girl at the time, maybe seventeen, but hell, I was barely twenty, so it weren't like I was robbing the cradle. Anyway, one thing led to another and soon we were both in love. We got married in San Cristobal de las Casas, beautiful little place by the way, and came back to America. Unfortunately, she's taken a liking to cheeseburgers, milkshakes, and all things potato. It's hell on her complexion, but I still think she's a doll."

Amadeus nodded and sipped his lemonade.

"I'm sorry, that might've been a little more than what you asked for. Tell me, son, you have a girl? Or a boy? That's okay, too. I got a cousin up in Lawrence, runs with a bunch of real funny fellas, but they're good men. Even had a van full of them come up here one year for caroling. Man, could they sing."

"No, I'm not gay. The girl I like now, she hates me. And there was this other one, but I'll probably never see her again."

"The latter," Clifton said, "those are the sweetest kind."

Zora returned with a blue-speckled braising pot full of roast beef and sloshing broth, along with potatoes, carrots, onions, and celery. She also laid out tortilla chips and a thick salsa. Amadeus was too hungry to be paranoid.

"She grows all the ingredients for salsa in a kitchen garden she keeps. She's got tomatoes, cilantro, onions, a little garlic. Don't you, hon?" Zora just nodded. After another trip to the kitchen she came out with plates and silverware. The knives, forks, and plates rattled and clinked as she set them upon the glass tabletop. She then plopped down in the chair, but motioned for them all to serve themselves.

"Why so surly?" Clifton asked, looking at his wife. She glowered back at him as he cut into the roast. The knife scraped against the pot's metal bottom. He set a big slab of meat on his plate then covered it with juices from the pot. Amadeus cut his own piece and took a bite.

"Wow, this is wonderful. Really. Best food I've had in a long, long time," Amadeus said, earnest as a schoolboy. The meat was tender and salty. He chewed slowly, savoring the food. As he chewed, though, he felt Zora watching him when she wasn't staring at her plate. Her dislike for him rose up like the steam coming off the mashed potatoes. Every time a fork scraped against a plate, Amadeus felt a sick feeling in his chest. He balled up a piece of napkin and rolled it between his fingers.

"Tell me about your family and your school, George. You a college boy?" Clifton said.

"I just finished," Amadeus said, "at Stanford. I studied computer science. I hope to head east for grad school, but I'm not really sure where yet."

"Well, if you're anything like your uncle, you'll do really well."

Amadeus nodded and scooped a heaping chipful of salsa from the bowl. Red chunks of tomato fell from the side. The first thing Amadeus tasted was the watery-freshness of the cilantro, then a little spice from the jalapeno chunks. Zora openly stared at him now. A vein on her forehead, the one right down the middle, was standing out. Amadeus knew the salsa wasn't that hot. He looked over at Clifton. He seemed oblivious as he chewed his food, a goat grazing in the middle of a firefight.

Amadeus ate quickly, hoping an empty plate would be a good excuse to leave, but when he finished his first serving, Clifton piled more on his plate. Zora watched her husband in disgust. Amadeus knew what she was thinking: how could he be serving food to a patricidal monster? It would be so easy, Amadeus thought, for people to hate him, especially if they didn't know him, if they only knew what they had read in the newspapers. The most recent he'd seen was a little capsule article about himself in the Opinion section of the pop culture website *Nuestro Tiempo Loco*. The article made three claims: one, Amadeus was a member of a Satanic death cult; two, the murder was a ritualistic killing; and three, that the intent of the killing had been to summon a demon.

Zora, after obviously kicking her husband under the table, finally threw down her silverware in disgust. It clattered on the plate as she stomped inside. Clifton looked at Amadeus, shrugged, and took another bite of his roast beef. A moment later, the screen door swung open with a clap and Amadeus was staring at a double-barreled shotgun.

"He is not George. He is Amadeus Brunmeier. He killed his father," Zora said to Clifton. "Mi amor, this man is wanted by the police. I saw his picture in the magazine not long ago."

"Those are lies. I didn't kill him. Other people did, bad people, and they wanted to set me up, to blame me for it. I'm going to reach into my pocket now, Misses McComas, because I owe your husband some money." With painstaking care, his every move watched by Zora, Amadeus retrieved the money Gravity had given him and counted out thirty-five hundred dollars.

"I can't take any of that. Not from you," Clifton said.

"I pay my debts," Amadeus said. He sat the stack of bills beside his plate.

Clifton looked from his wife to Amadeus and back. The gun in Zora's hand shook.

"Now, Zora, honey, lower the gun. You for one should know better than anybody that you can't trust everything the government says. George, Amadeus, whatever your name is, I'm not one to judge, but you need to leave. Now."

Amadeus set down his fork and knife. They clinked against the glass tabletop.

"I'm sorry for the trouble. Thanks for the food." He backed

away, toward the Pachyderm, thankful they had detached the dusting equipment earlier.

Back in the Pachyderm, he trembled and stuffed the piece of napkin into his mouth. The fibers separated, and he rolled them over his tongue, concentrating on the sensation. He took the Pachyderm back up but he felt spent, like he'd just finished a day of training with Gravity. Using the map, he found an isolated place to land. Safely landed, he threw the tarp over the craft. Under the light of the prairie moon, he fell asleep in minutes.

In the morning, he crossed the rest of the continent, watching as Midwestern fields changed to lush green mountains. Along the way, he scanned through various air traffic control frequencies. None made mention of his craft, just as Jones had promised. As afternoon became evening, he approached New York. After turning the landing over to the navigation system, he called Esther to let her know he was nearly there. She said she could get out for a bit, but she had a meeting later with an important client.

Esther's building, all glass, carbon composites, and solar panels, towered over the others. The Pachyderm's landing lights illuminated a woman in white who stood on the roof, her hair blown around by the descending craft. She shielded her eyes as she backed towards the stairs. After landing, he shut things down and hopped out. Esther greeted him with a powerful handshake then, looking him up and down, she said, "Come here," and pulled him in for a hug. She smelled like cigarettes and chai tea.

"You look a lot like your mother, you know that?" She gave him a sad smile. "I'm sorry about what happened."

"You knew my mother?"

"Long ago."

He changed the subject. "So you were involved with my father's research." She nodded."I need your help with a couple of things."

"I know."

"First, this." He pulled out the phone and told her he needed her thumb print and a blood sample.

"A blood sample? We haven't even had our first date yet."

Amadeus looked at her, his expression as flat as the tar roof beneath his feet. She laid a hand on his arm. "That was a joke. Jesus, kid, the world's fucked you up pretty good, hasn't it?" He smiled a little, but he didn't think it was funny. "Come on. There's a great coffee shop just a couple blocks away. You look like you could use some caffeine."

"You think the Pachyderm will be all right?"

"That thing is named after an elephant?"

"I didn't name it."

"Sure, it'll be fine. Only two other people have the access code to the roof; nobody's coming up here."

"I need to do something first." He climbed back in the Pachyderm. When he came out, he was wearing thick glasses, a fake beard, and the fuzzer around his neck.

"Are you serious?" Esther said. "You look like you just crawled out of some Williamsburg den of trust–funders."

He followed her down the stairs then to the elevator. The beard itched, like he had a bag of insects crawling on his face. When he glanced in the elevator mirror, he thought he looked like someone in a disguise. They didn't talk in the elevator. The street hummed with the sound of a million cars. Well-dressed people strode past shops and restaurants. After his month in Colorado, the city made him dizzy. Esther walked fast. Amadeus had always thought he was a fast walker, but he struggled to keep up, especially as his legs were stiff from his journey in the Pachyderm.

They reached the coffee shop, decorated faux-rustic with rough-hewn tables and wood paneling. Black and white pictures of prominent people hung on the walls. Esther ordered for both of them, two café americanos. As they waited for their drinks, Esther told her story.

"Your mother and I, we were roommates for a year at university. I wouldn't say we were close, but we kept in contact and would meet for drinks once or twice a year. Totally different lines of work, but we could still bitch about our bosses. Now that I'm the boss, I shudder to think about what people say.

"Anyway," Esther continued, "I always enjoyed hearing about her life. While I was busy smashing glass ceilings and making obscene profits for my employer, she would tell me about trying to balance a research career and a family. I had an entire division of a company, while your mother had a husband and, forgive me for saying so, a beautiful boy.

"You're probably wondering why I'm telling you all this. Well, I had met your father a couple of times and we hit things off okay. He knew I had access to some investment capital. Two years ago he propositioned me." She noted the look on Amadeus' face and laughed. "Just playing. Totally business. He told me what he was doing, showed me his research, and promised some pretty generous royalties. Spooky stuff, but the potential market for this tech was mind-blowing. I mean, teleportation? Trans-temporal communication? That's wild. So I agreed not only to fund him, but I put him in touch with another man who might be interested, a Czech by the name of Vesely Gustavius. You know Czechs put their family name first, right?"

"No, didn't know that," Amadeus said.

"There's a lot you don't know, isn't there," she said, not really asking. "So I agree to be a silent partner and set him up with Gustavius. When I asked him about other investors, he was kind of vague, said he had two more anonymous partners. I never pressed him for details. So your father would occasionally send progress reports, but one day I get an email. It's your father explaining that something has gone wrong, that he's had a terrifying, um, encounter."

"If I told you the problem, you'd never believe me."

"Amadeus, I did see the problem, and I still have nightmares about it. I think your father's honesty worked against him. He should've just kept quiet and either refunded our monies or kept going. But he kept talking about full disclosure, keeping things on the up and up. Anyway, after seeing what happened, Gustavius and I asked him to stop, told him we wanted to get out. This was just too much; we had our reputations to think about. Teleportation and maybe even talking to the dead was one thing; look at the Ouija board. But this monster stuff? No way. We'd be destroyed."

"Do you know where Gustavius lives?"

"He's a prominent Czech. He lives in Prague, of course."

"Do you think Gustavius knows who the other partners are? Because after him I'll still need one more fingerprint if we're ever going to open this file."

"I believe he hired someone to find out the identities of the other partners, but I'm not sure if they found anything. I recently received a message from him from a personal courier. He flew a man all the way here from Prague to tell me it was better if we didn't communicate electronically for awhile. He thought he was under surveillance. If you want his help, he might need some convincing. Maybe you can make a deal with him, something to make helping you worth his while; guarantees of royalties for any future developments, for example. Now that your father is, uh, gone, technically you own the intellectual rights to his work. But you need to ask yourself: are you sure you want to open these files?"

Amadeus nodded and laid the phone on the table.

"I'm afraid the wrong kind of people already have. I need to know what they know, and maybe find a way to prevent them from using it." Amadeus scratched his beard. "Can I get your blood now?" Esther nodded and placed her finger on the screen. He scanned it, then placed a clean lance in the glucometer. The lance pricked her finger and collected the blood.

On the screen, a dialog box appeared with Esther's picture

on it. "You've successfully collected information for Esther Elgers. Please press okay." Amadeus pressed okay.

As they finished their coffee, Esther gave him Vesely's address from memory. When he commented on her excellent memory, she recited pi to the thirtieth digit. When she saw Amadeus' slack–jawed expression, she said, "Memory tricks and mnemonic devices are one of my hobbies. I've trained myself to remember lists, names, and long strings of numbers as easily as putting on a pair of socks. Tell me something once, and I've got it. How do you think I got to be in charge of things?"

24

Back on the street, Esther started to hail a cab. Amadeus stopped her. "Do you mind walking?" he asked. "I'd like to walk a bit."

"I've got the shoes for it," she said, pointing to her flat heels. They walked north on Broadway, from the 30s to the 40s and through Times Square. Hucksters and bucket shops sold discounted tickets for plays. Video screens lined the sides of almost every building. Amadeus smiled and looked around, feeling less nervous and starting to enjoy the kitsch and energy of the place.

"Let's stop for a minute," Amadeus said.

"Aren't you the little sightseer," Esther said, but her voice was kind. They found a bench at Bryant Park.

"Tell me more about my mother," Amadeus said.

"Well ..." she started.

At that moment, glass crashed on 42nd Street, followed by a hurricane of screaming. A bus-sized version of the demon from the videos crawled along the glistening glass side of the MetLife building. Its mouth was as large as a double door. Yellow eyes covered its forelegs. The creature moved like a bear, powerful and a little awkward, its great claws digging into glass and steel.

Amadeus froze and stared. Esther grabbed his hand and pulled him towards the subway station. As they ran, Amadeus twisted his neck to watch the creature as it pounced upon a group of pedestrians. Even from where he stood, Amadeus could hear slurping sounds as the creature lapped up the blood along the sidewalk. "My father did this," he said to no one.

"Four four four eight," Esther said. Amadeus looked at her, confused. "For the roof. In case we get separated."

People fought and shoved to get through the bottleneck on the stairs to the subway, but the stairs weren't wide enough for all those trying to escape. Amadeus found himself shoulder to shoulder with frantic, panicked people. His body was jostled, knocked around like a soccer ball. Somehow the crowd came between Esther and him, separating them and sending them in opposite directions. He yelled for her to tell her to go on, but he couldn't see her and she probably couldn't hear him over the screaming crowd.

The demon had finished its first course and was creeping towards the crowd at the subway entrance when the bright red and yellow umbrella of a hot dog cart popped open. The creature howled and pounced on the cart like a dog pinning a mole, swallowing the umbrella in two bites. It roared in satisfaction, a sound like an arriving subway train.

The people pushed harder, trying to get to the stairs and into the subway. Amadeus felt a fist in his back and turned, ready to hit back, but with so many scared faces pressed so close together he couldn't begin to guess who had hit him. Probably an accident anyway. He imagined using the people around him to pull himself up, then walking over them, stepping on their shoulders as he scampered towards the stairs to safety, but he decided he'd probably end up trampled.

After flinging the remains of the hot dog cart down 42nd Street, the demon turned its attention back to the crowd and crept towards them, its tongue probing ahead of its body like an octopus' tentacle. The crowd let out a collective scream. Amadeus gasped for breath as a new wave of panic spread, causing people to push and push, harder and harder.

Each lungful of air carried the smell of sulfur, ammonia, and rotting flesh. The demon was close enough that he could see the folds and wrinkles in its smooth, grey flesh. The demon took a swipe at the crowd with its tree-sized paw and knocked ten rows of people away. They twisted through the air like paper trash in the wind, landing on the grass nearby. Suddenly he could breathe because he wasn't deep in the crowd, he was at the edge. He screamed and flailed his arms. The column of eyes on the demon's legs looked at him, then to the pile of people in Bryant Park. It went for the pile, pinning a group of men in suits, two under each paw, and began tearing at the soft flesh of their abdomens with its needle teeth. Their cries rang out like the stock exchange bell, their innards spilling out like ticker tape.

Sirens wailed and four-note car horns blared, as if the city were fighting the creature with noise. Flashing red and blue lights reflected off the windows of the surrounding buildings. Two SWAT trucks smashed into cars, pushing them out of the way, making a path for more police vehicles, which formed a line in front of the crowd around the subway entrance. More people pushed in. Amadeus was again trapped.

Spotlights shined on the creature from several directions. Gunfire rang out but, compared to the demon's bellows of anger and annoyance, the gunfire sounded like tiny firecrackers. The demon dropped the remains of the man in its mouth, released the others, and went for the police cruisers. The officers backed away. But instead of attacking the police, the demon focused on the flashing bars on top of the cruisers, pulling them off with its tentacle tongue. Lights flashed from inside its mouth. Pieces of plastic cracked and flew as it chewed. The police kept firing bullets into the creature, but it didn't seem to notice. It went from one cruiser to another, eating the light bars.

From the avenue, eight men with tour group passes hanging from their necks pulled handguns and began firing at the creature. A police officer looked at them, shrugged, and returned to his shooting. Gunfire crackled like water dumped in hot grease, and finally, as the creature tore at the last light bar, it began to falter and stagger. From a thousand little bullet wounds, black goo oozed onto the pavement. The demon stood up on two legs, clawed at the air, and wailed. All along the avenue, glass shattered, exploding onto the street. The demon dropped back down, took one half-hearted swipe at a SWAT van, knocking it on its side, then fell over onto the pavement and died.

The crowd was silent for a moment, then began to cheer and clap. Men cried openly. Almost everyone had a phone in their hand, capturing photos and videos of the spectacle. People circled around the monster to get a closer look. Amadeus looked around for Esther and called her name but heard nothing in response.

The demon's black tentacle-tongue spread out on the pavement like the roots of a tree. Blood dripped from incisors larger than Amadeus' legs. Even the police were too fascinated to tell people to get away. The eyes of the creature, ranging in size from billiard ball to basketball, still stared at the world. The irises were yellow, the pupils square like a goat's, and the sclera roiling red. Where it should've had ears, it had only stumps leading into the ear canal.

The creature's body quivered, and a spray of shit came from its anus, splattering the people unfortunate enough to be standing behind it. They screamed then began to sizzle. Somebody yelled out, "Acid!" Some firefighters tried to spray the acid-shit-covered people down, but it was too late; they had already boiled down to black piles of viscous liquid.

The mood changed as people cried and shook their heads in confusion and disbelief. Silence fell over the city; horns and sirens stopped all at once, as if everyone was too shocked to speak, to honk, to breathe. The world was watching, and what could they say? Within minutes, this event would be seen by millions. Amadeus thought about this and wondered how people would react. Then he remembered the farmer's wife and his own unfortunate legal status, and a realization of the danger he was in hit him like a spray of acid shit. If the world was watching, then someone was bound to pick him out of the crowd. He touched his face. His beard had slipped down under his chin Lincoln-style long ago. He pulled it back up and ran down 42nd Street.

25

Amadeus wanted to go straight back to the Pachyderm and get out of town, but he wouldn't leave before he found Esther. He jogged to her building. On the way, he thought about what happened, how on a random day, in America's largest city, a demon had just happened to show up sickeningly close to two people who were involved in his father's research. Hadn't Esther said Vesely thought he was under surveillance? If that was true, then Esther could be too. Amadeus shouldn't be a target; he dutifully wore his fuzzer. Only his friends in Colorado knew he was here. They must've been watching Esther. Most likely they saw some flying machine land on her building; that would be enough to send up some alarms.

The lobby was empty. Feeling exposed there, he took the elevator to the top floor, using the access code to unlock the door. He waited in the Pachyderm. On the flight computer he tried to contact Jones, then Esther. Neither answered, but when he dialed Lilly, her worried face appeared on the screen.

"I saw what happened. I'm so glad you're okay," she said.

"I was there," Amadeus said.

"I know. We saw you. Your beard slipped."

"Damn. Lilly, where's your father?"

"He locked himself up in his room a few hours ago, said he felt ill, more side effects. Where are you now?" Grassal came on the screen and waved.

"I'm on Esther's building, waiting for her to get back. I can't stay here. They were watching her, Lilly; it's like they were waiting for me to show up." Lilly nodded as he spoke. Grassal took the headset from her and put it on.

"Brother, glad you're okay," Grassal said. "But you need to leave. You've got about eight minutes."

"I'm fine, I'm on the roof."

"Trust me on this. You're just about to get tangled up in a first-class clusterfuck. I've accessed some street-level cameras near Esther's building. Go have a look over the edge."

"What?"

"Just do it," Grassal said. Amadeus peered down to the street below and saw four black police vans blocking the entrance. Police officers were streaming out the back. "Somebody recognized you. You've got to leave right now."

"No! I can't, not without Esther. She's in danger too." He spoke as he looked over the edge.

"Amadeus, this sounds bad, but you've got what you need. Get in the air. She'll be fine. Probably," Grassal said.

Amadeus got in the Pachyderm and started the engines. The cloaking paint took effect and all the exterior surfaces outside became translucent. "How much time do I have?" he asked Grassal.

"Five minutes."

"I'll call you back." Amadeus dialed Esther. This time she answered. "Where are you?"

"In the elevator."

"Get to the roof."

"Why?"

"Just go!" Amadeus hung up before she could say anything. He looked at the time. Two minutes. A minute later, the roof door flew open. Esther. Amadeus got out, grabbed her hand, and tried to lead her to the Pachyderm.

"What are you doing?" she said, wresting her hand free.

"We're leaving."

"I'm not going anywhere."

"Did you see the police outside?" She shook her head. "They must've got here after you did. Look, you've got to go with me. Some things you can't do on your own. That demon showing up, that was no coincidence, okay? You're in danger, it's my fault, and I want to help you."

"You're kidding, right?" Esther said. "You think I'm really going to leave all this behind?" She gestured to the building they stood on. "I already told you, this is my company, my life, and I still have a meeting to get to. I've done nothing wrong. I'm not afraid of the police. You go. Just leave me here. I'll be fine."

The door to the roof opened. A mustachioed policeman held up his pistol. "Freeze, hands up." Amadeus and Esther did as he said. He spoke into a shoulder radio. "He's on the roof." As he spoke, Amadeus noticed something red moving up the policeman's leg, over his torso and to his head. A laser sight.

"Oh shit," Amadeus said. "Officer, get down—" *Fwoop.* Blood sprayed from the back of the policeman's head before his body dropped to the ground. Esther screamed. Amadeus pulled her toward the Pachyderm. He heard more silenced gunshots nearby. Esther let herself be led and loaded inside. Amadeus pulled the door closed. Bullets pinged off the Pachyderm. None penetrated. The nanosteel really was bulletproof. In the copilot's chair, Esther rocked back and forth, arms folded across her chest, her breath coming in short gasps. He threw the vertical thrust levers forward and the Pachyderm shot up into the air. With as much speed as he could muster, Amadeus flew out of Manhattan and to open water. He flew with all the lights off. To anyone watching on satellite, the Pachyderm would look like nothing more than the glimmer of a wave. Thermal imaging, though, he wasn't sure about. Several minutes had passed when Amadeus finally spoke.

"Do you believe me now?"

"Oh my god," she said. "Oh my god. He was alive then he

wasn't. I don't believe it. That was something else, it had to be something else. He's not dead. It was a trick."

"That was no trick," Amadeus said. "I hate to say it, but I know what it looks like when somebody gets shot. Now, do you understand why you can't go home, at least not for a while?"

"This is your fault, Amadeus. You brought this into my life, you and your father with his ... his fucking experiments. And now, what? I just put everything on hold? What will they say? That I just disappeared? That I took off with some, some murderer? They'll make it look like you killed that cop. Why did it have to be like this? I was supposed to have a few more prosperous years and retire into a peaceful life of travel and cocktails and casual sex. Now? What now?"

"I'm sorry, Esther. Every single day I wish things were different. I would trade anything in the world for things to be the way they were. But they're not. I can only work to make things the way I want them to be. That's all."

Silence fell over the cockpit. Several minutes passed. Amadeus focused on the map, though he was just flying low over the ocean with no particular destination set.

"No, I'm sorry. You're the one who lost your father. It's just a career, right? I still have assets," she said, but to Amadeus she sounded resigned and a little sarcastic.

"You know you can't go back, right? Not until this is all over?"

"I guessed as much. If they kill cops, they certainly wouldn't have any problem killing me. But why?"

"I've been trying to figure this one out. Maybe it's because we know about the demon gates. The world knows about the demons now, or at least that one, but so far that's it, and maybe that's how they, whoever they are, want it. And they don't want us to talk. Do you have anywhere you can go? I can take you there."

"I've got a second house in the White Mountains. There's my sister's house in Rochester. And I have a cousin with a beach house."

"All those are probably no good. They'll know about all of those. Is there anybody from long ago, somebody you don't have an obvious connection with? I think that might be best."

"Hmm. Actually, I've got an old, old boyfriend in Nantucket ..."

26

As they flew over the black water of Long Island Sound, the only noise was the hum of the engine. Esther stared out at the lights of the city. Amadeus held the yoke like it was a life buoy, devoting all his attention to the task of flying, a task made only a little difficult by the high ocean winds. He asked her to find her friend's house on the map, as well as an isolated place to land.

Nantucket made Amadeus think of his great uncle. He and his father had visited him once. They'd flown by commuter plane and rented a car when they arrived. Amadeus was young then, eight or nine. Mostly, he remembered his uncle wearing a blue plaid bathrobe at all hours of the day and smoking sweetly choking tobacco out of a deer antler pipe. He died a few months after they visited.

"On the east side of White Goose Cove, land there," Esther said, bringing Amadeus out of his reverie. She had been looking at the map. "Approach from the ocean, keep the lights out and we should be able to slip in no problem. Once we land, I can walk to my friend's, it's only a couple of miles."

"By yourself? At," he looked at the clock on the navigation system display, "three in the morning?"

"This is Nantucket we're talking about here. It's mostly rich people."

"I know. It's their kids I'm worried about. I know what

they're like." Amadeus thought of Davy attacking him on graduation day, back in his old life. "I'll walk with you. Would that be okay?" Esther nodded. "It's the least I can do."

"Shh," Esther said.

Amadeus made a wide arc and came upon the island from the south, flying low, one hundred meters above the waves. Ahead, a line of red flashing lights stretched across the shore like Christmas lights. He zoomed in on the map. The lights came from the New England Wind Farm. He took the Pachyderm up to three hundred meters and over the turbines.

"Land ho," Amadeus said. He waited. Esther said nothing. "That was supposed to be a joke."

"I know," Esther said. "It just wasn't funny."

"I guess not."

They flew into White Goose Cove and landed in a clearing. He didn't like landing without lights, but they couldn't risk being seen. With two hours until sunrise, Amadeus wasn't worried about anyone stumbling upon the Pachyderm during the night. Even if they came close, they probably wouldn't see it.

"My friend's house is pretty close, on Madaket. West of here, I think." She hopped down and started to walk.

"Hey, wait up just a minute," Amadeus said. "I still need a minute to shut things down." But Esther kept walking. Amadeus yelled after her then. "What the hell?" Then she turned around.

"What the hell?" she said, shaking her finger at Amadeus. "What the hell? Really? You want to know what the hell? I'll tell you what the hell. I was almost eaten by a monster today. I find out some mysterious people want to kill me. I'm forced to leave my entire life behind. And now I've got to bang on the door of a man I haven't talked to in over a decade and ask if I can sleep on his couch until, until, when? When, Amadeus, when?"

"I'm sorry, I don't know."

"So that's what the hell." She started walking again. He followed her through the noisy Nantucket night. Crickets sang, frogs chirped, and the wind made the tall sea oats wave and rub against each other. After about forty minutes of silent walking through sleeping neighborhoods, Esther pointed out a house. "That's the house. I really don't want to do this, but there's not much I can do, is there?" When she rang the doorbell, a thin, bald man peeped out the door. He recognized Esther and smiled.

"Darling," he said. "You're the last person I expected to see on my doorstep at four in the morning. It's been too long since the last time this happened. Who's your little friend?"

"An old friend's son. David, I hate to ask you this, but can I stay with you for a while?"

"Um, yeah, well, you see, I would but I've got someone really special here and I think that may not be the best idea. Sorry."

"Your ego's still as big as Boston, isn't it? I'm not here because I want to get back into your bed. I just need your help."

"This isn't about the Manhattan Monster, is it?" She nodded but didn't say anything else. "Fine. Okay. God, I totally misread that situation. Apologies. Come on in, we'll have some coffee. I'm awake now ..."

"I really am sorry to wake you, I know it's early," Esther said.

"It's okay. Would your little friend like to join us?" David asked. Amadeus wanted to punch this guy in the mouth.

"Not particularly," Amadeus said. "Esther, can you give me the address?" He pulled out his phone. She sighed and waited until he was ready.

"Vesely lives in the Mala Strana near Legii Bridge. His apartment is above a bank, number three-oh-two. Vetezna Street. Two-oh-three Vetezna Street. Czech is a damn confusing language and the addresses aren't much better."

Amadeus repeated the directions back to make sure he had everything.

"Oh, Prague is such a fabulous city," David said, looking

befuddled. "It feels like a city from a fairy tale, only with more drunk people. Do go to the town center and see the astronomical clock."

"Yeah, sure, I'll do that, since I'm not actually going for anything important."

"Amadeus," Esther said, putting her hand on his shoulder. "I know this isn't your fault, not completely. You're doing your best, and it's all very confusing. So, thank you, I guess, and good luck." She hugged him. "Give my regards to Gustavius."

"I will." They went inside. Amadeus turned away and began the long walk back to the Pachyderm.

27

He called Jones and told him what happened and what he planned to do. "But I've got one question: is the Pachyderm good for a transatlantic flight?"

"I don't see why not," Jones said. "Stay high, keep an eye on other crafts' flight paths, and you'll be fine. Please verify that the logger is running; it's a minor distinction, but you'll be making the first transatlantic flight ever using a craft of this type. Worst-case scenario, you can do a water landing. The Pachyderm should float. Excessive salt water could make the verticals malfunction, but you'd still be able to hydroplane your way to Iceland or Greenland or wherever is closest for you. Just make sure you've got a full charge."

"Okay, Jones, thanks."

"And Amadeus," he said, "I'm glad you got Esther out of there." Just before the screen went blank, Jones leaned forward with a shaking hand to switch off the video. Five hours later, Amadeus sat on the eastern edge of Newfoundland, squinting against the late morning sun, staring at the Atlantic and thinking about his life. Waves crashed against the rocky shore, washing away the kelp.

Amadeus decided to take a nap. He was thankful to be so far north; the weather was nice and cool, and he slept poorly when it was hot outside. The thought of sweating and sticking to the vinyl of the seat made him shudder, the way some people shudder when someone runs their fingernail across a chalkboard. He fell asleep hoping weather in the Czech Republic would be equally pleasant.

Amadeus awoke two hours later to an alarm announcing his fuel cells were fully charged. Wiping the sleep from his eyes, the muscles in his body feeling like brittle rubber bands, he ran through his pre-flight checks. Satisfied, he instructed the navigation system to start the route. The turbofans whooshed to life. As their speed increased, the sound changed from a whoosh to a steady hum. Moments later, the Pachyderm lifted into the sky. The rocks of the shore below became a shapeless, lumpy grey mass.

He flew over the violent ocean and into, and then above, a pillar of clouds. With clouds below and blue skies above, he realized he was leaving his home continent for the first time. Strange, he thought, that his family had never traveled abroad. It wasn't like they couldn't afford it, they just weren't travelers. Amadeus thought that he wasn't either; if he'd had his way, he would be at home with his father, enjoying the final summer before his working life began. But that path, with its promise of a perfectly normal and perfectly boring life, was gone, along with the last of his immediate family. At least, he reminded himself, he still had people in his life who cared enough to help.

All this time, he hadn't even thought of Lilly, hadn't had enough time. New York was all business until the monster showed up. Crashing in Kansas and having a shotgun shoved in his face didn't lend itself to wistful romantic thoughts, either. Now, though, with nothing to see under him but the swirling silver clouds, and under that the churning black Atlantic, he thought about her, and what he could do to make himself more desirable. That occupied him for about fifteen minutes, but he still had a long trip ahead. Why hadn't he loaded any movies onto the flight computer? He settled for the radio. The only thing he could pick up was a station from Iceland. The music made his heart move, he had never heard anything like it; the singers' voices soared and swirled like the clouds he had seen earlier, the music largo, moving like an ice floe scraping against a giant string. With the sounds of Iceland filling his head, he reached the edges of the old world.

28

Several hours and one recharge stop later, he was flying over green fields, villages, wind farms, and tidy highways. He'd always imagined he would be terrified of visiting a foreign country, but now, in spite of everything that had happened, he found himself mildly excited. Most of his ideas of Europe were formed in childhood, castles and rivers with the occasional fire-breathing, villager-eating dragon. Maybe it was time to refine that understanding. Despite what he'd said to Esther's friend, he decided that maybe he should do a bit of sightseeing. His time was short, but he may never come back. He had heard people say a change of scenery had done them good; maybe it would work for him as well.

Prague grew closer. He searched for an isolated place to land. He guessed he wouldn't have the luxury of landing directly on top of a building like in Manhattan. In the pictures he had viewed, the buildings had red-tiled, sloped roofs. According to his map, a small forest north of town offered reasonable cover and a short distance to the nearest tram station. Without local currency to purchase a ticket, he'd have to walk to town, but it was only a few kilometers south along the bending Vltava River. His legs and body demanded exercise.

The Pachyderm landed without difficulty, though an inspection of the exterior showed the barn crash and the bullet marks had chipped and scraped away quite a bit of the cloaking paint. From a distance, Amadeus could see streaks and spots of metal that seemed to float above the ground. Fortunately, he still had the cloaking tarp. Amadeus had said to Jones it wouldn't do much good in New York, but Jones had insisted he keep it. Now Amadeus was glad he had.

The forest was mostly light underbrush under a big canopy of bent oaks and old ashes swaying with late-summer leaves. No obvious trails ran into the clearing, but Amadeus remembered the direction of the river and set off that way, stopping occasionally to leave marks on trees with his knife. One tree he didn't mark already had an old, almost overgrown carving; Russian letters inside a heart, a Soviet love affair from long ago. Eventually he came to the highway. Cars sped along like darts, leaving a swirling dust trail behind him. He ran across the highway, then across the railroad tracks, and walked to the path that ran along the river. The river was brown, slow, and bits of trash floated atop its waters, but Amadeus found it peaceful anyway. The houses across the river were small and clustered together, not spread out like the ones he was used to back in America. He passed a power substation. A nearby sign read "Roztocka 242." The language, with all the accent marks, was confusing. He tried sounding out some of the words, but they stumbled along on his tongue. He hoped nobody would notice him as he walked along muttering to himself.

The houses changed to cramped, sprawling apartment blocks. The streets so far had been empty, but on the sidewalk ahead of him, two men walked, their arms thrown over each other's shoulders. They staggered towards him. Amadeus considered crossing to the other sidewalk, but decided that would look strange, so he just kept his eyes fixed on his feet. They were talking, laughing, but he had no idea what they were saying. To him, their words sounded like a misfiring engine. They passed without incident.

He checked the map on his phone. Downtown lay across the

bridge, but Vesely Gustavius' apartment was on this side of the river, four more kilometers. His stomach complained. So far he had found no restaurants or currency exchanges. He ignored his stomach and walked on. An hour later, when the crowds had thickened and brown destination signs listed popular landmarks in several languages, he guessed he had reached Prague proper. Unlike the area outside of town, here the streets were narrow and clean, the buildings freshly painted. At the corner, under a multi-lingual sign showing the direction to the Charles Bridge, a man sat drawing caricatures.

On down the street that ran along the river, he found a currency exchange. He went inside and exchanged one hundred dollars for about two thousand crowns. Outside, he went to the first restaurant he saw. The restaurant featured a bilingual English and Czech menu. He ordered goulash. His waiter had a curled, upturned mustache. The goulash was rich and salty, and he was full well before he finished. Afterwards, he laid his money out on the table, trying to pick out the right amount. The waiter laughed at him and showed him the bills and coins to use. Amadeus left an adequate tip.

His belly full, his body limber from the walk, he strolled toward Vesely's apartment. After half an hour, he reached the building. The bank on the first floor had already closed for the day. Going around the side of the building, he found the resident's entrance open to allow in the warm summer air. A row of steel mailboxes with engraved brass nameplates sat in the wall. Amadeus found Vesely's name beside 302. The complete lack of security gave Amadeus an apprehensive feeling as he climbed the wide mahogany staircase. He ran his hand along a rail smoothed and oiled by a thousand other hands and was struck by the feeling of being a young man from a young country. He'd been to plenty of historic New England towns, but when contrasted with the gothic permanence of even something as utilitarian as the Charles Bridge, they all seemed like rickety shacks thrown together by upstart colonists. And

Prague was not only old, but well-preserved, like a taxidermied animal. On the way here, he had read that Prague was spared most of the hell that befell Europe during the second world war.

He reached the third floor and went down the hallway to 302. Amadeus knocked on the door, and it creaked open. He stepped back and called inside. "Mr. Vesely? Hello?" He received no response. He called again, but still nothing. Glancing over his shoulder then back down the hall, he pushed the door open and slipped inside.

29

Inside, the house stank of burnt plastic and sulfur. He stepped into the sun-lit front parlor, with its white couch and elaborate wooden mantle, and walked to the stainless steel kitchen. His steps were careful, and he took care not to touch anything. "Mr. Vesely, sir, hello? Hello?" Still silence. Down a hallway with black-and-white photos of Mr. Vesely in Rome, Mr. Vesely with a beautiful woman on a boat, and Mr. Vesely with a skinny man standing at the base of a gigantic, three-spired temple. The temple looked vaguely familiar, and when he examined the bottom of the picture he found an inscription that read, "*Angkor Wat w/ Laroux.*"

Amadeus felt his heart thumbing against his chest, felt his pulse in his head. This intimate look into a stranger's life was sickeningly thrilling. At any moment, he expected someone to attack him with a blunt object. He looked in two more rooms down the hallway. Both were tidy and minimally furnished. Someone lived here, but barely.

At the end of the hall, two doors stood closed. The door on the right opened into a black-and-white tiled bathroom. Fresh-cut irises sat atop the sink. He pushed the other door open, peered inside, and recoiled from the scene before him. Involuntarily, he pulled the door shut as he backed away. He wanted to unsee what he had seen, to run screaming out of the apartment and to never look back. Then he thought of his father, his goal, and his job. He pushed the door open and stepped into the room.

Behind the glass-topped desk, in front of French doors that led to a balcony, was the headless torso of what had probably been Vesely. The arms were gone. The chest was ripped open, the organs removed. The wall by the window was smeared with blood. An arm lay nearby, chewed and discarded, the tissue from the bicep and forearm gone, leaving only the chubby hand. The room stank of death.

Amadeus stood at the threshold, trying not to vomit. He realized a human hadn't done this, couldn't have done this. A demon had been here. But that would mean someone had brought it here, had controlled it. His skin prickled and the hairs on his neck stood up.

Okay, he decided, get the fingerprint and blood and get out. But what about the other partner? He'd have to search. Vesely was his only hope. Kneeling by the bloody mess of Vesely's hand, he pulled the phone out and opened the scanner. Wincing, he grabbed the cool, dead hand and placed the thumb against the scanner. He pricked the finger with the lance to get the blood sample. A dialog box appeared on the screen. "You've successfully collected information for Vesely Gustavius. Please press okay." Amadeus pressed okay.

Vesely's hand was only a little stiff. He was freshly dead. Not yet full rigor mortis. Whoever, whatever had killed him, Amadeus had just missed it. What if they were watching his apartment? He shuddered and felt sicker, as if he needed another reason not to stay.

Stepping over Vesely's entrails, trying to avoid leaving bloody footprints, he searched the desk. The filing cabinet was filled with manila folders, neatly labeled in English. The man had no computer. Gravity would've liked him. Amadeus flipped through and pulled out folders marked "Investments," another labeled "Partnerships," and one labeled "Brunmeier." Each was at least a centimeter thick. He took these. Amadeus flipped through the other folders, but nothing else caught his interest. In a side drawer, Amadeus found an address book. He put that in his backpack as well. Now he was a murder suspect and a burglar.

Just as he unzipped his backpack, he heard a woman's voice. "Gustavius? *Ahoy?*" Had he closed the door? Amadeus zipped up the bag. She called again, only louder, closer.

"Gustavius?" Amadeus could hear doors down the hallway opening and closing. She followed the same pattern he did, checking each room. He hoped she was slower. Surely she would assume he was the murderer, even if he wasn't covered in blood. Could he force his way past her? That wouldn't work. He looked around ... the French doors. He opened one and slipped onto the balcony. No fire escape, but like so many other buildings here, this one had plenty of ledges. He hoped they weren't just for decoration.

He climbed over the railing and onto the ledge. The ledge wasn't quite as wide as his foot was long, but he could stand with his feet sideways. The wind ruffled his clothes, but he kept his balance. Once he and his backpack were fully on the ledge, Amadeus reached over, pushed the door closed, then edged sideways along the ledge, hugging the wall, out of view of anyone in the apartment. Just after he closed the door, he heard the woman's scream cut the day like a razor. On the street below, people shuffled about but didn't look up. He thought of the layout of the apartment and remembered the window in the shared hallway. Yes, it was all the way on the other side of the building, and he was exposed there on the ledge, but if caught climbing on a ledge outside the scene of a murder, what could he say? He was cleaning pigeon shit from the ledge?

While normally uncoordinated and awkward, he felt agile and focused, unconcerned with falling. He made his way around the building to the window in the hallway and peered in. The door to Vesely's apartment was closed. He pulled the screen off, set it on the ledge, tossed his backpack in the hallway, and crawled inside. When he took his first step down the stairs, Vesely's door opened. A young woman came out. She grabbed his shirt and spoke to him in blubbery, rapid-fire Czech. She had dark hair.

Amadeus put up his hands and took a step backwards. The woman kept going. He pointed to his mouth and ears and shook his head, as if to tell her he was a deaf mute. In a move that surprised himself, he pulled her close and hugged her, patting her back, then took her arm and led her down the three flights of stairs and out to the street. She hardly looked at him. Outside she seemed to relax. She again tried to talk, but Amadeus just pointed to his ears. People passed by, staring with uncurious eyes. She kept crying, and he stood there beside her, wanting more than anything to run away.

He tapped her shoulder and made a gesture for telephone. She looked at him, quizzical, then appeared to realize that yes, she had a cell phone, and she should probably use it. Nearby, a wooden bench sat under a tree. He guided her over by the elbow and helped her sit down. She called what he guessed was the Czech equivalent of 911. He stood up and started to inch away from her, slipping away like the daylight, slow and gradual, but she grabbed his shirt and pulled him back down. He looked at her and pointed to an invisible watch. She shook her head.

She made a slashing motion across her neck. This somehow made her look younger. He shrugged and again started to walk away. This time she held onto his belt and pulled him back. He smacked her forearm, just hard enough to make her let him go. Freed, he found himself running towards the tram. As he ran, some people took pictures of him. He thought for a moment his fly was unzipped. Without stopping, he looked himself over. Fly zipped. No blood. Nothing, he guessed, but a wild look in his eyes. Just before he reached the tram platform he heard sirens. He ducked into a store selling postcards of the astronomical clock and the Charles Bridge. He pretended to browse but felt like a lurker, felt the eyes of the shopkeeper watching him. At least he didn't look like a gypsy. He had read about gypsies but hadn't seen any. When the sirens passed, Amadeus bought a bottle of water from the cooler. This time he counted out the price without assistance. The coins felt big and strange in his hand, like play money. At the tram platform, he bought tokens, then sat on a bench. At his feet, broken glass. Other parts of the city had been so clean; this surprised him.

The tram arrived and took him on a slow tour back through the north of the city along the river, the same way he had walked. The route looked different this time, less threatening, but he guessed that was from familiarity. The tram was half-full, and though most people were occupied with books or digital devices, he felt watched, but he reached his stop without incident and crossed the highway. He waited just inside the forest until the road was clear of cars, then pushed through the thick layer of brush along the road and into the stand of towering oaks and alder. A bit of sunlight filtered through the thick canopy.

He followed his marks and found the winding path that led over the stream and to the tree with the old carving. As he examined it for the last time, he heard yelling and a clanking sound from the direction of the Pachyderm. Fists clenched, he ran towards it and found a man in a faded green sweater attacking the Pachyderm with a tree branch. Little dents and scrapes covered the sides, one of the windows was shattered, and bits of the craft showed through the cloaking paint. The tarp was piled nearby.

"What the fuck is this?" Amadeus said, spreading his arms out in an involuntary reaction. The man was older, his face covered in grey stubble, his hair cropped short. He sneered at Amadeus, wagged his finger at him, then turned back at the Pachyderm and said something in Czech, his words a slurred blur. Amadeus thought he looked drunk. As if to confirm this thought, the man staggered and moaned. He used the stick like a cane, trying to support himself. He spoke again, realized Amadeus couldn't understand him, and went back to his work, slamming his stick against the right front turbofan.

"No!" Amadeus said. Gravity's training took over. He ran forward and tackled the man, taking him by surprise. Dried leaves flew up around them. When they hit the ground, the man bellowed, his warm, sour breath hitting Amadeus' face. Amadeus started to punch him. The man went slack, then suddenly freed his arm from under Amadeus' leg and swung. Amadeus leaned back, easily avoiding the clumsy punch.

The man arched his back and rolled. Amadeus was knocked off. The man got to his feet and ran for his stick. Amadeus pulled himself up and dove after him. Amadeus' right shoulder rammed into the man's lower back. Again the man fell.

Amadeus pinned him. The man howled. Amadeus wanted to get off him and let him go, but he had no idea what the man would do. Rather than keep punching him, Amadeus held him down, his hand on the man's forehead. The man struggled, tried to get free, couldn't. He went slack in defeat.

"Go," Amadeus said. "Go, go." Surely the drunken bastard knew go, Amadeus thought. "Go? Okay?"

"Okay," the man said. Everyone knew "okay." He had a cut on his forehead, and blood ran into his eye.

"I'm gonna let you up now, but you try any stupid stuff, you're going right back down. Okay?" The man said okay again. Amadeus wished he could ask him why he would want to beat on the Pachyderm, but he supposed he would never know.

Slow and careful, like someone balancing an egg on a spoon, Amadeus let the man up. He crawled to his feet, brushing bits of leaves from his pants and sweater. Then he smiled at Amadeus and pointed at the ship, going on a small tirade, about what, Amadeus had no clue. Amadeus took a step forward and pointed to the road, interrupting him, and said, "Go." This time he listened, shuffling away with his head low, looking like a beaten dog.

Amadeus watched him leave then set to examining the Pachyderm. A porthole was shattered, but it was small, no bigger than a paperback book. He wondered if he could duct tape a pressurized cabin. He suspected he'd find more problems after firing everything up. He did. The servos that controlled the pitch of the right front turbofan had stopped working. When he took the Pachyderm up, it flew with the grace of a drunken fruit bat, even with assistance from the navigation computer.

He landed and called Jones. "Got problems," Amadeus said.

"Don't we all. Go on," Jones said, looking like he had just woken up.

Amadeus explained what happened.

"Poor bastard," Jones said, his face turning away from the camera, as if looking down at his shoulder. "But you found what you need?"

Amadeus nodded. Jones said nothing more on the subject. He seemed untroubled by this news. Instead, he talked about the repairs, said he'd check today's flight logs for errors, then he'd send the necessary parts as soon as possible. Until then, Amadeus would need a better place to hide the Pachyderm. Jones gave him some coordinates far out of town, ten kilometers from any houses but only a couple kilometers from the highway.

"You can hitchhike back into Prague," Jones said.

"Hitchhike? Are you kidding me? Nobody hitchhikes. You just can't ... it's dangerous."

"You just flew an experimental aircraft over the Atlantic Ocean and you're telling me you're worried about hitchhiking? Kid, I used to hitchhike from the east coast to the west coast on a whim, no money, and this was back when the newspapers were full of stories about hitchhikers being murdered and raped, usually in that order. Plus, you're in Europe. Things are different there. You'll be fine."

"If you say so," Amadeus said, not really feeling like he'd be fine. He'd rather walk all the way to Prague than hitchhike. Who hitchhiked, anyway, he wondered, besides old people and characters in books? Who knew what people were capable of? One of them had already made a holiday of smashing his craft.

Jones double checked exactly what parts were required. Amadeus then asked about using duct tape to fix the window. Jones yelled at him.

"Are you ignorant? If you're going to fix something, do it right. Don't duct tape it. Jesus. That sounds like something your father would do, a half-ass quick fix. The parts are coming, and you're going to get everything back to tip-top shape."

Amadeus said nothing, just let Jones finish his rant.

"Two days," Jones said. "I'll let you know later where you'll need to pick up the parts. I'll send all the tools you'll need. For now, get to those coordinates and make your way back to Prague. Understood?"

"Yeah, I got it," Amadeus said. "I still don't know where I'm going next, but I've got some files from Vesely's office that might be able to help."

"Figure it out," Jones said. Amadeus thought he'd been strange, different. He assumed that Jones was upset that the Pachyderm had been damaged, as if this were Amadeus' fault. He thought of the note, then Gravity. Jones isn't what he seems. Was Amadeus being paranoid, or was Jones really up to something?

30

He flew the wounded Pachyderm to the coordinates Jones had given him, covered it with the tarp, and set himself by the road with his thumb out. Within twenty minutes, he was sitting in the passenger seat of a middle-aged man's Peugot, listening to Liszt. The man had tried to talk to him, ask him a couple questions in halting English, but the conversation died soon after that.

The green countryside blurred outside the window. Amadeus wondered if this man had any murdering tendencies, and decided he didn't. He seemed sincere enough. He said he was an engineer. That made Amadeus feel better.

The man dropped him in downtown Prague, beside a tram stop, though Amadeus didn't know which one. He thanked the man and offered him some money, but the man smiled, shook his hand, and drove away.

Downtown with no place to go, Amadeus decided to do some sightseeing. He went to the Old Town Square and, out of morbid curiosity, a torture museum. After leaving the museum, the heat of the street and the crush of the people made his head spin. His stomach rumbled, and he set out for food. Like the restaurant before, the places here had menus in both English and Czech. He chose one at random, a dimly lit place, faux-rustic, with some classical piano music playing on the sound system. The waitress handed him a menu, but he didn't look at it. Instead, he asked her what she liked to eat, hoping she spoke English.

"The pickled cheese sandwich is very delicious," she said, smiling at him.

"Really? Pickled cheese?" Amadeus asked.

"Sounds not so good, but the taste is very delicious."

Amadeus said that would be fine. His food arrived; the bread was crusty and the cheese oily, pungent and, Amadeus decided, very delicious indeed. Shredded cabbage and cucumber gave the sandwich some crunch.

After he finished, he checked his phone for affordable accommodations. He crossed a square where church spires tried to impale the clouds. He tried several guesthouses, explaining at each that he had lost his passport, and finally found one that would let him stay without it.

In his dim room sat a small bed and a low wooden writing desk. He spread his pilferings from Vesely's out on the table. First, he leafed through the folder marked "Investments." Lots of financial data, and what appeared to be company profiles. While scanning one of these pages, most of which were written in Czech, he found his father's name. After that, he found Esther's name, and two others: Quinton Laroux and Edward Ross. In his notebook, he wrote these names down. The second name sounded familiar. He typed it into his phone. His jaw dropped with recognition as he read the search result summary.

Edward Maximilian Ross, 35, is the controversial American computer scientist, VC investor, and founder and CEO of Tivooki Systems. For the past eight years he's been ranked among the world's 500 wealthiest people, though the exact amount of his fortune is unknown. Ross is best known for an advanced storage technology that allows free, unlimited data storage for all internet users. While admired by many, critics point out that forty percent of the world's digital data is stored on Tivooki

Systems servers.

Mr. Ross has a history of misanthropic statements. Last year, while accepting an award from the National Science Foundation, Ross caused an outrage when he said the human race was "like a plague of locusts upon the earth, consuming her resources and leaving nothing but a trail of empty shells." Ross also maintains a small, highly-trained security force which insiders estimate numbers around fifty people.

Quinton Laroux returned no results. Who, he wondered, doesn't even show up on an internet search? Everyone shows up somewhere. But the man had to be well-off if he was able to operate as an investor in his father's research. It didn't make sense, this Laroux guy, totally anonymous, unknown. Unless ... he wanted to remain unknown. Amadeus knew you could pay people for such a service. He continued searching but didn't find anything more. Laroux was a shadow, a whisper, totally invisible.

Could he get access to Ross? If so, what would he do? And how could he find Laroux? He needed some help, so he called Grassal. Grassal's tiny image appeared on the screen. Crutches leaned against the desk.

"Agent Delgado here."

"I need all the information you can find on Edward Maximilian Ross. What he's like, how to find him, whatever you can find. There should be plenty on him."

"The Tivooki Systems guy?"

"That's right, and there's a man named Quinton Laroux. I couldn't find a thing. Maybe you'll have better luck. But I just want you working on this. Don't tell Lilly or Jones."

"But ..." Grassal said.

"That's the way it has to be right now. Just you and me until we know more. Any word from Gravity?"

"Nothing. Like he just disappeared."

"Okay, I'll contact you soon. And Grassal?"

"Yeah?"

"Thanks, brother."

31

Amadeus was in a cold room that stretched into forever, but he could only see a few meters before everything faded to black. Metal beams supported an obscured ceiling. In the dark distance, he heard a clicking sound, like a dog walking on hardwood. He called out, but the words from his mouth were foreign and undecipherable. A breeze blew, and his clothes waved like they were on a laundry line. When he looked down, his clothes disintegrated and his body had withered down to nothing but grey skin stretched over extruding bones.

The clicking grew louder, more rapid. Amadeus ran his hands over his body, trying to assure himself he was still physical. His teeth felt loose. He pulled on his front teeth and they came out in his hand, followed by a spray of brown blood like chocolate syrup. The clicks became scratches, and the scratches came from all directions, growing closer and closer.

Amadeus woke with a start and sat upright in his bed, panting as if after a sprint. Around him was the familiar room of the night before, with the little desk, and the crisp white sheets bunched up at his feet. Their wrinkles reminded him of the stretched skin of his dream. He ran his hand over his torso, relieved that he still had a little pudge on his stomach. His face, though, seemed bonier than ever.

Pulling himself out of bed, he checked his phone and found a message from Jones. He read the message. "Package arrives today. Lilly is bringing it. Meet her at the airport this evening, Lufthansa flight number 5321. She should land around seven p.m. your time. Don't let her out of your sight. It's a dangerous world out there for a girl like her." A girl like her, Amadeus thought, surprised Lilly was making the trip.

Yesterday, he had decided to find a translator for Vesely's documents, but he couldn't just drop a folder full of stolen financial statements and memos on a translator's desk. His solution was decidedly low-tech—he would copy by hand everything that looked important, replacing each name with the first letter of the first name, shifted right by two, so Tommy became "V", Ross became "T", and so on. Save for names, addresses, and a few technology cognates, Amadeus couldn't understand a word of what he was writing. And now, excited and a little nervous at the prospect of Lilly joining him in Prague, he continued this task, working until late morning.

At the front desk downstairs, he rang the bell. A man came out, not much older than himself. He had auburn hair and thick-rimmed glasses. The glasses had no lenses. In English, he asked what he could do for Amadeus.

"I need some business documents translated from Czech to English. Do you know where I can find someone that could do that? It's just for me, so the English doesn't have to be perfect."

The man smiled. "I study English for many years. I can do it." Amadeus asked him his rate. "Three hundred and fifty crown per page, every fourth page is only two fifty."

"I have twenty-four pages. They're all handwritten, but the writing is neat. Can you have them done by tonight?" Amadeus asked.

"I could do by tonight, but this makes hurry hurry job. Can you pay a little extra, say two hundred crown? Maybe then I could finish tonight."

Amadeus nodded and said that would be fine. He handed the man the documents. "What's your name?"

"I am Jan, just call me Jan, like January. I was born in January."

"Okay Jan, great. I'll be back later tonight."

32

At the airport, a digital screen reported Lilly's flight was delayed. Amadeus bought a copy of the Prague Post, settled into a coffee shop, and started on the crossword, deliberately ignoring any actual news articles. Three hours later, crossword completed, he stood at the international arrivals gate holding a little cardboard sign he had made. Of course she would recognize him, but he thought it might be a nice touch. People streamed out, pushing luggage carts. He held the sign above his head and caught a flash of red hair. There she was, struggling to push a cart piled high with soft-sided suitcases. All around him, people embraced as if trying to prevent the other from floating away.

"Lilly," he said, waving his sign. She finally saw him. She strode over and threw her arms around him, pressing her body against his. He wasn't expecting that. As he held her, the image of Vesely's mutilated body crept into his mind. "Good to see you. But I can't help but wonder why you would come here."

"Why wouldn't I? That's the question. What better excuse to go to Europe than to deliver parts and tools? You need parts, I need a vacation, and Grassal's mobile enough to help my father for a couple of days. It's a perfect match. A win-win-win. And since I'm here, you can show me around."

"Now?"

"Come on, Amadeus. I've only got a couple days. At least let me enjoy myself?"

They stood in silence for a few moments. The people around them had faded away and soon they stood alone outside the gate. Lilly waited with her arms crossed. Finally Amadeus gave her a noncommittal answer. They left the terminal, Amadeus pushing the cart and half-listening as she talked about the long flight, the singing stewards, the pig slop they passed off as food, and the weird feeling in her head. She said she was too tired to sleep and hungry enough to eat a goat or a sheep whatever they ate here.

"We'll drop this stuff off and then I'll take you to a place I know."

After several attempts, they found a taxi that could accommodate all their luggage. They still ended up riding with heavy suitcases on their laps. At the guesthouse, Amadeus stopped by the desk, but Jan said he wasn't finished yet; he needed until the next day. They left and went to the restaurant. On the street outside, someone bumped into Amadeus.

"Excuse me," a man said in English. Amadeus looked into his eyes as he brushed past. The man had shoulder-length brown hair, and his eyes were almost entirely black: sclera, retina, and pupil, the only exception being a thin ring of pale blue iris.

"You're excused," Amadeus said, ignoring the whisper of panic in the back of his mind.

"Pickled cheese?" Lilly said after Amadeus ordered for her. He had the mustachioed waiter again. Outside the restaurant, a string quartet played something modern and repetitive. A candle flickered on the table. "Sounds like heartburn."

He promised her she would like it. The encounter with the man outside had left him unsettled, but he wasn't sure why.

"And beer?"

"Everyone else is drinking. I think I saw some schoolchildren with beer in their lunch boxes."

Lilly laughed before she spoke. "This city, it looks amazing. I've never been out of the States. Well, I went to Calgary once, but that hardly counts."

"Can I see your passport?"

She pulled it out of her purse and handed it to him. He glanced at her picture and suppressed a laugh.

"Amadeus! Never laugh at a girl's picture, you could give her a complex."

"You, you look so ... young." In the picture, she wore thick-rimmed red spectacles and neon yellow braces. While he examined the passport, the mustachioed waiter brought two bottles of beer and glasses. Amadeus started to drink from the bottle but the ever-patient waiter wagged his finger at him, grabbed the beer bottle, and poured it into the glass for him.

"Are you trying to get me drunk?" Lilly said.

"No. Why would I do that? Besides, you probably need the carbs after a long flight."

"Carbs, right. If you say so. But sometimes bad things happen when I drink." Amadeus took a swig of his beer and wiped his mouth with the back of his hand. He was enjoying her company, and he thought things were going really well, but ... something felt off.

"Okay, I'll bite. What happens when you drink?"

"Well, the first time I drank beer I was ten years old. Daddy had left a can of beer in the fridge, so I grabbed it, hid under the bathroom sink, and drank the entire thing. I puked about a minute after I finished it."

"Under the sink?"

"No, in the toilet. I'm not an animal," Lilly said, twirling a strand of her hair. "But it's been all downhill from there."

Their sandwiches arrived. Amadeus was hungry, but he waited for Lilly to take the first bite. She picked up her fork and knife and cut into the sandwich. The waiter started to show her how to eat it, but Amadeus waved him away.

"Just use your hands," Amadeus said.

Looking exasperated, Lilly shrugged and took a big bite of the sandwich. Pieces of oily cheese and shredded vegetables slid out the end and onto the plate, sending tiny droplets of oil onto Lilly's white shirt. The splattering food brought to Amadeus' mind a flashback to Ramona's shop. His mind played through the entire scene, right up until the end, when he had stood over the man who had been incapacitated by Gravity's seizure grenade. That man had had the same black eyes as the man who'd bumped him on the street.

"Oh my god," Lilly said, her mouth still full, "it's wonderful." She took her time, sipping her beer after each bite. Amadeus ate fast, finishing his beer before his sandwich. During the meal, his chest began to constrict, his hands grew sweaty, and he was sure other diners were making discreet glances in their direction. He'd been careless and reckless just walking around like this was an ordinary night. Even if he was mistaken about the man, and he probably was, someone else could have recognized him and called the police. Maybe another American, maybe someone from near Vesely's house. He tore off a piece of napkin, balled it up, and rolled it between his fingers. Lilly narrowed her eyes at him. He stopped.

"Everyone is looking at us," Amadeus said. Lilly glanced around, then furrowed her brow.

"You're imagining it. No one's looking at us."

"We need to leave now," Amadeus said. "Quickly." Lilly started to protest but Amadeus' look convinced her to guzzle the rest of her beer. He flagged the waiter down, paid, and left a generous tip. Outside, Amadeus looked around. No one seemed to be paying them any attention. They hurried towards his guesthouse in silence, passing the Charles Bridge on their way. Lilly gazed at the statues as they passed.

"All these dead saints," Lilly said. "I wonder if it was worth it."

"If what was worth what?"

"Dying for whatever they died for. You do or say something

to piss off the Big Power, you get yourself killed, and a couple centuries later they build a statue for you. Then the tourists come and take selfies with you."

"These statues probably don't even look like them," Amadeus said.

"Nobody even knows who they are or what they did, they just see some old guy covered in pigeon shit that looks pretty on a bridge."

Lilly stopped, put her elbows on the balustrade, and looked out at the city. Nearby, a man sat with an easel, sketching charcoal caricatures. A little fluorescent light illuminated his work-in-progress.

"It's so old, this city, this continent," Lilly said. "But I wouldn't want to live in the old days. People talk about the good old days but they forget about things like fleas, raw sewage, and plagues. Can you imagine what this place smelled like three hundred years ago?"

"Probably pretty bad," Amadeus said.

"You know what else smells bad?" Lilly asked. Amadeus' eyes darted around the crowd but saw nothing that looked out of the ordinary. So he leaned toward Lilly and made a show of sniffing her. She smirked, then smacked his shoulder.

"No, what?"

"My father."

"Umm."

"Not smell, I mean he's just acting kind of strange, distant, like he's hiding something. He *is* up to something, I just don't know what. I've caught him on the phone several times. Whenever I walk in, he shuts the screen down. I have never known him to do that. He just doesn't hide things. So when he does, it's terribly obvious."

"Lilly, I'm sure it's nothing," Amadeus said, thinking about Gravity's note. "This is your father we're talking about. He's probably trying to figure this thing out, just like we are."

"I'm sure he is, that's probably it, but he's never been like this."

"It's a stressful time. Maybe he has a girlfriend."

"He scares women away. I told you about the nurses. He can be a pretty intense guy. All I'm saying is ... well, I don't really know. I just wanted to tell you. What do you think?"

"So far he's done more than anyone else to help me. Not to downplay what you and Grassal are doing, but still. I trust him; I kind of have to."

"That ... means a lot to me. I wish I could say the same." She placed a hand on his. Amadeus felt heat rising to his face and was glad of the dark. "I know that sounds like a horrible thing for someone to say about their father, especially after you just lost yours. I'm sorry."

"It's okay," Amadeus said, understanding now that they had a common bond beyond a desire to unravel a mystery. "Let's make our way back, but maybe take the long way. There are some things I'd like to show you."

33

They walked over cobblestone streets and through alleys that didn't feel like alleys. After passing under an archway, they stopped at the base of the astronomical clock. Its orange and blue circles and strange symbols reminded Amadeus of a deck of tarot cards.

"Those are zodiac signs?" Lilly said.

"Yeah, I think so." He had read about the clock on his way to Prague. "You see the four figures? On the far left, the guy with the mirror, that's vanity. Beside him, a Jew. When this was built, Jews weren't particularly popular, usury and all that. The skeleton there, that's time, and beside him, a Turk. The king gouged out the clockmaker's eyes after he finished so he couldn't make another."

"That's a hell of a thank you, isn't it?"

"Medieval gratitude. Lilly, I'm still thinking about what you said about your father."

"Maybe I'm just imagining things, but I really think something's going on."

"Anything else I should know about?"

"Someone recognized you in New York, right after the demon ate all those investment bankers. They connected that with your father's murder, Ramona's murder, and the dead cop on the roof. You're a popular villain right now."

"Great," Amadeus said, looking over his shoulder. "That's just great."

"I'm sorry, I should've told you this when I first got here, but I just wanted us to, you know, enjoy my time here and pretend that things were normal, that I was just here to visit an old friend, and that you weren't connected with three murders."

As Lilly spoke, Amadeus' eyes slid across the crowd. A familiar figure stood across the street, a barrel-chested man with shoulder-length brown hair. Amadeus turned his face away, for all the good it would do.

"Lilly, don't look now, but not far from us is the same man I bumped into earlier. He's across the street. Wait. I'll turn you around." He put his arms around her and twisted her in the direction of the man. He whispered in her ear. "Have you seen him before?"

"Oh my. Yeah, I've seen him. Twice."

"Then let's get out of here."

They walked down a tight alley to another street. Crowded pubs and souvenir shops lined the way. Wooden puppets and red-faced men stared out of the shop windows. After a block, they turned down another side street and ducked through an open door to the foyer of an apartment building.

Amadeus' hands began to shake. In the dark, he recalled the mutilated body of Vesely Gustavius, the metallic blood smell, and the terrified woman in the hallway.

"Lilly, I don't like it in here. I really want to get back on the street."

"We're hidden. What's the problem?" Lilly peered out the little glass pane on the door.

"I just, this, the dark," Amadeus said.

"Shh." Lilly dropped her voice to a whisper. "He's coming down the street."

Amadeus sat up and glanced through the window to the street outside. The man strolled through the night, his hands in his pockets. His lips were puckered like he was whistling.

Though the foyer was cool, Amadeus felt a film of sweat growing on his forehead. He wiped it away. The black-eyed man leaned close to a window across the street and gazed in. From upstairs, Amadeus heard jingling keys.

"Shit," Amadeus said. A moment passed, and they exchanged a glance. "We'll go upstairs."

Before going up, Amadeus looked out again. The man was still across the street, hands behind his back, looking in another window, not even trying to be discreet. The dark staircase had landings on each half floor. They crept to the first landing, Amadeus following Lilly. Footsteps approached from above. On the second-floor landing they stopped.

"What if they question us?"

"Kiss me hard," Lilly said. Amadeus hesitated. "I know you don't have to fake it. Just do what you wanted to do back in Colorado." Amadeus pressed his lips against hers. Lilly stepped back and he pressed her against the wall. She tasted like beer. He ran one hand down her leg, over her jeans; she bit his lip and pushed his hand away. The footsteps grew closer, closer. Lilly tugged at a handful of his shirt. The person muttered something as they passed by on their way downstairs. When the sound of the steps faded, they bolted up the stairs to the second floor. At the rear of the building, a green sign showed the way to the back exit.

"There's our way out," Amadeus said.

"Don't get the wrong idea. That was just a distraction." Flickering fluorescent lights lit the hallway, the wood floor scraped and worn from years, centuries, of footsteps. Each door had a brass mail slot. On the other end of the hall, a swinging wooden door led to a narrow stairway, winding and dark.

As Amadeus pushed the door open, heavy footsteps started approaching from the front stairs. They slipped into the back stairwell. Amadeus stopped the door from swinging behind them. With each step they took, the stairs groaned in protest. They gave up trying not to make any noise and ran down. At the bottom, Amadeus gripped the back door's handle. He turned the knob back and forth, he pushed and pulled, but it wouldn't open. In the dark, he ran his hand up and down the door frame.

"Deadbolt," Lilly said. She found the latch, turned it, and flung the door open. Lilly ran out first, then Amadeus, who pulled the door closed as he left.

"Walk fast, don't run," Amadeus said. "If we can get to the main street, we can lose him in the crowds."

They started back towards the Old Town Square. Every few steps, Amadeus glanced over his shoulder. He didn't see the man. As they pressed their way through the crowds, Lilly began to giggle, just a little at first, but after a moment she was doubled over with her hands on her knees. Amadeus looked at her, puzzled, then felt it too, the relief, the release, the escape. Their waning adrenaline propelled them through the floodlit night, laughing all the way.

When they returned to the guesthouse, Amadeus waved at Jan and told him he'd be down in the morning for the documents. Jan looked at Lilly and gave Amadeus a knowing wink. Amadeus just shook his head. Upstairs, Lilly flopped down on the full-sized bed and stretched out her arms. Amadeus wondered if they could both fit into the bed, and if so, where that would lead.

"I know what you're thinking, so don't even ask," Lilly said.

"It was that obvious?" Amadeus saw no point in trying to deny it: he wanted her.

She smirked then tossed a pillow onto the woven rug by the radiator. "There's your bed, flyboy."

"That's cruel," Amadeus said. But only minutes after he covered himself with the airplane blanket Lilly had taken as a souvenir of her flight did he fall into the black sleep of the exhausted.

Sometime before dawn, Amadeus' own screaming startled him awake. His body jerked and he hit his head on the warm metal of the radiator. He expelled a string of curses then put his hand on his head to soothe the pain as he got to his feet. He fully expected Lilly to be staring at him with sleepy green eyes, but she was still asleep, rhythmically breathing in the stuffy air of their room and wrapped up in a tangle of sheets. He thought about waking her, but decided to let her sleep off the jet lag. For now, he padded down creaking stairs and found Jan at the desk.

"Good morning," Jan said. "You had a satisfying night?" His hair was slicked back with pomade. Amadeus thought he looked like a man who'd just stepped out of a wind tunnel. Jan offered him coffee. Amadeus declined with a smile.

"I slept, I'll say that," Amadeus said, leaning on the counter. Jan frowned and appeared genuinely disappointed for Amadeus. "Yourself?"

"I wished for good night, but it never happened. I had nightmares, first since I was child."

"Nightmares?"

"Your friend or associate or whoever he is, he is crazy man. Rich, too. Maybe he is writer, man who constructs fictions. He mentioned to make profit talking to dead people and doing teleporting. Maybe he is crazy rich writer. Who knows? I just make translation."

"You're finished, then?" Amadeus asked.

"I am finished, yes," Jan said. He handed Amadeus the original document and a folder of typed, double-spaced sheets. "I made marks on original, I hope is okay."

"It's okay," Amadeus said. "Here is your payment." He handed him a small stack of notes he had set aside, folded, in his wallet. "Now, two more questions. One, where can I hire a driver, and two, what would it cost for you to forget I was ever here?"

34

They drove along a road beside the tracks. Amadeus liked the feel of the wind on his arm, which hung out the window. For a driver, Jan had called a friend of his. This friend had arrived an hour later, blasting Czech metal from the tinny speakers of his old Bongo delivery truck. On a map, Amadeus had pointed out to Jan the place he wanted to go. Jan had explained the job to his friend and apologized that his friend didn't speak any English. "But for driving, he is okay," Jan had said.

Now the unshaven driver was singing along to an angry song. The stale smell of cigarettes lingered like a bad rumor. He offered the opened pack to Amadeus and Lilly. Lilly took one. Amadeus sighed.

"What would your father say?" Amadeus said.

"My father is an asshole. I'm due for a little rebellion. Didn't you wonder why he sent me instead of using FedEx?" Amadeus said nothing because he hadn't actually thought of it. "I told him the only way I'd continue our present arrangement was if he let me bring you the parts. I had to get out of there, if only for a couple days."

"And if he would've said no?"

"I would've taken the Jeep and never looked back."

"It's that bad?"

"It's getting that way. Have I ever told you about the panic room?"

"Um."

"Guess not. Remember the door in the hangar with the round handle, like on a ship?" Amadeus said he did. "That leads to the panic room. Down there he has enough supplies to live for three years. Three years! And he says it's for me. Fuck that, if the world dies, I don't want to stick around. What's the point? But he says it's to protect me. I said if he wants to protect me, his plans should include considerations for my brain as well as my body. I told him I would go crazy down there."

As she spoke, she tried not to blow the smoke in his face, but with the windows down, the cigarette's fumes flowed in all directions. Amadeus said nothing more, only rode the waves of the wind with his hand and gazed at the passing landscape.

"That's odd. You told me he scared off nurses. Is that really the only reason you've stayed? I mean, to me it sounds like he wants to keep you locked away."

"I don't want to talk about it. Just because you had to sleep on the floor doesn't mean you can interrogate me."

"Come on, Lilly, talk to me."

"No."

"Lilly ..."

"Fine. You really want to know me? Okay, here it is: I was in juvie for two years. I burned down a convenience store."

"Jesus. Why?"

"I had my reasons. They had it coming. Is that enough for you? Have you satisfied your curiosity?"

"Okay," Amadeus said. "I got caught shoplifting once."

"Aren't we just a regular Bonnie and Clyde?" Lilly was silent for the rest of the drive.

Half an hour later, they reached the spot, about fifty kilometers out. No houses nearby. Only the desolate road and a nearby forest. The driver spoke in a perplexed tone, probably asking why they would want to be let out here, as he helped them unload the heavy suitcases. He handled them with care, as if they were full of snow globes. When the driver pointed to the forest, Amadeus said, "Camping." The driver appeared to know this word, because he smiled, looked at Lilly, and gave Amadeus a wink before he hopped in his truck and drove off. Amadeus blushed.

All four suitcases had wheels, but pulling them over the bumpy ground of the forest floor made them both strain. Lilly, as she pulled her two, grunted and grumbled. They reached the Pachyderm after an hour.

The Pachyderm still sat under its tarp, undisturbed in its temporary forest home. Amadeus pulled the tarp off. Lilly hopped inside and started playing a jazz recording Amadeus found slightly grating.

"Coltrane?" Amadeus asked. He had already opened all the cases and was inspecting the parts.

"Charles Mingus," Lilly said. "The Black Saint and the Sinner Lady, good stuff. Mingus was one of the few jazz guys to actually do full arrangements. People called him the heir of Ellington. He was an asshole, though. Had temper tantrums."

"You don't have temper tantrums," Amadeus said, only half-listening to her.

"I'm a balanced girl, with a totally normal life. Just like you."

"I had a normal life." He began to unpack the replacement parts and lay them on the tarp he had spread over the forest duff.

"You were never normal," Lilly said. "But maybe you're not as weird as I thought."

He narrowed his eyes, then smiled. "I'll take that as a compliment. Can you get me the calipers from the toolbox?"

"Do I look like your bitch?"

Amadeus scowled.

"Just playing," Lilly said as she handed him the calipers. "Um, this might be an awkward question, but ..."

"All questions that start with 'this might be an awkward question' are going to be awkward questions," Amadeus said.

"Shoot."

"Have you ever been in a relationship with a woman?"

Amadeus blushed as he thought about Regina, an English major he used to pay for sex. Amadeus had met her through friends, and he used to pay her one or two awkward visits a month during his last two years at UConn. Amadeus reasoned it was both ethical, since she spent the money on rare illuminated medieval manuscripts, and economical; based on what his friends with girlfriends said, visiting her was a far cheaper way to meet his needs than to get into a committed relationship. Besides, Amadeus liked that they both knew exactly where they stood with each other: she provided a service, and he gave her money for it.

"Yes, I mean, I've been with women. Well, a woman. Several times. I'd rather not talk about it." Lilly didn't seem satisfied by the answer, and Amadeus didn't want to elaborate, so he said, "She died."

"Oh. Sorry." Lilly examined her wrists as if her veins were interesting headlines.

"It's okay. Now, will you help me with this compressor?"

35

By nightfall, Amadeus had replaced the damaged parts. Lilly had started to read the translated documents but had fallen asleep. The papers had slipped out of her hands and onto the floor. He thought she looked like a student on the night before a final exam, exhausted from last-minute cramming.

Amadeus turned on the exterior lights, put away his tools, and started the engines. They sounded good. The Pachyderm was in the air before Lilly woke up. When she did awaken, they were several hundred meters off the ground. She looked out the window, screamed in surprise, then began to laugh.

"Jesus, I had forgotten where I was." From her bag, she pulled out a black knitted cap. "It's cold in here," she said.

"It's cold outside." He allowed the Pachyderm to hover as he checked the map for their next destination. He realized he didn't have a next destination. "Did you learn anything?"

"Sorry, I fell asleep before I even read them. What is it, like five in the morning back in the States?"

"Who knows? Would you like a city tour?"

She smiled and Amadeus set off towards Prague. Flying without lights, he circled around Prague Castle, its lonely spires illuminated by yellow sodium lights. By this time, most visitors had left. Lilly pressed her face against the window to gaze at the complex below. Amadeus took the Pachyderm down until they were level with the top of the cathedral.

"I wonder if any maidens were ever locked in the tower," Amadeus said.

"I know how they feel," Lilly said. Below them, the red tile roofs had become shaded black by the night, while the streets were lit up like a circuit board.

"What would he do if you didn't go back? At least not when you were supposed to?" Amadeus asked.

"The first thing he'd do is shut down the Pachyderm. You know he has remote command and control capability. After that, who knows? But we'd be stuck here."

"I didn't know that."

"You think he'd just let some kid he kind of knows run off with his multi-million dollar ego trip without a kill switch? You're funny."

"Hmm," Amadeus said. At that moment, something occurred to him: his father had trusted Jones enough to send Amadeus to him, but what if his father hadn't known Jones as well as he had thought?

The morning was cool, and they went for one last stroll in town before heading to the airport. They arrived early at the airport and found a little table to have coffee.

"If Grassal or I learn anything else, or you need to talk to us about what's going on with my father, we'll need to bypass any monitoring. Don't use your main email account." She handed him a slip of paper with an address and a long string of random characters. "Grassal, that clever boy, set up an encrypted chat channel on an anonymous server. You could use the Pachyderm flight computer to access it, but that's probably unwise. If you have to, go through a proxy. If there's anything sensitive we need to discuss, I'll send you something in your main email and put the word 'friend' in the subject line. You see that word, read deeper. Look for a subtext. Assume everything. And jump on the chat."

"Got it. Thanks for bringing the parts." Amadeus grasped her hands in his. She didn't pull them away. "It was good to see you."

She smirked. "If you see that big black-eyed bastard, punch him for me. Can you do that?"

He nodded.

"And Amadeus? Thanks for showing me around. I ... had a good time."

Two hours and three cups of coffee later, Lilly was bound for America and Amadeus was in a cab headed southeast.

36

Back in his guesthouse, Amadeus stretched out on the bed and leafed through the documents Jan had translated for him. One in particular caught his attention.

The Brunmeier investments are likely to be a total loss. Eight months ago, he offered to buy me out for five million dollars. A pittance. At the time I chose to stay in. Maybe I shouldn't have. Too late now, the offer was withdrawn. And after seeing what he created, with no hope of a return in the near term, I have no choice but to stay in. To put my faith in a crazy man. Why do I do this? Because he is less crazy than Ross. The things Ross says ...

This is more than a business decision. This is a defense of humanity. Perhaps I can take a deduction for humanitarian work. Jokes aside, I must stay in this dire business to act as a counterweight to Ross. He is a very powerful man, but I have resources as well. Maybe Esther is more clever than me. She has, to use an English expression, risen above the fray. She refused to become involved. She said the less she knew the better off she would be. Perhaps this worked. Sometimes I think ignorance is better! But no, I am always the curious cat.

Ross desires to be the only investor in Brunmeier's research. Fortunately, Brunmeier made a clever contract and said no single person could have a majority stake; he created a balance of power. One consolation in an ocean of grief. Yet I feel the balance shifting.

If only Laroux would come out of that malarial jungle one more time, we could work something out with Brunmeier to push Ross out entirely. This would be the sweetest relief. The last meeting was a disaster. But all Laroux wants to do is build schools and remove land mines in Siem Reap, waiting for Brunmeier to finish his work. He believes in Brunmeier and his research, that Brunmeier will lay the foundation for a legitimate teleportation system. The idea is so intoxicating. And maybe by the time our grandchildren have grown into adults, the idea will be realized.

But the finish time is so far away, there is much work to be done, and Brunmeier appears distracted with this business about talking to dead people before they are dead. I have always had my doubts about this direction of the research, and I've always urged him to focus on more practical aspects such as the transportation. He must forget this spooky business and focus on the task at hand. But Laroux, when he does make his opinion known, says talking to the past is an idea with merit, that it will allow us to heal, to say the things we never got to say. But I think this is just a Frenchman's guilt over his ancestors' colonial adventures.

Amadeus put the paper down and called Grassal, who answered on the first ring.

"What have you found on Laroux?" Amadeus said.

"A couple of old news articles in French. I translated them as best I could. Laroux used to be CEO of a French telecom. One day he just decided to resign and start working on development projects. Also, and I had to dig for this, I learned he gave a small fortune to a few charities. Some people accused him of embezzling the money from his old company, but they found him innocent."

"Good. I mean, good that he wasn't guilty. Is he in Cambodia now?"

"As far as I know," Grassal said.

Amadeus explained what he had learned. "This is starting to come together. Did Ross kill Vesely?"

"It's possible. Maybe Ross set it up, paid someone to do it for him, or had his security goons do it. Assuming our information is solid, we can assume it wasn't Esther. There could be other people involved, like Gravity suggested, but after what I've just read, that doesn't seem as likely. As for Laroux, he seems like a do-gooder not particularly interested in either profit or the implementation details."

"Unless that's a cover," Grassal said.

"I can't say why, but I doubt it. According to what Vesely wrote, Ross wanted complete control over the research. Vesely and my father kept that from happening. What if, since Ross couldn't buy everyone out, he looked for a different way?" Overhead, the ceiling fan shuddered, making a repetitive clicking that made Amadeus think of Morse code, as if the fan were sending him a message.

"Which means ..." Grassal said, and understanding began to flood Amadeus' brain.

"Which means that Ross could be my father's killer," Amadeus said. He smacked the bed, once, twice, then again and again. His heart began to race and his fingernails dug into the synthetic leather of the chair. An animal moan escaped his lips.

"Amadeus, buddy, calm down. Breathe." Amadeus listened to his friend and took one deep breath, followed by another. He kept this up for half a minute. A sensation of control flowed over him, mingling with his rage, like the snakes of a caduceus wrapped around a staff.

"Okay, thanks for that. I'm good now," Amadeus said.

"You sure?"

"No."

"Thought so. There's one more thing. Gravity left me a cryptic voicemail yesterday. He said that he was trying to pull back the curtains and reveal the actors but he lacked the proper weights. Strange dude."

"Hmm. For now, just tell Jones that I'm going to Cambodia to find Laroux. He's the last one we need. Maybe he can tell us more about Ross. It's falling together."

"Like an equation. But ..."

"But the big picture is still out of focus, like a camera lens that's a little off."

"And when you find Laroux?"

"I'll adjust the camera and maybe frame the shot."

"Good luck, brother." Grassal shut the connection down, leaving Amadeus to imagine the ways he would murder Edward Maximilian Ross. After allowing several fantasies to play out, he changed his focus to the task at hand: Cambodia. He imagined a river running through a jungle, but that was all. On the flight computer he studied the two legacies of Cambodia: 1,000 year-old temples from a lost empire, and a million unanswered questions.

Amadeus developed a flight plan.

37

To recharge both the Pachyderm's batteries and his own mind, he stopped first in Turkey, and then the next evening, before making the last leg of his flight, he found a landing and recharging site on a mountaintop near the Soon Valley in Pakistan. Red and white flowers covered the valley, swaying in the wind like the surface of the sea. He thought the flowers seemed familiar, but he wasn't sure why. He crushed one in his hand. Sticky goo oozed out. Scrubby forests surrounded the field. According to the map, the nearest village lay eight kilometers away. He threw the tarp over the Pachyderm just in case, now that so much of the paint was missing. Covered, the Pachyderm just looked like a translucent shimmer of red, white, and green. Amadeus crawled inside and slept until sunrise.

In the morning, fog lay over the field. He was shaking dew from the tarp when something caught his attention. A group of eight black silhouettes stood on the edge of the field, watching, motionless. Amadeus squinted and saw the silhouettes were women in burkas. He waved; he couldn't help himself. They didn't wave back, didn't react, didn't move, only stared, black statues standing sentinel. Amadeus kept the women in his peripheral vision as he finished his exterior inspection. Back in the Pachyderm, he started the turbofans. Just as he did, a little boy popped out from behind one of the women and began to jump up and down, waving both his arms as if trying to shoo a swarm of insects. As Amadeus took off, the boy bounded towards where the Pachyderm had been. Even from the air, Amadeus could see the smile on his face.

That day, he passed over India, Bangladesh, Myanmar, and Thailand. When he crossed over into Myanmar, raindrops began to streak across the windshield. The wind battered the Pachyderm, rocking it back and forth, arrhythmic like a sputtering engine. As much as he could do so safely, he read up on his destination: Cambodia. At Siem Reap, millennia-old temples stood as evidence of the once-great Khmer empire, an empire eventually beaten back like an unruly bear by the Thais. As Vesely had noted, the French had colonized the country, and according to what he read, the legacy of the French lingered like a carving on an ancient tree. If the French legacy was like a carving on a tree, then the Khmer Rouge regime and the forced relocation, reeducation, slave labor, and famine that came along with it, was the lightning that struck the tree and reduced it to a charred stump.

His stomach turned.

His father had told him they'd lost relatives in the Holocaust and, given recent events, he could personally attest to the barbarity of man, but this information surprised him; he didn't recall learning about it in school, as if some genocides were more important than others. The worst part: Pol Pot had died under house arrest, in his own bed, and not at the hands of those whose lives he destroyed.

Justice, he thought, should never be left to chance or committees.

For a landing site, he found an uninhabited area called O Ta Yu less than twenty-five kilometers outside of town. As he had done in Prague, he would land, cover the Pachyderm, and walk to the nearest road in the hopes of catching a ride. He scrounged through the supply box for an umbrella. Grassal had said he packed one, but Amadeus couldn't find it. He did find a waterproof bag, which he filled with extra clothes and money. He put his phone into yet a second waterproof case.

While he was tempted to drop below the clouds and get an aerial view of the temples, he knew the rain wouldn't stop the sightseers. People might see parts of the Pachyderm where the paint had been scraped off. The last thing he needed was some pictures of the Pachyderm's outline hovering over Angkor Wat ending up on the internet. So he stayed high until he reached O Ta Yu. There he dropped below clouds, confirmed that the area looked uninhabited, and made a vertical landing, going down fairly fast, as he was sure the air here was clear enough to see for at least ten kilometers, despite the rain. Looking at the ground below, he found a little clearing beside a stream, partially covered by vegetation. The Pachyderm sat down easy enough, but the ground below was uneven. Amadeus found himself leaning, though not enough to tip over. As before, he threw the tarp over the Pachyderm and set out towards the road.

The jungle was thick with green humidity. The rain felt like small weights slapping against his body. Amadeus had never seen or felt anything like it. The heat, rain, and writhing vegetation enveloped his body like a damp sleeping bag. Within five minutes, he was dripping wet, thankful he had brought a waterproof bag.

Every few meters he made a mark in a tree with his field knife. In the Czech Republic, he had been thankful for the markings he had left, even if he hadn't really needed them. Maybe they were training for this. Of course, he had had no idea he would end up hacking his way through a steamy Cambodian jungle in a ruthless rain. But who could know the future, who could foresee such things as betrayal, murder, and traveling around the world? Certainly, Amadeus thought, not me. No, I'm just the poor schmuck who has to run around and fix problems and atone for other people's sins. What if the right thing, though, wasn't really the right thing? What if all this was a mistake? Amadeus pushed these thoughts out of his head.

What happened, happened. Thinking about it would not change it. He had no way to go but forward, out of this jungle, out of this predicament, and onto what he hoped could be a normal life, a life without warrants, assassins, or inter-dimensional demons.

When he reached the road, it appeared to float in a sea of jungle, a straight, flat surgical cut through the green, like someone had unrolled a great spool of tape, crushing everything underneath it. No signs, driveways, or cars disturbed the silent stretch. He stood sodden beside the road, waiting for someone, hoping chance would send him a ride. Chance did not abide. He started south, towards town, following the route he had studied before landing, watching raindrops assault the road, for a split second upon impact mingling with the standing water, then exploding upward like an unfortunate trekker stepping on a mine.

After half an hour of walking, a strange contraption rolled towards him: an old motorcycle was pulling a little red-and-blue trailer behind it. The trailer was painted with loud colors. The drenched driver wore no helmet or glasses, just a purple shirt and hair slicked back from rain and wind. Under the canopy, two bench seats faced each other. In one sat a young man with a backpack.

"You look like you need a ride, my friend," the young man said, his accent Indian. "You are going to town?" Amadeus nodded. "Ponleak, do you mind if we add another passenger?" Ponleak was the driver.

"Is okay, but you pay little extra. Fuel very expensive," he said.

The young man nodded, then to Amadeus, he said, "My *tuk tuk* driver is an obstinate dude, always telling me how expensive fuel is, that if I want to go anywhere extra, I pay extra. So it goes. Do you mind to pitch in on our fare?" Amadeus said that was fine as he climbed in, glad to be out of the rain, even if shelter had become meaningless by this point. Amadeus thanked the young man for the ride and introduced himself as Wesley Oliver.

"Hello Wesley Oliver. I'm Salaman, but just call me Sal, like Sal Paradise," he said.

"Who's Sal Paradise?" Amadeus asked.

"Who's Sal Paradise?" Salaman asked, feigning offense. Amadeus started to apologize but Sal cut him off. "You're joking, right? You travel to Cambodia and you ask me who Sal Paradise is? You've heard of *On the Road*, right?"

"I've heard of it," Amadeus said, sounding unsure.

"Look, Wesley, we must fix this egregious gap in your appreciation of the spiritual journey. At my guesthouse, I actually have a copy I keep with me, I like to re-read sections now and again, but for you, the strange, soaked, and please take no offense, sadly ill-read, American, I assume you are American, that I find walking down a lonely stretch of highway, I think that is the perfect opportunity to give my copy away as a Gideon would give away a bible, for I do consider *On the Road* my bible. Do you take offense? I do hope not, for I want you to experience the joys of such a wonderful book ... and by one of your countrymen, of whom you are ignorant! Oh no, this is a deplorable oversight that must be rectified."

Amadeus nodded. He had seen *On the Road* in his father's collection of books, and his father had even once recommended it to him, but Amadeus had never read it.

"And if I may ask, what were you doing in the jungle, anyway?" Sal asked. Amadeus shifted in his seat.

"Hiking," Amadeus said. "I set out from Siem Reap this morning, but lost my map along the way."

"Hiking? Alone? In this jungle? You are a crazy man. You are lucky you did not find yourself blown to small pieces. Even today, there are still landmines. I hope you stayed on the paths."

"I was careful," Amadeus said.

"A crazy man is never careful, only lucky. And you are a crazy, lucky man."

"I don't feel lucky," Amadeus said, telling the truth. "I feel ... hungry."

"Then we shall eat dinner together. I know a wonderful place. You can go to your guesthouse for dry clothes, then we can meet for dinner. Where are you staying?"

"Um ... downtown. In the backpacker area."

"Which one?"

"I forget," Amadeus said. "It was on my map."

"Are you near the night market?"

"That's right."

Sal yelled at Ponleak. He turned around, a soggy cigarette hanging out of his mouth. The *tuk tuk* veered a little to the right. "Drop this gentleman off at the night market." Ponleak nodded as he turned around, righting the direction of the *tuk tuk*, narrowly missing a Lexus SUV as it barreled down the rutted road.

38

The road into town changed from uninhabited jungle to a strip lined with shacks on stilts, front yards full of brown water, and little stores selling liters of fuel from plastic bottles. Women sat on their front stoops, waiting out the rain. Signs written in a curved, unknowable script advertised services and products he could only guess at. Amadeus realized his mouth was gaping. He had only seen such houses in pictures and documentaries. The shacks seemed to be thrown together from packing crates and leftover corrugated iron. Here and there sat piles of garbage, drenched by the rain. Closer to town were more concrete structures. Sal looked at him and raised a knowing eyebrow.

"One would think with all us people coming here, some of the money would be spread around. But this country," he lowered his voice, "is still a clusterfuck, even with all the NGOs and well-meaning travelers. And I know a clusterfuck when I see it."

Ponleak drove slowly over the marginally-paved main street, making quick, stomach-turning swerves to avoid the brick-filled potholes. As he did, the *tuk tuk* groaned, and Amadeus and Sal slid from side to side. Amadeus clutched his bag in his lap. Sal did the same, holding onto a handle that came down from the roof. Sal pointed out a bank on a busy street corner. "Can you meet me there at, say, seven o'clock?"

Amadeus decided that yes, he should meet Sal for dinner, if only to get more information about the town, to find out where the expats hang out, and start looking for Laroux. Amadeus said seven o'clock was fine. That would give him time to find lodgings and change into some dry clothes.

Off the main road and onto an unpaved side street, Ponleak drove even faster. Mud flew up from the back wheels of the *tuk tuk*. They finally arrived at the night market. Even in the early afternoon, the neon sign for the market was lit. Amadeus hopped out and produced a soggy ten-dollar bill from his pocket. "That should cover it?"

"That's a little too much."

"Don't worry about it. Saved me a lot of pain."

"Suit yourself," Sal said, pocketing the wet money. "See you at seven, my crazy friend."

From the market, Amadeus followed signs pointing him to a cheap third–floor room with air con. Behind the desk, incense wafted from a little red structure which housed a gold Buddha statue, a bowl of rice, and a *maneki-neko*, its plastic paw perpetually waving. After a shower, his first in days, under a sky streaked mournful orange, he set off to find the bank.

They sat in an open-front restaurant, under the breeze of ceiling fans, and ate fish curries. Amadeus had thought he wouldn't like it, but it was the combination of spicy pepper and sweet coconut that changed his mind. He was tempted to order a second one. Instead, he ordered them both a bottle of beer.

Sal told him his story: he had been studying in the United States but returned to Brahmapur, India, when his mother became sick. She had recovered. Now he was waiting another six months for a new education visa. He decided to spend that time here. When Amadeus asked him what he studied, he smiled.

"I know it's a cliché thing for an Indian person to say, but I study computer science and programming. American education is not cheap, so I support myself by running an information propagation company."

"Like marketing?"

"Marketing on steroids, injected with adrenaline. Think heat-seeking missiles with a self-replicating payload of targeted messages. A group wants to get their word out, I make sure that message spreads like a plague. I make viral seem like a common cold. High-tech word-of-mouth. And what is your trade?"

"So you're a spammer."

"I should be offended, but I'm not. In a way, I do spam. Only more sophisticated and targeted. Plus, I have standards. I don't do pharmaceuticals or quackery. Mostly ideas and beliefs."

Amadeus told him he had been studying geography, but he too had had family troubles.

"The world is a strange place, my crazy friend. That's why I like programming; so many potential solutions, and the best ones are usually the simplest and most elegant. The world is messy. You can see that all around us. There is no one, easy, elegant solution. I wish getting countries to change were as easy as writing beautiful code, adding a few functions, or developing a clever campaign, but sadly it is not possible. But enough about me, why did you choose to come here? Are you interested in the temples?"

"Yes, temples, but I'm looking for a friend ... of my father's. His name is Laroux."

"Laroux. Hmm. Is he a Frenchman? There are many in this town. I heard of one group that went out into the jungle maybe, um, fifteen years ago, they started a colony, took their Cambodian wives with them. A woman told me a rumor that their children are the most beautiful children in the world."

"Yeah, he's French, but I don't know about the jungle colony. I think he's doing charity work," Amadeus said.

"There's a bar in town you might check, called the Gecko Café. Many French expats hang out there." Sal gave him directions. As they finished their dinner, they talked about their university time. The hour grew late, and Amadeus said he was going to ask around town about Laroux. They shook hands. Sal gave him his copy of *On the Road*. "I wrote my email in the front, if you ever want to catch up with me."

"That would be nice," Amadeus said. "Thanks for your help."

39

At the Gecko Cafe, Amadeus sat at the table next to a girl typing on a tablet computer. Beside her sat a book with a French title. Her hair was the same brown as the dusty street outside. "Excuse me, do you speak English?" he asked. She shot him a cold look and returned her attention to her work.

"Hey, I'm really sorry to bother you, but I'm trying to find someone."

"Aren't we all," she said.

"It's important."

"So is what I'm doing."

"People could die if I don't find him," Amadeus said. "I saw you had French books and I thought you might know him."

"I'm from Quebec. You think I know every French person in this town?" She looked up from her laptop, stared straight ahead at the bar, took a deep breath, and said, "Who are you looking for?"

Amadeus pulled out his phone and showed her Laroux's picture.

"You know, I think I have seen him around. He stays out in the jungle, near the Fuckoff Temple."

"Fuckoff temple?" Amadeus said. He started typing a search query into his phone.

"You're way too earnest." Amadeus thought about the name

for a second then smiled. "Let me have another look." She squinted, zoomed in on the image. "Yeah, I really do recognize him. He runs an orphanage or charity or something." Amadeus asked if she knew where he could find Laroux. "No, I do not. Where have I seen him ... not here, but maybe ..." She thought for a moment. "That's right. At Le Bistro, the most expensive place in town. He has dinner there sometimes."

"Where is that?"

"Do I look like a guidebook? Just walk down the main street and you'll see it. Would you leave me alone now? I'd like to get back to work."

"You're working?" Amadeus asked.

"No, I just sit in a bar with my computer hoping to be distracted by a dashing Yankee."

"Any luck yet?" She just smiled and shook her head.

"Not yet. One day, one day."

He found Le Bistro and looked in, but he didn't see Laroux. He went in, caught the eye of a waitress, and flashed her Laroux's picture. She recognized him. Amadeus asked her when Laroux came in, how often.

"Every day around dinner, maybe seven, seven thirty. He is regular like clock," the waitress said, her skin unblemished by age or makeup. "And he always leaves big tip."

"Do you know what he does here?"

"Something good," the waitress said, but that was all she knew.

Amadeus returned to his guesthouse, turned on the air con, and spread out on the stiff white sheets. He watched a gecko on the wall then slept until late morning the next day. When he stepped outside, the heat hit him like a wall. He turned around, went back to his room, and spent the afternoon under the air conditioner, reading *On the Road*. At six forty five, he went to Le Bistro. Outside the restaurant, a row of *tuk tuk* drivers reclined in their little trailers. No foreigners besides himself.

Amadeus pulled out his book and waited. At exactly seven thirty, a man in a white linen suit and matching hat strode into the restaurant. All the waitresses smiled at him when he came in. He gave them a little bow and sat near Amadeus. Amadeus watched him as he adjusted the place setting before him. He seemed approachable enough. After the man had placed his order, Amadeus went over to his table.

"Excuse me, are you Quinton Laroux?" Amadeus asked. Laroux gave him a tight smile and nodded.

"And you are?" he asked.

"My name is Amadeus Brunmeier. I think you knew my father."

"Knew?" Laroux said, arching his thin eyebrows.

Amadeus explained everything that had happened so far, his father, the demon, Vesely. He withheld his hypothesis that Ross was his father's killer. Laroux nodded as he listened, his forefinger pressed against his cheek. After Amadeus finished, Laroux said he was sorry to hear about his father. "He was a man of astounding qualities."

"I really need your help."

"Tomorrow morning I will show you something, but not now. Even with such sad news, tonight is still a beautiful night. Do you hear that?" Amadeus listened but he wasn't sure what he should be listening for. He heard some *tuk tuk* drivers laughing and vehicles sputtering down the rough street.

"That is the sound of hope, of progress. People laughing, living their lives. The evening is a time for peace and happiness. What I will tell you will bring you just the opposite. So, let us meet first as friends sharing good news in a sad and beautiful country. Tomorrow, tomorrow morning, you can tell me more and we will figure out how I can help you with this awful business. Tonight, would you like to dine with me?"

Amadeus nodded and got up to collect his plates and silverware. Laroux waved for him to sit back down as he called for the waitress. Laroux told Amadeus about his decision to leave the corporate world behind. "Sharks, vultures, and plutocrats. My life felt as cold and empty as a prison cell. Now I help people. I know my purpose."

Before sunrise, Amadeus met Laroux outside Le Bistro. He stood beside a *tuk tuk*, speaking to the driver in Khmer. Amadeus hopped in, telling Laroux about his situation on the way. Fifteen minutes later, they were crossing the causeway to Angkor Wat. Amadeus ran his hand over the cool sandstone balustrade as they walked. Even in the dark, Amadeus could make out the long wall and the spires of the temple, rising from inside the walls like giant inverted pine cones. Once inside, they stood by the reflecting pools with other visitors and watched the sun rise over the temple.

They climbed the smooth stone stairs. The temple smelled of moisture and moss. Amadeus wanted to linger and examine the long wall carvings which depicted writhing armies of Khmers, Thais, Chinese, and Chams engaged in eternal stone battle. Laroux told Amadeus there would be time to view these later, but now he would show him something that would help him explicate his story better. Amadeus followed him to the back of the temple.

"This relief," Laroux said, "depicts the Churning of the Sea of Milk." The relief showed two groups of warriors pulling on a giant snake. The snake was coiled around a mountain. Just above eye level, a four-armed figure stood atop the mountain. The mountain sat on a turtle. Above the scene, a thousand fairies danced and flew. Below, just as many fish twisted and swam.

"This is a Hindu creation story of demigods and demons cooperating to gain the elixir of eternal life. On this side are the asuras. Think of them as slightly less sinister Christian demons. And on that side are the devas, or demigods."

Amadeus leaned in close to examine an asura. "The demons don't look that different from the demigods."

"That's because they represent the two sides of human nature. Sometimes asuras can become devas, depending on the choices the asuras make. This whole story is a metaphor for spiritual practice. The ocean is our mind, and the waves represent our thoughts and emotions. The mountain, stoic and calm, is concentration.

"Here in the middle," he continued, pointing to the four-armed figure, "is Vishnu, one of the highest gods in Hinduism, overseeing everything. Vishnu is also incarnated as the turtle at the bottom. The turtle holds things up and keeps them from sinking, and also represents spiritual practice, withdrawing into oneself.

"They're all pulling back and forth on Vasuki, the giant snake. The snake is coiled around the mountain. As they pull back and forth, they make waves in the ocean, and after initially releasing a dangerous poison, they soon gain great treasures. At first, the demigods promised to share all the treasures with the demons, but when they find the elixir of eternal life, they will break their promise."

"So the devas lied to the asuras."

"That's right. And they had Vishnu's help. You probably want to know why I'm showing this to you," Laroux said.

Amadeus started to speak, but Laroux continued before any words escaped his lips.

"I know it's a little confusing. We'll come back to the story in a minute. For now, let us keep walking." They set off down the pavilion. Each support pillar had a dancing deity and flowing patterns carved into the rough stone. Their footsteps reverberated down the corridors. They reached a doorway, climbed some steep steps, and entered the upper courtyard. Laroux continued.

"A few months ago, Vesely and your father convinced me to come to New York for a meeting. I hadn't spoken to anyone for several months, but they both said this was urgent, that things had gone awry. I arrived late and walked in on an argument.

The atmosphere was more tense and bitter than anything I have ever experienced. Your father, Vesely, and Ross were there. Esther was not. The moment I walked in, your father said there was something I must see. And he showed me a video of a monster, crawling out of one of his contraptions. I assume you have seen this?"

"Yes."

"After watching, I did not know what to think. I wanted to ask your father some questions, but before I had a chance, Ross stood up and began to give a speech. How did he start?" Laroux put his finger to his cheek and looked at the ceiling. "He said we faced a scenario very similar to the story of the churning of the sea of milk, and that much of humanity had become like the asuras: prideful, arrogant, ignorant and violent. Yet, there were also devas in the world, people like us, pulling the snake the other direction. We all needed each other, at least for a while because, as with the churning of the sea of milk, we stood to gain great rewards that we couldn't even begin to imagine. Yes, we might find vile poisons. Yes, there would be struggles, and yes, people would die. But in the end ... we would become something approaching gods."

Nearby, a family was having their photos taken with local women dressed in traditional gold and red costumes. Little metal orbs hung down from their clothes, jingling as they moved.

"He said, and I'm paraphrasing, that a new age was dawning, that our civilization had grown decadent, lazy, and apathetic, oppressed by its own creations, and the time had come for a new age of man. It was time to transcend our primitive roots and to make a great leap into the future. If there were monsters, then there were monsters. Sometimes epochs ended in cataclysm. The last part of his speech, though, I can quote. Ross leaned forward, looked around the room, and said, 'This is the end of the iron age, and we are its heralds.'

"At that point, your father stood up, called Ross a maniac,

and tackled him. Vesely and I pulled your father off. Ross fumed with anger. Your father said that he would stop his research, that he would rather teach high school physics than risk allowing demons and monsters to run amok. I told him he should continue, but only after taking time to build in appropriate safeguards. Vesely agreed.

"When Ross saw that he had no support, he offered to buy us out for what, even for a roomful of already-wealthy men, was a staggering amount of money. Both Vesely and I shook our heads. Your father, he looked so relieved at that moment. I know your father had said no one person could have control over the research, but the amount of money offered by Ross was more powerful than any contract. Yet we both stood firm and said no to Ross and his insanity. After we made our decision, Ross shook his finger at everyone and told us we had made a mistake we would regret until our 'ever-quickening dying day.'"

Amadeus reached in his pocket for some paper but found none.

Laroux sat on the stone stairs leading to the highest part of the temple and sighed. "Immediately after the meeting, I returned here, wanting to get back to my work. I have not heard from Ross since."

Silence settled between them like the fog of evening. After several long moments, Amadeus heard himself speaking.

"I think Ross killed my father."

"Hmm," Laroux said. He closed his eyes and placed his forefinger against his cheek. "This creature you speak of, you say it was in New York while you were there?"

"It showed up near Esther and me when we were walking downtown. It ended up eating some investment bankers."

"No huge loss there," Laroux said, smirking. Without meaning to, Amadeus remembered the smell of sulfur and rancid meat and the image of the avocado-green puddles of dissolved people. He wondered if the authorities had burned the demon's body or taken it to a research lab. Hopefully the former, more likely the latter. And Vesely was dead by the time you reached Prague?" Laroux put his hand on his shoulder and held his gaze. "Amadeus, do you see a pattern here?"

"Um ..."

"The creature in New York, that was no coincidence. Who could possibly know where you were going, especially if this craft can travel undetected? How much do you trust this man Jones?"

"No," Amadeus said, "it's impossible. Someone was watching Esther, waiting for me to show up. Jones wouldn't do that. He was my father's friend!" Amadeus remembered Gravity's note, Lilly's suspicions, even the way Jones' demeanor had changed, but pushed all this out of his mind.

Laroux gave Amadeus a sardonic grin and said, "Tell me: what are in these protected files?"

"The last three years of research results, as well as the latest schematics and operational materials."

"Let's talk about what we know. One, someone has previously gained access to your father's research and has figured out how to weaponize it. Two, some other party appears to be tracking your movements, and would like to recover the biometric data. From this, I see two possibilities."

Pausing as if to collect his thoughts, Laroux pulled a handkerchief from his pocket and dabbed sweat from his brow. Though the sun had only just risen, the air was growing heavy with jungle heat. He continued.

"The first possibility is that some group has convinced or compelled Jones to use you to acquire your father's latest research. Perhaps it is Ross, or whoever has weaponized your father's research, or even another party. Or maybe Jones wants the research for himself, perhaps intending to sell it to the highest bidder. The other possibility is that someone has infiltrated Jones' data systems to such a degree that they know both what you're doing, and why, and that Jones is mostly blameless. Is it possible Jones' systems or physical security were compromised?"

"It's possible," Amadeus said. "But Jones had said he had, and I quote, 'Taken momentous steps to stay under the radar of the leering eyes of the world.' Jones knows data security, or at least is willing to pay for it."

Even though signs indicated, in several languages, that smoking was strictly forbidden in the temple area, Laroux lit a cigarette and took a long drag.

"You said Jones lives on a compound. And it at least is partially self-sufficient. Doesn't this seem strange? Here we have one man talking about instigating an apocalypse and another living in a place designed for just such an occasion. What does he say about the outside world?"

"He says it's a dangerous place full of awful people; he barely lets his daughter leave, and when he does ..." Amadeus suddenly wondered if the black-eyed man had been working on behalf of Jones, keeping an eye on his daughter.

"And Jones is just happy to help you, to let you fly his very expensive prototype machine all over the world to help you collect all our blood. For this, he expects nothing in return?"

"Um ... he said he needed a test pilot."

Laroux took a long drag on his cigarette and flicked the ashes into his palm.

"Amadeus, I think you're being used."

Amadeus felt sick rising up from his stomach. He focused on it and forced it back down. His hands shook. He hadn't felt like this since before his graduation speech. If only he had some paper to chew.

"But why did they send a demon to kill me? And why use a demon to murder Vesely?"

"Maybe the demon in New York wasn't meant to kill you. Maybe your opponents didn't want Vesely to speak with you. Who knows? But about one thing, there is no maybe: they will be here soon. They follow your craft, your movements. And now that you've found me, they have everything they need. But it's not your fault. How could you know?"

In the distance, a monkey howled with either delight or fear. Amadeus couldn't tell the difference.

40

Amadeus opened his phone and, with a tiny screwdriver and tremendous care, removed the RF transmitter and an even tinier GPS chip. The phone rebooted without problems. He asked Laroux for his fingerprint.

"You must understand the risk of carrying this information on your person. You become an even more attractive target. If you lose possession of it, your opponents—who have already utilized this technology—will have a complete picture of the Brunmeier gate research program. Not that it will matter to you, since you will be dead. Are you prepared to take responsibility for that?"

"If I want to stop the people who murdered my father, I have to. Worst comes to worst, I'll destroy this thing, smash it under my foot."

"You're a confident boy," Laroux said.

"I wasn't always," Amadeus said.

Laroux smiled at him. "I haven't told you yet," he said, motioning for the phone, "but I thought your father was a wonderful man. He really did have grand aspirations. The world is a darker place without him." He placed his thumb on the touch screen, pressed scan, allowed the lance to prick his finger, then handed the phone back to Amadeus.

"I seem to hear that a lot, but you know what I think now? I think this is all his fault. If he would've stuck to his original research, none of this would've happened."

"Death does things to a man," Laroux said. "He becomes a stranger to himself."

Amadeus said nothing, just looked at his feet.

"But the fear of death, in the sane man, makes him do even more momentous things. Look around you, Amadeus. These temples were built so the ancient Khmer kings could have immortality. They wanted to last through the ages. Few remember their deeds, but everyone sees what they created."

They descended the smooth stairs and walked back across the great sandstone causeway that once supported kings, armies, and elephants. The sun had burned away the mist and the day had grown hot. Amadeus noticed his forehead and arms were covered in a thin layer of sweat. He also noticed that since the nausea had passed, his stomach was growling. He eyed the food vendors set up in the shade near the temple.

"You mind if we stop for food?"

"Ah, the food here, it's probably bush meat ... but I would like to eat too."

The second they started walking towards the vendors, a Khmer woman in an apron waved a menu at them, calling in nasal tones, "You eat my restaurant, you buy from me. Best food in Angkor Wat."

"Okay, let's go eat her restaurant," Laroux said, giving Amadeus a sly grin. Amadeus shrugged and followed her to her restaurant, which was nothing more than a few tables covered in red-checked table cloths and a food cart. Amadeus ordered pad thai, Laroux beef lok lak.

"The shade is nice," Amadeus said, trying not to touch the sticky table cloth. He put his foot up on the chair across from him as he waited on his breakfast. The sounds around them, the calling of the restaurant women, bird songs, a gentle breeze rustling the tree above him, these lulled him into a peaceful state. He thought he could sleep.

Laroux was smoking a cigarette and looked like he was contemplating the mysteries of the universe. Amadeus appreciated that Laroux could let him sit in silence. Their food arrived and they started to eat. "Bon appétit," Laroux said. Amadeus started on his pad thai. The noodles were rich and greasy, and he didn't spend enough time chewing. A couple minutes into their meal, Laroux squinted and craned his neck to peer at something nearby.

"Amadeus," he said, "some men are staring at us, at you. They're dressed like Chinese tourists, but something seems off. Don't look now. Sink down in your seat a bit." Amadeus sunk. "That's good. In just a moment, we're going to get moving. We'll go out behind the carts. Back there are some trees and paths. We can cut through there, and then go out the back way, behind the temple."

Laroux left some money on the table, enough for the meals and a generous tip. Keeping his head down, Laroux scuttled away from the table and between the food carts. Amadeus did the same, but he spun around to look. When he did, he knocked a big wok off the food cart. Rice, noodles, and hot oil splattered onto the well-trampled ground.

"Ahh!" the food cart lady yelled at him. "My food! You ruin my food."

She smacked Amadeus' butt with a wooden spoon as she yelled at him in a torrent of English and Khmer. Laroux turned around and told him to hurry up, but the lady blocked his path. "You break you buy!"

The Chinese tourists pulled out cameras and began taking photos. Flash bulbs went off as Amadeus defended himself.

"We must run now," Laroux said, shoving a handful of dollars into the free hand of the food cart lady. That seemed to satisfy her, but the tourists were on their feet, pointing, laughing, high-fiving each other. Laroux took off into the woods. Amadeus followed close behind. He knew he shouldn't, but he looked back. Through the space between the food carts he could see four men running after them.

"They're still coming," Amadeus said.

"Then keep running."

They dashed along a bare brown dirt road, striking in contrast to the green forest all around them. Every footfall kicked up a cloud of dust. Laroux cut onto a smaller path through a stand of Banyan trees. The roots reminded Amadeus of veins bulging from the ground.

Amadeus looked back. They were growing closer. He heard them yelling to each other. When the trees thinned out, Amadeus could see the temple to their right. Laroux stumbled over a tree root. Amadeus pulled him up by the arm.

They came to a high wall made of pockmarked grey and maroon laterite blocks. Splotches of green moss covered the lower blocks. Along the wall, two hundred meters to the right, directly behind the temple, was the rear exit. Laroux pointed to it.

Someone fired a gun. The report thundered through the quiet jungle. Monkeys howled in agitation. Ahead of him, where the bullet had struck, Amadeus watched a cloud of dust sparkle in the late morning light. While looking at this, Amadeus stumbled, catching himself just before he lost his balance. More gunshots *pftwted* in the dirt beside him. Amadeus' heart tried to outrun him, smashing against his chest, forcing blood through his veins. They sprinted for the exit.

"Outside," Laroux said, between gasps of breath, "will be motorcycles, drivers waiting on passengers. We will buy one. No *tuk tuk*, only a moto. Or steal one. Whatever is easier." He said something else in French. Amadeus didn't understand, but it sounded like cursing.

The entrance of the back gate was flanked by rectangular columns. They bounded up the stairs and ran through the stone portico. On the other side, just as Laroux had said, a few Khmer drivers reclined in the back of their *tuk tuks*, smoking cigarettes. They gave Amadeus and Laroux a half-interested look, apparently unperturbed by the gunshots

One man stood beside his bike, talking on his mobile phone. Laroux ran to him and shoved a wad of U.S. dollars into his hand. Surprised and visibly vexed, he looked down and started counting the money. As he did, Laroux hopped on the motorcycle and stomped the kick starter. The motorcycle sputtered but didn't start. The driver started yelling while trying to pull Laroux off. Amadeus pushed the driver. He staggered and fell onto the dirt. Amadeus muttered an apology. The other drivers hopped out of their *tuk tuks* and crept towards them. One held a crescent wrench.

Laroux tried again. No joy.

Amadeus heard footsteps clobbering stone as the men passed through the gate. The Khmer drivers pointed at them, then at their guns. Laroux kicked the motorcycle one last time and it wheezed to life. Amadeus hopped on and Laroux took off. Gunshots cracked behind them. Amadeus turned to see the drivers with their hands raised above their heads. One writhed in the dirt, clutching his arm. Laroux opened up the throttle and the motorcycle whined in protest. They left a trail of smoke and dust.

Amadeus again turned to look. The men had taken a *tuk tuk*. One was driving, another leaning out the side, aiming a pistol at them. He fired. *Ping!* The motorcycle's mirror shattered. They raced on, though Amadeus doubted the bike was going over 70km/hr. They fired more shots, but the distance between them was growing and their shots became less accurate. The road changed from dirt to asphalt and the ride became less bumpy. Laroux downshifted and the motorcycle lurched, carrying them even farther away from the men and their heavy *tuk tuk*. Soon they were out of sight of the men.

Eventually they came to a fork in the road. Laroux chose the left fork. Amadeus tried to talk to Laroux, but he couldn't yell loud enough to compete with the engine. Instead he just held on and hoped for the best.

After following the left fork for awhile, the forest changed to fields and rice paddies. Behind them was only an empty stretch of road. He hoped the men had chosen the right fork. Amadeus patted Laroux's shoulder. Laroux gave him a thumbs-up and shifted to a higher gear, giving the little engine a break. The road turned and ran along a blue-green lake. Pink lotus flowers floated on calm water.

The wind ruffled his hair as Laroux drove them past the lake and through more fields going to who knew where. They passed through some small villages and soon the rice paddies changed back into jungle. Laroux turned off the paved road, onto a brown dirt path that cut through the woods.

"We will hide out for a while," Laroux said. He drove slower, taking care to avoid the ruts and potholes. Amadeus thought the speed was still much too fast for such a road. This was the middle of nowhere, miles from anywhere. Amadeus wondered what they would do if the bike broke down. At least he would have time to figure out his next steps. This had to end soon. Somehow, he would take the fight to Ross ... if only he could find him. Laroux hit a deep rut, jarring Amadeus' brain. The bike sputtered, coughed, and finally died.

A chattering sea of green and brown surrounded them, the dirt path their only lifeline to the outside world. Laroux looked around and nodded. He seemed confident, like a man in his element. Amadeus, however, felt anxiety constricting his breath.

"I know where we are," Laroux said. "Don't worry. We need to stay low for a while anyway. You can be sure our visitors are searching every road and guesthouse around Siem Reap. Maybe a half-day's walk from here, I have a friend who lives at a little hermitage. Isolated, unknown to most foreigners, and most importantly, safe. Besides, we don't really have much choice," Laroux said. "Eventually, they will give up. Maybe they will think you left. So long as the little modification you made to your phone works."

Laroux took off walking, pumping his arms like the middle-aged ladies he used to see walking down his road, the little pink weights in their hands swinging back and forth. Amadeus shrugged and followed.

"Please, tell me more about your airship. You say Jones built this?" He turned off the road and started down a little unmarked path into the jungle.

"That's right, he used nanosteel. It's the only one of its kind."

"So he knows exactly where his craft is at all times?"

"Lilly says he tracks the airship, so yes. It's his investment."

"Can he control it?"

"Hmm," Amadeus said. "I've never seen him do it, and he didn't mention it. But there is an automated navigation system, plus the fail–safes."

"And what do the fail–safes do?"

"They take control of the craft in emergencies," Amadeus said, feeling foolish as the words left his mouth. Jones could shut him down at any time.

"If this is the case, you must be a fox, clever and full of guile," Laroux said. The jungle around them was a wall of thick green. He heard some rustling overhead. A grey monkey flung itself from one tree to the next. The monkey seemed to be following them.

"Right. I can't let him know what I know."

"In the times of kings and courtiers," Laroux said, "the fool was often the one who knew the most. Since he was usually of common stock and unable to attain office or property, people confided in him; he was only a fool, after all. Yet, in many courts, the fool became very powerful. Why?"

"Because he had information, and everyone underestimated him," Amadeus said.

"Exactly," Laroux said. "And because people underestimated him, he was the most dangerous courtier of all." The monkey howled and made his next jump.

"Now I need to play the fool, let Jones think I'm still the same stupid kid that showed up at his compound." He noticed an aching pressure in his bladder. "Sorry, but I've really got to piss. Hold on." Amadeus stepped off the path and started looking for a nice tree to stand behind. He couldn't pee within sight of Laroux. He selected a downed tree that would provide him some privacy. He put his butt on the tree and swung his legs over. Just before he planted his feet on the other side a monkey screeched.

Amadeus froze. A chill ran up his spine like a whisper. He looked down at the ground. Inches below his right foot was a rusty metal canister, partially covered by years of jungle growth. A little spur stuck up from it. Amadeus gasped. He had almost stepped on a land mine. He felt a little stream of piss drip down his leg.

He flung his legs back over the tree, scrutinizing every place his feet would land. On the other, hopefully safer side of the tree, he unzipped. As the remaining urine flowed out, relief and gratitude flowed in. He had been lucky. He thanked the monkey for its warning as he returned to the road. There he told Laroux what he'd seen.

"I should have warned you. Most are gone, but a few of the damn things are still around. I'll let someone know later," Laroux said, his voice nonchalant, as if he were talking about a squirrel infestation.

41

They trekked through a green tunnel of jungle. To Amadeus, everything looked the same, but Laroux seemed to know where he was going, and Amadeus followed without question. The image of his foot, hovering inches over the land mine, replayed over and over in his mind. He had seen people in Siem Reap, mostly older men, on crutches and in wheelchairs. Some were scarred by burns, others missing arms, legs, or hands. He hadn't understood why. Now, though, he knew. He had almost joined their mutilated ranks.

"We're almost there," Laroux said.

"Why land mines?" Amadeus asked.

"Fear. Control. Terror," Laroux said. "The people who ordered the mines laid are unfit to be called human beings. But the people who laid the mines? They were mostly poor, uneducated country people. They did what they were told. It's all very sad. But you know the worst part?"

Amadeus shook his head.

"This country never saw any answers, anything like a truth and reconciliation committee. A few people were put on trial, but you could never try everyone involved. The people you see in town, the ones with the scars, they are the visual reminders of the insanity of bad things that happened even before they were born. I came here hoping to help heal this country. I believe you cannot heal without forgiveness, but here people only want to forget. Who am I to say what is right, what is wrong? I am just a foreigner here, an outsider. I do my little works, and I see that it helps, and that is enough."

Laroux sat down on a log and lit a cigarette.

"One day, Amadeus, this will be a wonderful country. In so many ways, it already is." He flicked some ash behind him. "Have you ever been to a Buddhist temple?"

"On a school trip, once," Amadeus said, "but it was in upstate New York. It probably doesn't count."

"Of course it counts, but this one will be unlike anything you have ever seen. We are almost there, maybe another hour or so. When we get there, just remember to take your shoes off."

"Got it," Amadeus said. "Shoes off."

The day grew late, the jungle around them a little darker. The air smelled faintly of jasmine. Finally, in the distance, Amadeus saw the faded gold spire of the hermitage rising out of the trees like a jousting lance. The hermitage had a gold frame and white plaster walls and was no bigger than a taco stand. On the porch sat a bronze cauldron that held several sticks of burning incense, the source of the jasmine smell. In the center of the temple, on a wooden platform, a seated gold Bodhisattva held a lotus flower in his left hand. His right hand was raised, palm out. Vines climbed up the outside walls of the temple like clutching fingers.

Nearby was a little house, built in the style of the temple. Facing the house, Laroux called something in Khmer. The door opened, and a man in an orange robe stepped out. His head was shaved and his shoulders a little stooped. When he smiled at Laroux, he flashed a mouthful of yellow but intact teeth. Then he put his hands together as if in prayer and gave them each a little bow. Laroux returned the bow and nodded for Amadeus to do the same.

"This is Rithipol," Laroux said. "He's the caretaker of this temple. He doesn't have much English, but he tells me my Khmer is passable, even if I sound like an injured duck." Laroux then said something in Khmer to the monk. Rithipol smiled then put his hands under his armpits, making like he had wings, and said, "Quack, quack."

Everyone laughed, and they went inside, where Rithipol served them vegetables, rice, and two big green coconuts he hacked open with a machete. Laroux and Rithipol chatted for few moments. Laroux told Amadeus he was explaining their situation. "He said you can stay here and be a monk, if you wish," Laroux said. Rithipol made a buzzing sound, pointed at Amadeus, and ran an invisible electric shaver over his head. "He also says we can stay as long as we need. And that after we eat he wants to show us something."

"I appreciate the offer, but enlightenment will have to wait. I don't have much time," Amadeus said.

"You'll have even less if these people, whoever they are, catch up with you."

"I suppose you're right," Amadeus said. "But if we can get to the Pachyderm, we can get out of here, no problem. All I have to do now is get my friends out of the Jones compound, figure out how the demon gates work, and stop Ross from ending the iron age. Easy stuff, right?"

Laroux smirked then spoke to Rithipol.

"He says he saw the New York monster on television and he is pleased to meet demon bait. He wants to know when you'll start fighting them."

"Tell him I haven't killed any yet, but I'm working on it."

Laroux did, nodding as he listened to Rithipol's answer. "He says you can fight without killing. He also says he thinks you're a smart boy, even if you don't speak Khmer, and that he thinks you'll have much success. But you must believe you can." Rithipol spoke a little more. "He sees you're very nervous and have a lot of worry. Your mind, your fear, and your doubts, he says, are the only things holding you back. Seems cliché coming from a Buddhist monk, doesn't it? But he's right, Amadeus. You can stop this."

Something in Amadeus' stomach twisted and turned, a slithering eel beating against the lining, trying to gnaw its way out. Outside, monkeys shared their secret knowledge about the coming night. Rithipol said something else.

"He wants to know the last time you watched the news," Laroux said.

"A couple days ago. There's a television here?"

"He says he normally only uses it to watch soccer, but there's news we must see." Laroux spoke a little more. "But he wanted us to eat before we saw it. He won't tell me what."

"I don't like the sound of that." Amadeus nodded at the monk. He had a feeling that whatever he was about to see would be bad. Terrible. The monk slid open a rice-paper door, revealing a water-buffalo-sized television.

"Hi-def," Rithipol said. He turned the television on and flipped through several channels of Khmer karaoke before stopping on the first news channel he came to. On the screen were images of a burning city, military trucks, and overweight citizens hefting guns over their heads. Then it flashed over to footage of not one but several demons. They looked like the one from New York as they stalked through the city, far from the camera, turning over cars and knocking over lamp posts. The footage jumped to a convoy of three desert-brown humvees and a tank firing on a group of four demons. Alerted, the creatures ran towards the convoy. Along the way, one dropped and another staggered then fell, but two reached the convoy and pounced on the humvees. The soldiers retreated to surrounding alleys, firing as they ran. The tank turned and shot a round into one only meters away, splattering demon goo against a building.

The cameraman ran backwards. The image jumped and jerked, but he kept it focused on the one remaining demon as it tore the humvees apart like a kitten mangling a roll of toilet paper. All the time, voices had been talking over this, but they weren't in English.

"Can we get an English channel?" Amadeus said. "Where is this?" Rithipol nodded and flipped to the BBC.

"America. Huntington, West Virginia," Rithipol said. He nodded to the anchor speaking on-screen.

"—and the destruction is widespread. Military sources tell us they estimate the number of creatures still alive at ten, though these numbers are unconfirmed. So far the military reports they have killed nine, including the four shown on the dramatic footage released by the local news channel. One Huntington resident told reporters they had seen a group of four crawling out of the Ohio River.

"Though citizens were warned to stay in their homes, a large number have formed vigilante groups and are working with the military. Our military source said, and I quote, 'We need all the help we can get.'

"Now we're going to switch over to a live feed from cameras atop the county courthouse and another building." The screen split into two images showing the small city from high above. Several demons ambled along the avenue. In the side streets and alleys, groups of civilians, soldiers, and military trucks waited for their chance to shoot.

Outside the little house with the big television, Amadeus heard a helicopter flying overhead. The whooping sound grew louder before fading out.

"We haven't received any definitive casualty reports yet. Initial estimates are in the dozens, though as you can see this is far from over." The anchor put her hand up to her ear and listened. "I have just received word that the U.S. Air Force has deployed drones." She pressed her ear again. "It appears that approximately five more of the creatures have emerged from the river ... uh, okay, right. The local news has a live feed. We're switching now."

A reporter stood on the bridge. He wore a flak jacket and spoke with a twang. "They're coming out of the river, over there." He pointed. "Larry, zoom in on that." The camera refocused and showed a demon with its back legs in the water. It stepped out onto a boat ramp and shook itself, just like a wet dog. Then it screamed and took off running towards the city center. The howl distorted the sound coming from the television speakers. Amadeus put his head in his hands. He didn't want to watch any more, but he knew he needed to watch, to see what he was facing, what he had to stop. The eel in his stomach tried even harder to escape. He took several deep breaths and calmed himself.

At first, all three of them had watched the images with looks of horror on their faces, but Rithipol had gotten up from the wooden floor and busied himself by removing and washing their unfinished dishes.

"There's another problem," Laroux said. He spoke to Rithipol more. "He says the police are looking for two art thieves accused of killing three guards and two drivers. Rithipol tells me the police think it was us. They are using search helicopters."

"For fuck's sake," Amadeus said.

Amadeus didn't sleep that night, but it wasn't for lack of trying. His body felt as if he had been thrown down the steep stone stairs of the big temple he had just visited. His mind raced through all the scenarios, possibilities, and uncertainties. He cried some, too. Eventually he fell asleep. Rithipol woke them before dawn and gave them plastic bags of cooked rice and vegetables for their journey.

"Good luck," Rithipol said in English. He stood on the porch of his little jungle house and watched them as they set off down the path into the forest. The trail eventually joined a dirt road. After sunrise, they twice heard the helicopters flying overhead. Both times they ducked under the thick green leaf canopy. Amadeus scrutinized every inch of ground before each step. As they walked, Amadeus described where he had landed and the road he had taken into town. Laroux said he knew where they needed to go. Soon, Amadeus heard cars in the distance. The wind blew. A dust cloud rose up on the road. Again they stepped off the road and watched as the vehicles, two trucks, drove by. Amadeus shuddered when he saw police logos on the side.

"They know we're in this area," Laroux said. "Maybe they are using satellites. Maybe Jones told them where we are. Who knows?"

After another hour of walking, they came to a paved road lined with houses. The houses were wood-sided shacks on stilts with little wooden ramps or stairs leading up to the front door. Looking up and down, Amadeus recognized this as the outer area of O Ta Yu. Now they were close. He could feel unseen eyes watching him. He wondered if these people had heard about the murdering, antiquity-thieving foreigners. He wished for a hat to pull down over his face, to provide cover not only from their eyes but from the beating, draining sun. His shirt was drenched, his entire body felt slimy and sticky from sweat, humidity, and fear. They came to a fork in the road. The road in both directions looked the same as the one before. Laroux asked which way they should go. Amadeus shrugged.

"Are we on the west or east side?"

"East, I think," Laroux said.

"Then we go left," Amadeus said. They started down the road. Here was more traffic, mostly motorcycles and the occasional *tuk tuk*. Whenever they heard a car or truck or helicopter, they would step off the road and stand under a house. The shade felt good, though some places smelled like rancid eggs. Twice, women came out of their house and looked at them, but they never told them to leave.

Soon the houses gave way to jungle. Amadeus knew they were getting close; he remembered this stretch of road from his ride with Sal. The helicopters came more frequently. They spent more and more time hunkering and hiding. Finally, just before he thought he would collapse from the heat, Amadeus found the notch he had made in the tree.

"This is it," Amadeus said, hearing vehicles and helicopters coming from all sides. In the distance, he could see vehicles approaching fast, taking up both lanes of the road. Amadeus' heart raced faster than a motorcycle. Laroux ducked into the woods. Amadeus followed.

"How far?" Laroux said.

"Maybe two kilometers," Amadeus said. Laroux nodded and began to run. Amadeus took the lead, afraid Laroux would take a wrong turn.

From the road, the whine of the engines grew louder. Overhead, two helicopters were hovering, watching, searching. Even with the distance between them and the road, Amadeus heard shouting, orders being barked, men getting ready for the hunt. Amadeus' feet flopped and plodded as he ran. He knew the path was safe, but he watched his steps anyway, as if another land mine would appear from nowhere. Amadeus looked over his shoulder. Laroux trailed close behind him. Even farther back along the straight path, the thick green forest walls shivered. The police or army or whoever were close behind.

Just ahead, he found another of the marks he had made. Laroux stumbled. The motorcycles drew closer. They came to the shallow creek, water splashing up as they dashed across. A tree on the opposite side bore another mark. After the creek, the path narrowed. Tree roots as big as oil drums covered the ground. Amadeus hopped from one tree root to another. He hoped the roots would slow the pursuing motorcycles.

They raced through the green tunnel of the path. Some shots sounded, but they seemed far away. The motorcycles grew louder and louder, but they no longer sounded like motorcycles. The sound was a deep *whoop whoop whoop*. Amadeus looked up through the leafy canopy. A helicopter passed overhead.

"Those," Laroux yelled, "are Apaches, old American military equipment. They have guns. Big guns."

"Is that what we heard?" Amadeus said.

"Probably," Laroux said. "How far?"

"Less than one kilometer?" Amadeus said. Ahead the trail ended and opened up into a rice paddy, knee deep with water. A water buffalo stood in the field, watching them with uncurious eyes.

"Across that field and to the right."

"I will stay behind you," Laroux said, scanning the sky.

They sloshed through, running as fast as they could. The silt floor of the paddy was slippery, squishy underfoot. Just as they passed the water buffalo, three motorcycles rode onto the narrow strip of high ground that separated one paddy from another. Amadeus looked over his shoulder.

The one in front crashed. Trying to avoid it, the other two swerved and became bogged down in the muck. The two stuck drivers pulled out their guns and fired. Bullets splashed into water around Amadeus and Laroux, who stumbled and cried out. Amadeus helped him to his feet. More gunshots. They ran. The drivers chased. The helicopters made a fast, wide arc around the field, faced them, and opened fire. A line of water flew up like a fountain's spray.

They were almost across when something tore through the back of Amadeus' shirt. He didn't feel anything, but even if he did, he wouldn't have stopped. He had only one thought in his mind: forward motion. Nothing else mattered. Only running. Escaping. Getting to the Pachyderm and flying away from this nightmare.

They reached the other side. Amadeus saw the last marker. They darted back into the jungle. His lungs burned. Gunshots cracked. Monkeys screamed. Sweat stung his eyes. Laroux wheezed and coughed but kept up, a trooper's trooper.

Suddenly he felt something underfoot, a bulge, solid. By the time he realized it was not a land mine, he had already lost his balance and tumbled forward. His face slammed into the hard-packed earth. He felt hands in his armpits, being pulled up.

They ran again. Breath came in gasps and gulps. At the gnarly old banyan tree that marked the edge of the clearing, he saw the faint distortion of the tarp. If he hadn't been looking for it, he wouldn't have seen it.

"Over here, we'll get underneath it," Amadeus said. "Follow me and stay low."

"Underneath what?" Laroux asked, looking around. Amadeus crouched down, Laroux did the same, and they duck-walked through the high grass. Soon, Amadeus lifted the side of the tarp and pushed Laroux underneath. He crawled in behind him. Laroux chuckled when he realized they were underneath the Pachyderm. This could hide them, but not for long. He stood up and slid the side door open. Laroux followed. Amadeus hopped in the chair and hit the switches for auxiliary power. He hoped that when he started the turbofans the tarp would fly away. By this time, he was sure the motorcycle guys were in the field, though the gunfire had abated.

"Is this the—the—what is it called?" Laroux asked between breaths.

"It's a second-generation experimental variable-pitch turbofan prototype craft. It's called the Pachyderm." Amadeus felt a little pride then, but a fresh barrage of gunfire burst that bubble. He took a deep breath and closed his eyes, seeing the take-off in his mind. In a matter of seconds, he was ready and had started with the preflight tasks. He fired up the turbofans and the tarp flew away, revealing the field around them. Then a grinding, grating sound made his heart slam against his ribs. Diagnostics showed an obstruction in the right rear turbofan. He tried first reversing the flow then shutting it down and restarting it, but nothing worked. He'd have to pull the tarp out by hand. Gunfire slammed into the Pachyderm and, out of instinct, Amadeus hunkered down in his seat.

"I will fix this," Laroux said. He opened the door, holding his side as he did. Blood seeped from between Laroux's fingers.

"No, no, you're bleeding, you're not leaving," Amadeus said.

"Just give me a minute."

"Yes, I am bleeding, and I am leaving because you don't have a minute. I'll pull the tarp out so you can go. I will surrender to them and bribe my way out."

"Laroux ..."

"There's no time. You've got a job to do." Laroux reached into his pocket, removed a phone, and spoke a command into the phone's microphone. "Now say your name."

Amadeus cocked his head, but did as Laroux asked. The phone chimed. Laroux then tossed the phone to Amadeus. "You might need this. Godspeed, Amadeus," Laroux said.

With that, Laroux jumped from the Pachyderm and began pulling the tarp free. He turned and made eye contact with Amadeus just as the gunfire started. The tarp tore loose and flapped in the wind. Bullets ripped through the tarp, spinning Laroux around and hammering against the Pachyderm. Blood splattered on the glass. Amadeus cried out. Laroux fell to the ground.

Amadeus slammed the vertical control lever forward, harder than he knew he should. The Pachyderm shot straight up, the pressurization valves hissing as it did. Bullets pinged against the nanosteel frame of the Pachyderm. Below, Laroux was sprawled out like a man who had just finished a marathon, his bloody torso partially obscured by the tarp. As the ground shrank beneath him and the Pachyderm entered the clouds, Amadeus began to sob.

42

An hour later, Amadeus opened the Pachyderm's communications software and contacted Jones, who listened impassively as Amadeus related what had happened. "What about the bio-lock? You can open the files now?" His oversized pupil had grown even bigger, but that could've been a distortion caused by the camera lens.

"There's a problem," Amadeus said, ready with the lie he had practiced. "The computer was damaged. When they were chasing me, I fell; the screen is cracked and it won't start. Maybe ..."

"How could you be so careless?" Jones said. Amadeus bit down on his tongue and tried not to begin a verbal tirade that would end up blowing his front. Jones paused when he appeared to interpret the expression on Amadeus' face as worry. "But that's okay. The screens are fragile but those solid state drives can take a beating. I'm sure we can extract the data when you return to the bunker." Amadeus gave Jones an apologetic grin. Jones seemed to believe his story. "And Amadeus, there were more demons. Dozens dead. Check the news on the computer for the details."

"That's terrible to hear," Amadeus said.

"You need to come back here as soon as you can." Jones was playing him like he was a timpani, but this song was a duet.

"I'll be back in a few days. It's a long flight home."

"Be careful. I'd hate to see any more misfortune befall you. I'm ... glad you're okay."

Amadeus broke the connection and Jones' face faded out. Next he connected with Grassal.

"How's the leg?"

"Great, man. I've ditched the crutches and I'm using a cane now. We ran out of pain pills, but Jones has some medical chronic he shares with me. That helps a little; it still hurts, but I just don't care."

"What about your friends?" Amadeus said.

"My friends? What friends?"

Amadeus wondered if Grassal was stoned now. Amadeus widened his eyes and tried Lilly's secret word again, hoping he would figure it out. "You know, the friends you and Lilly talked about. Have you heard from them?" Amadeus said.

Grassal got it. "Maybe I should check on them."

"Damn right you should. Okay, nice talking to you. Take care of that leg."

Their video connection shut down. Expecting that anything he did on the Pachyderm's systems would be monitored, Amadeus removed the phone Laroux had given him. The screen was locked, but when he said his name, the home screen appeared. The user interface was familiar, with icons for a web browser, music player, email client, and cryptocurrency wallet. Opening the browser, Amadeus removed the slip of paper with the chat channel's address and passphrase from his wallet and accessed the chat room. Grassal's status indicator showed he was already in the channel. Amadeus began to type.

[AB2101]: *Bad shit going down, G. QL is dead. HJ is in on this. I just haven't figured out how.*

[Greasemonkey]: *Damn. Lilly said her father was acting strange. What should I do?*

[AB2101]: *That's up to you. You can leave CO or you can try* to intercept Jones' communications. Right now I need to get a good look at Dad's research.

[*Greasemonkey*]: Less suspicious if I stay. But since I'm here, I'll put a backdoor on the bunker's security system. It'll be my own little insurance policy. You saw what happened in West Virginia?

[*AB2101*]: Some of it. How did it end?

[*Greasemonkey*]: With press conferences. The president came on, said this was an act of terrorism, and those responsible would be found out. He talked about how the university in Huntington was known for early research on kipium, though the president never said that was the reason Huntington was attacked. Then, within minutes, a video was released by the BBC of our friend Ross. He said that while he wasn't responsible for the Huntington Incident, we should use this opportunity to reflect on our way of life, then went on about some mythological Hindu stuff.

[*AB2101*]: Laroux said that at their last meeting Ross gave this big speech about the churning of the ocean of milk. It's a creation myth, but it's also a story of demigods and demons. Crazy guy thinks he's a demigod. But Laroux says Ross doesn't really understand the myth, he just likes the imagery. What is the government doing?

[*Greasemonkey*]: Whatever the government does. They said they have people working on it and they expect another attack within the next two weeks.

[*AB2101*]: I've got to think ...

[*Greasemonkey*]: Not much time for thinking. Besides, you might hurt yourself. Strange stuff going on here, too. The contractors have been taking supplies down and working on the panic room. Before all this, I thought it was Jones being paranoid. Now it makes sense. Jones said it was just routine maintenance. I think that's bullshit.

[*AB2101*]: I think you're right. Where is Gravity?

[*Greasemonkey*]: He sent you and me a postcard from West

Virginia with his signature. No message, just a winking smiley
face. Maybe he's playing detective and trying to make some
money. The Chinese did put out a multi-million dollar bounty
on whoever can find the people responsible for the attack.

[AB2101]: *Well, the Chinese can afford it. I can't say for sure*
when I'll be back. Do what you need to do ... and keep in touch.

Amadeus exited the chat channel and turned off Laroux's
phone, then took out the other phone and turned it over in his
hand. He opened the bio-lock software then used that to
decrypt the files. A status bar told him to wait as the
information loaded. While he waited he chewed his thumbnail,
biting it down to the quick.

A little green light flashed on the screen and a new window
opened. There they were: hundreds of directories, labeled and
dated. Amadeus found the directory called "Schematics." The
small screen showed several dozen CAD files and one directory.
He opened it. Inside, he found another directory entitled
"Lorentzian Wormhole/Transitional Portal Prototype;"
everything one needed to know about building demon gates,
even down to the probability of encountering a demon in each
frequency range.

He scrolled through the other directories and found one
called "Detection." He opened it to find a single text file three
paragraphs long. The further he read, the more excited he
became. By the end, he had almost jumped out of his seat.
There, in bold, twelve-point Arial font, his father had written
that "in this particular application, before and after electron
bombardment, kipium emits electromagnetic interference in the
UHF spectrum that affects common consumer electronics for
up to three kilometers away. Frequency increases with
proximity. Analog cordless telephones and police scanners are
especially susceptible to this interference. The effect is even
stronger after bombardment. Mitigation is possible ... but not
desirable at this time."

"Beautiful! Dad, you're a genius," Amadeus said. He started laughing, laughing in spite of everything that had happened, laughing at this simple solution, at the absurdity of his long errand. Then he felt the guilt crushing down on him; if he had known about the frequencies in the first place, he never would've needed to make this errand, and maybe Laroux and Vesely would still be alive. Why hadn't his father told him? Amadeus put his hand on his forehead. Despite his excitement, he felt a headache coming on, felt a weight crushing down on him, on his shoulders, on his body, like he was deep, deep underwater. For a moment he wondered what the weight was, and then he knew: He was the turtle beneath the mountain. And the world rested upon his back.

43

For three days, as he made the return flight to the States, he formulated a plan. The engineering would be easy: with a parabolic dish and a cordless phone, he could develop a device anyone could use to locate a demon gate and destroy it. But what baffled him was the human factor. How could he share his findings with the world?

While he mulled over this problem, he watched news analysts react to an intelligence leak that suggested demon gates would appear in several major cities around the world. Ross was one of these analysts, speaking over video chat from an unknown location; Amadeus guessed Ross' wildly controversial opinions would be great for ratings. An Indian intellectual pointed out several errors in Ross' understanding of the churning of the sea of milk and said that his use of the story was a "bamboozlement of sacred mythology." Ross maintained that he was only attempting to interpret these events as he understood them, and to urge humanity to see itself both as it was, and as it could be.

Ross was dressed in a well-tailored suit and could have been any of the investment bankers in New York. But instead of talking about returns and derivatives, Ross spoke about death and rebirth. He called the lecherous demons of humanity an infectious algae plume, the world a sea. He said that now everyone must unite and face the threat, and that as the sea churned, the world would cleanse itself of its "many diverse poisons" and would receive in turn great elixirs of happiness and serenity.

While Ross spoke, he was polite and respectful, even while he was shouted down by everyone who spoke with him. Amadeus remembered reading that the Khmer Rouge were also generally considered very polite. Ross' smile never wavered; Amadeus had seen this expression before on the faces of both actors and the self-proclaimed righteous: ideologues, demagogues, fanatics. He wished he could reach through the screen and strangle him, this monster who had murdered his father. And the gall, the nerve he had, to force his apocalyptic wet dreams upon the world.

Yet, a small part of Amadeus suspected that this was all some kind of deception by Ross. Despite his smooth delivery and apparent utter conviction, Amadeus wasn't completely convinced that Ross actually believed what he was saying. Ross was a computer scientist, entrepreneur, and venture capitalist, and his past behavior belied the tin-foil philosopher image he had created for himself. And, as others had pointed out, the ideas rolling off Ross' tongue were so disjointed and outlandish that Amadeus suspected Ross had simply pulled them out of his ass.

In public addresses, leaders from around the world pleaded with whoever had unleashed the creatures. Their messages were variations on a few themes: some threatened, some exhorted, some even offered money, power, and dialog. The President of the United States offered open negotiations, while at the same time matching the death bounty offered by the Chinese for the culprit's head. Governments also called on their people to remain calm, but that was like telling a dog not to lick its own genitals. In developing countries, riots and looting broke out like malaria epidemics during the rainy season. Religious fervor swept the world like a dust storm; mass conversions took place blocks away from stonings and suicides. Some people tried to organize vigilante groups like the ones from Huntington. A vast majority of people, not knowing what else to do, simply went on about their daily lives.

With the leak of the document that suggested demon gates would soon appear in major cities, the reaction was understandable, according to analysts. The world had watched as Huntington, a city of 50,000, was nearly destroyed by two demon gates and, according to the last count, twenty-three demons. Killing these had taken a majority of the 101st Airborne, one brigade from a private military corporation named Securaux, and not a few well-armed citizens. If hundreds or, as the document implied, thousands, of these were loosed upon the world, what hope did the world have?

Yet, Amadeus knew that he could offer them hope ... but first he needed to confirm his hypothesis. For that, he would need a demon gate. The two from Huntington had been destroyed. The ones created by his father had probably been stolen. Unless he happened to find a prototype the attackers had somehow missed, he would have to build one on his own to test the device he had named the Gate Crasher.

Amadeus again tried to call Grassal, but no one answered. He tried the chat channel, but no one was there. He tried Lilly and even Jones. Four times a day, he dialed Colorado, but the compound was incommunicado. The phones rang; his messages and emails went unanswered. Amadeus tried not to think of what had happened. He hated himself for thinking it, but his friends would have to wait.

Amadeus landed in the woods behind his old house. From the air, everything had looked normal. The house was intact, the driveway empty save for the first fallen leaves of autumn. Stepping out, the air was almost cool. After the heat of Cambodia, this felt like standing before an open refrigerator. All around him, grasshoppers chittered and buzzed. With great caution, he approached his house from behind. He felt like a trespasser, even though this was his land. At least, he thought it was still his, but he wasn't sure.

Yet, none of it felt like home. He wasn't sure why; maybe it had something to do with the boards over the windows and the yellow police tape strewn around the yard like party streamers. Or maybe the crudely painted red cock-and-balls that now decorated the back of the house. He wasn't sure who had boarded all the windows, but he was glad they did. At least he and his father still had some friends out here.

The yard was empty and overgrown. Climbing hydrangeas threatened to consume the house. The gate at the end of the driveway was chained and locked with a padlock. His hopes for an untouched basement lab rose, but he cut them away as he would one day prune back the hydrangeas.

With a spare lawnmower blade retrieved from the mostly-pillaged garden shed, Amadeus pried the boards off the basement window and crawled in. The house was dark, but slivers of light shone through slits between the boards. After disabling the main internet connection, he flipped the main breaker and squinted against the light that flooded the basement. Amadeus was glad he'd convinced his father to configure auto-pay for all the utilities. With the power back online, computers whirred to life, their green and blue lights flashing and winking. The overhead lights showed the aftermath of the attack.

Oscilloscopes and electronic components lay on the floor. The workbench had been turned over. Amadeus looked closer at the computers. Though they were running, the monitors showed BIOS screens. All the data storage had been removed, and was now presumably in the possession of their attackers' employers, or a law enforcement evidence locker. So many years of work, gone. At least he had his copy.

Amadeus looked around for blood and other evidence of the attack. Many bullets had been fired, but there were neither shell

casings nor blood. Either the police had cleaned things up or …
no, they had killed his father. He couldn't have made it through
the attack. The aftermath had been cleaned up. That was all.
Without a doubt. His father was dead. He could feel it in his
bones, in his heart.

Outside, darkness crept in like a thief. Amadeus performed a
quick sweep of his own house. A thin layer of dust covered
everything, and the faint smell of mildew hung in the air.
Broken glass still littered the hallway. On the dark mahogany
mantle above the hearth, he lingered for a minute looking at
pictures: his parents' wedding picture, a candid shot of the three
of them taken somewhere in Maine, and a press photo of his
father accepting a prestigious award from the Academy of
Sciences. These photos seemed out of place. This wasn't a
home anymore; it was a memorial. He didn't want to accept it,
but now, looking around, he had no choice. He was still angry,
but his life would go on. At least for a little while.

Amadeus' stomach growled. He had eaten almost all his
energy bars and cans of tuna during his return trip. In the
kitchen, the bowl of fruit had rotted away. When he opened the
refrigerator, the stink of rancid meat made him queasy. Pulling
his shirt over his nose, he threw it all into the trashcan, tied the
bag tight, and set it outside. In the cabinets, he found plenty of
dried squid, as well as canned peaches, pears, and precooked
spaghetti. This last, his father had said wasn't food, but
Amadeus liked it, and had insisted they include it on their
regular grocery delivery list. He ate some syrupy peaches and
cold spaghetti and felt better.

Back in the basement, Amadeus went into the crawlspace
and found the kipium in a box of plumbing supplies, right
where he had left it. The thick glass housing felt heavy in his
hands. The electric blue light emitted by the kipium gave
Amadeus' hands an alien glow. He wished that this material
had remained unknown, but that cat had clawed free of its
proverbial bag several years ago.

Amadeus set to work. First he examined the list of subsystems attached to the schematics. Each subsystem on the list was linked to a page containing a diagram, along with schematics and technical documentation for each of its components. After some study and searching, Amadeus realized that the components were all vaguely familiar. Only when he stepped out of the lab and into the basement did he realize that most of the items on the parts list were stored on the shelving lining the walls. Some components were even already partially assembled into subsystems. Most of what Amadeus had assumed were obsolete electronics and abandoned projects had actually been assorted pieces of an inter-dimensional portal.

Going down the list, he laid out each of the necessary components. For each subsystem, there was documentation on how to run a diagnostic test to verify functionality. Working slowly and methodically, talking to himself, and grumbling when he couldn't find some part, Amadeus made progress. After he soldered, fastened, screwed, and bolted each subsystem together, he ran each test. In most cases, the tests failed the first few times, but between the excellent documentation, detailed error messages, and Amadeus' sheer stubbornness, he was soon satisfied that he had both the necessary parts and necessary knowledge to build a demon gate.

And so, late into the night he soldered, scrounged, screwed and bolted parts together, ignoring the fatigue that made his fingers clumsy and his thoughts muddled. For a few components he couldn't identify, he transferred the specifications from the schematics into the 3D printer, which slowly but accurately created the missing component from the aluminum feedstock Amadeus fed into it.

Just before four in the morning, after he nearly pierced his hand with the drill press while making a mount for a flange, he realized he needed rest. He thought he would be too wound up to sleep, but as soon as he lay down on the cot his father kept for "inspiration naps," fatigue pulled him under.

44

He stood on a stage before a crowd of millions. Everyone was shouting angry and unintelligible words at him. He tried to placate them, to offer assurances, but his efforts only raised their vehemence to another level.

Amadeus replayed this dream in his mind as he stood in the kitchen savoring yet another can of sickly sweet peaches. He tried to tease out the dream's meaning. That he was trying to help these people was obvious, but something about the dream struck him as incongruent. As he swallowed a peach, he realized it: in his dream, he felt no fear. While all those eyes had been focused on him, he had not felt a single shred of anxiety. Instead, he had felt calm, competent and, for the first time in a long time, in control.

Before resuming work on the demon gate, he found an old analog cordless phone among his father's collection of scrounged, obsolete devices. He plugged it in, left it to charge, and, with the imagined eyes of the world upon him, went back to work. By lunch time he had welded the external frames together. He turned the last screw to secure the circuit board to its housing, then double-checked that the spheres were watertight. With a digital multimeter he verified all his solder connections. Finally, he re-ran the self-tests for each subsystem. Everything checked out. He set his phone to record video and flipped the switches on the control box that sent power to the system. He then typed the commands on the keyboard connected to the control box that initiated the startup sequence.

In the space between the gate's two pillars, an orb of light blossomed, just like in the videos his father left. This he had expected. He hadn't expected the smell of rotten meat and sulfur to fill the room. When the orb grew larger, howls and moans filled the air. Amadeus felt his skin prickle as his brain told him he wasn't meant to hear such sounds. He told his brain to quiet down.

When a gnarled claw reached out of the gate, Amadeus turned off the switch on the control box. The orb and the claw remained. He tried again, flipping the switch on and off. Nothing happened. The claw became an arm. The stink increased. Soon the creature's arm lashed out at the air. The demon howled like a teapot on the boil. This one was different than the others. This demon had a head with many eyes and a spade-shaped crimson snout. A black tongue lolled out the side. The demon pulled itself out farther.

The control box still didn't work. Amadeus ran to the gate and, just before the demon got its back legs out, began pulling wires from one of the pillars at random. Suddenly the light disappeared and the demon shrieked as it fell to the floor. Amadeus covered his ears, but too late. The howl assaulted his eardrums. Amadeus couldn't hear anything but high-pitched ringing.

When the gate closed, the demon's hindquarters were severed. It pulled itself towards Amadeus with its front legs, snapping, howling, and off–balance, all mouth and fury. His mind shut off and his body took over as he grabbed a fire extinguisher from the bottom of the workbench. He raised the extinguisher high and smashed it down onto the demon's skull. His attack had no effect on the demon except to piss it off further, if that was possible. The demon swiped at his legs, but Amadeus jumped back.

Amadeus tried again, this time harder. Under the weight of the extinguisher, the demon's head hit the concrete floor, but it immediately jerked itself back upright. Amadeus realized bludgeoning wouldn't work. He looked around the lab before he remembered the saber hanging above the lab door. As he started to back away, the demon lunged at him and took a swipe at his calf. Amadeus felt something tear. He fell and scampered backwards, pushing himself with one leg.

The jeans on his left leg were shredded and bloody. Amadeus didn't feel anything until he stood up. When he put weight on his left leg, white light appeared at the edges of his vision and he felt dizzy. He imagined what would happen if he fell again, and that thought propelled him out of the lab and away from the demon. He limped outside and grabbed the saber from the wall. Its curved blade glinted under the fluorescent lights of the basement. He held the grip with both hands.

The demon crawled towards him, trailing black blood and what Amadeus guessed were intestines. Just when the demon's head passed through the door frame, Amadeus pulled the door shut, trapping the demon's head and a foreleg. Leaning on the door, holding it shut with his body, he slammed the saber down on the demon's neck. It howled and snapped at him. Amadeus hacked again and again. Each hack and chop brought more blood, more howling.

At first the demon fought with tremendous energy, its one free talon moving at electric speed, but soon it became clumsy. Finally, with one last, two-handed swing, Amadeus brought the saber down into the nape of the demon's neck. The demon twitched for a moment then fell still. He had severed its spinal cord. Amadeus crumpled to the floor, gasping for air. He drew his legs up and began to rock back and forth, waiting for the adrenaline to give way to pain.

Amadeus poured water over the laceration on his leg, washing the blood and unattached bits of tissue away. The cleft-shaped wound on his calf was about five centimeters long and one or two centimeters deep. On the kitchen table sat a pair of latex gloves, an industrial-sized first aid kit, and his mother's old sewing basket. He examined the wound again. More bits of skin, fibers from his jeans, and some black flecks still remained. With sterilized tweezers he picked everything out, dumped iodine on the wound, and smeared a tube of clotting agent over the whole mess.

He needed stitches, but he expected a hospital would be hazardous to his health and dangerous to his plans. He threaded a needle then, holding the needle with pliers, and sterilized it over the gas flame of the stove. He pinched the flesh together, pushed the needle in one side, then pulled it out the other, wincing as the thread rubbed against the inside of his skin. Tears streamed down his cheeks.

Fighting every pain-avoiding instinct he possessed, he pushed the needle through to the skin on the other side. He repeated this eight more times until the wound was closed. He cut the thread. By the time he finished, everything was blurry, but he managed to cover the stitches with gauze and to wrap tape around his leg. He focused on slowing his gasping breaths and trying to figure out why he hadn't been able to shut off the gate, but logical thought eluded him, and soon darkness settled on him like a fog.

Amadeus awoke on the kitchen floor sometime the next day. His head hurt almost as much as his leg. Pulling himself up to a sitting position, ignoring the pain, he checked his work. A small red cloud of blood had appeared on the gauze, but the clotting agent seemed to have done its job. He shifted his body until he was on his knees, then he managed to stand up. At first he was unsteady, but once he figured out the ways he could move his wounded leg, he was able to get around easy enough. As he pulled himself up, he realized he had been reckless, had underestimated just how dangerous this work was.

With the help of a high dose of pain pills, he returned to

work. He added a simple fail-safe switch on the right post of the demon gate and on the control box. To figure out why the control box hadn't worked, he decided, was a diversion from the main task at hand, that of confirming that the Gate Crasher would do just what he expected. Clearly, he already had a working demon gate. The throbbing wound on his leg reminded him of this fact with every beat of his heart.

So he started on the Gate Crasher. His father had observed that during and after electron bombardment, charged kipium emitted electromagnetic radiation in the UHF spectrum. This radiation caused the interference with cordless phones, and this interference varied as a function of distance. In his experiment, Amadeus had only to confirm this observation. He smiled, thinking that if this worked it could go down as the simplest counter-terrorism tool ever developed.

Considering the experimental design, he thought that holding the phone to his ear would be okay for this test, but he needed to collect as much data as he could. And though he wanted to take his time to plot the data, perhaps create a visualization, activating the demon gate could have alerted anyone who was both aware of this vulnerability and paying attention, so he only had limited time. For now, he decided, he would record two things: his position relative to the gate, and audio from the phone. He'd need as many recordings of both as he could collect. When he had more time, he could run the audio through a frequency analyzer and plot that against his location.

Though the parabolic dish was optional, Amadeus estimated this would increase the effective range to at least two kilometers. In the kitchen, he found a big plastic bowl he and his father used to use as a popcorn dish. He drilled a hole in the bottom and slid the antenna through it. His final product looked like some child's idea of a space ray gun, complete with duct tape.

Before he turned on the demon gate a second time, he ran a line with a power switch outside the lab room. This way, if another creature decided to crawl through, it would be locked inside.

Amadeus checked the remaining memory on his phones; between the two, he had enough for several hours of high-definition video. After readying Laroux's phone to log his position and to record audio from the cordless phone, he took a deep breath, started the video recording, and began to speak.

"I'm Amadeus Brunmeier, and my father developed the technology that led to the creation of demon gates. Inter-dimensional demons were an unintended side effect of his teleportation research. Someone found out about this side effect, stole his technology, weaponized it, then murdered him. Today, I'm going to document a method to detect demon gates." He went on to explain the details and conditions of the experiment.

With the lab door closed and barricaded with a heavy air compressor, he sent power to the demon gate, then put the cordless phone to his ear. He heard a steady tone. Inside the lab, in the center of the demon gate, an orb of light began to grow. He provided voiceover for the video recording.

"The sound just barely comes through, but it can be heard. Listen." He held the phone's microphone up to the cordless phone's speaker. "We're right beside a demon gate, maybe three meters from the kipium housing. I've just initiated the startup sequence. That tone you're hearing is interference in the UHF spectrum." He hobbled upstairs and went outside. The sound began to change to a rapid-fire clicking.

"Now I'm about twenty meters away. As I get farther from the gate, the frequency decreases and the wavelengths get longer." He hobbled farther and farther from the house, aiming his makeshift parabolic dish at the house the whole time. "If I aim the dish away from the gate," he pointed it in the direction of the Pachyderm, "the signal strength decreases."

One painful kilometer away from the house, he guessed he heard about ten clicks per second. Farther away, the frequency was just a little bit less. He guessed that the frequency increased exponentially within a certain range. This also suggested exponential decay, and while he couldn't verify that now, with better instrumentation, he suspected the detection range could be very large. After walking in two concentric circles to collect more data, he decided that the experiment had been a success.

Back in the house, he heard a familiar howl coming from the basement. Still recording, he left the Gate Crasher clicking away on the kitchen table, hobbled down the stairs, and flipped the kill switch for the gate. The lab door had remained shut, but two demons were snarling and slamming themselves against the window, smearing fluid against the glass as they did so. Both looked just like smaller versions of the Manhattan Monster. Amadeus held the camera up to the window to get some footage. He kicked the creature he had killed last night.

"See this creature?" he said, focusing the camera on its carcass. "Even though only part of its body emerged, it very nearly ate my leg before I killed it. As for the other two, I can't do anything about them. Maybe they'll starve in there, or eat each other."

Turning the camera back on himself, he took a deep breath and delivered his closing monologue.

"Today, I have demonstrated a simple method for detecting demon gates. Use what I've shown you to build your own Gate Crasher. No one can do this alone, but together, we can stop future attacks."

Before he left his home, Amadeus copied the encrypted research files and the biometric keys onto two small memory cards, along with backups of all of the data from his experiment. He tucked one card into his wallet. The other, he buried in a watertight plastic container in his backyard. Finally, he deleted the schematics from the phone. Carrying the Gate Crasher, both phones, and a backpack full of canned peaches and precooked spaghetti, Amadeus set off for the Pachyderm. He would complete his plan from the sky.

45

While flying west, Amadeus considered several scenarios for distributing his plans. His basic premise was that demon gates would be placed in several major metropolitan areas throughout the world and activated at about the same time; the intelligence leak had implied as much. To detect these gates in time would require dozens, maybe hundreds, of people in each location, each with their own Gate Crasher.

In the first scenario, he contacted government leaders and told them he knew how to locate demon gates. They had the resources and they were desperate for a solution. Yet some half-remembered history lessons told him that relying on the government would be a mistake. Too much bureaucracy, too many channels for information and decisions to flow through. He imagined objections, debates, and rhetoric flowing like so much sludge. People would be destroyed not by the ideology of a madman but by the slow machinations of contrarian politicians looking for political capital. Another concern: what politician would risk aligning himself with Amadeus, who one pithy journalist had called the "poster boy for privileged patricide?"

The next scenario he considered was seeking the help of some larger organizations. Multinational corporations had the resources and maybe the motivation, but the possibility existed that their efforts to maximize shareholder value might slow their response. With enough time and influence, perhaps he could convince a group of non-profits to organize enough people, but he had neither.

No, he couldn't rely on just a few large organizations. He needed to address people directly. But how could he reach them without exposing himself to arrest ... or worse? How did anyone bypass the gatekeepers and give their information to the world? The answer was like the picture window a bird slams into: right in front of him but invisible until impact.

He would build a simple website with video, instructions for making a Gate Crasher ... and his own version of the story. That was good, he decided. Give the information straight to people who could use it. And maybe, just maybe, take the first step toward clearing his name. But he faced two issues: the internet was populated by billions of websites, a vast majority of the non-pornographic sites run by marketers, propagandists, and teenagers. How could he convince anyone his footage and plans were genuine? Two, even if his footage seemed credible, how would people find out about it?

After a moment's consideration, the answer came to him: Annie. She'd freelanced for the *Times of America* and had said she had a good relationship with a couple editors there. Through her, he could reach millions. More importantly, if the *Times* ran his story, he would have the most important ingredient: credibility. But did she think Amadeus had murdered her brother-in-law? That didn't matter; the only thing that mattered was Annie taking the time to watch the video and read his account. He could even give her the location of a fully functional demon gate (complete with demons) to corroborate his story. If she ran his story, the information would propagate. Information propagation ... as Amadeus chewed on this phrase, another face came to him: Salaman from Cambodia and his "marketing on steroids" business. He checked his bag; there was the copy of *On the Road* with Salaman's email address in the front. Perfect. He would contact him as well and ask for his help. A plan and a backup plan.

But first he needed a place to host his website, a place uninvolved with and ideally antagonistic to Tivooki Systems. He remembered a company his father had dealt with called Privihost; their anonymous, distributed hosting service catered to privacy activists and the paranoid. Their flagship product was distributed, encrypted storage and log-less hosting; they even offered a free trial. Amadeus laughed out loud. Hovering less than a hundred meters over an upstate New York lake, he began to write his story.

After two hours, Amadeus had used Laroux's phone to build a simple website from a template. He was proud of his site: it had the videos he had recorded, as well as detailed instructions for developing and using the Gate Crashers, data on structural weak points of the gates, and a version of his story. The copy began:

My name is Amadeus Brunmeier. I know how to destroy the demon gates, but the world thinks I murdered my father. Here's what really happened ...

Amadeus concluded by imploring people not only to make their own Gate Crashers, but to make mirrors of this website, because once it went live, he expected it would only last for a little while. He pressed publish. After a breathless moment, he received a message that the site was now live. He clicked the link to view the live version, and there it was: his best hope for, well, everything.

He next tried calling Annie, but couldn't get through. Instead, he sent her a message with a compressed copy of the website. He then sent a copy of the site and a brief message to Sal. Almost immediately after he sent this last message, the navigation system alerted him to an incoming call. He answered, and a familiar face appeared on the chat screen.

"Amadeus, my boy, you are clever," Jones said. "But you're also terribly misguided. I'm in a real bind here and I'm incredibly sorry to tell you this but ... I have to kill you," Jones said. "You tried harder than anyone expected." The call disconnected before Amadeus could say anything. Everything in the Pachyderm powered down. Amadeus felt his stomach twist as the Pachyderm lurched to the side. Instinct took over. He stowed the phone in a waterproof bag, pulled a helmet on, and opened the side door. Amadeus had imagined such a scenario more than a few times. He wasn't ready, but he knew what to expect.

The Pachyderm fell towards the lake below. Using the manual controls, he closed the foils over the turbofans, slowing the descent somewhat. Amadeus drew himself up into a ball in the cargo area and braced for impact.

The crash roared like an apocalypse, jarring Amadeus' body hard onto the cabin floor. His head hit against something and his vision went white for a long moment. Water rushed into the cabin, throwing Amadeus around like a rag in a washing machine. He thrashed, fighting to regain his bearings. The Pachyderm was on its side, the open door below him. He had an air pocket, half a meter high, shrinking quickly.

Still holding the waterproof bag, Amadeus took in a deep gasp of air and dropped into the water, pulling himself out from underneath the Pachyderm and into the open water. Disoriented, he realized the sunlight was below him. He flipped and swam towards it. He was deep. His lungs screamed for oxygen. He swam harder. Air bubbles rose around him. Every muscle in his body ached as they sacrificed their oxygen for his starving brain. Finally he broke through and splashed out the top. He gasped until he was dizzy. Thankful for his childhood swimming lessons, he looked around.

The lake that had almost killed him was rather peaceful. Bubbles from the sinking ship fizzled around him. Birds chirped in the surrounding forest. He wondered if anyone had seen the crash. The nearest shore lay almost a kilometer away, but a couple of trees growing from a small island nearby promised a place to rest. He swam towards the trees and worried about Grassal and Lilly.

Closer to the island, his feet scraped the bottom. He trudged his way out of the silty water and onto the weedy island. He stretched out and caught his breath. His body shook. The sandy ground underneath felt solid and reassuring. The longer he sat still, the more pain filled his body, like a cup under a leaky faucet, gradually growing full. Sitting under a tree, he felt detached, unwillingly lulled into rest. He knew he should be in much, much more pain, but all he knew was the ground beneath him. He really wanted to sleep, but he also suspected that was a bad idea.

The sky glowed fire orange with the first hint of sunset. Amadeus heard the whine of a small engine. Faint at first, like the tinnitus that had stayed with him, it eventually grew louder as it drew closer. The sound was a boat motor. He thought that if he lay flat, the scrubby trees could hide him, but he knew that wouldn't work. Instead, he limped back into the water, went out a few feet and sunk down, keeping only his face above the surface. He knew his hearing was still not as good as it should be, but he knew the boat was closer. If he could hold out until darkness, he could avoid whoever was out there ... unless they had scanning equipment. He remembered that some fishermen used a simple kind of radar technology to find clusters of fish. Would he show up as a man-sized carp?

At the same time, Amadeus thought, he had no idea where he was. And even if he did reach a town, he was still a wanted man, the message to his aunt notwithstanding. If he went into town, soaking wet and beat up like a punching bag, he would be at the mercy of the authorities. He'd read of riots and looting due to news of the impending demon gate attacks, and he expected the police would be on edge. Now, he suspected, was a particularly bad time to be a vagrant, especially one wanted for murder. Nevertheless, he was in bad shape, and he needed help.

Just as the sun dropped behind a mountain, Amadeus gave up. He was tired of running, tired of evading and hiding and lying. He would have to trust the boat people and hope that his videos and plans would convince them he was someone worth saving.

The growling engine was closer now. A searchlight scanned the water. In the dim evening light, Amadeus finally saw the source of it: a small pontoon boat. The light danced over the water but refused to fall on the island. Amadeus stood up, waved his arms, yelling until the light finally settled on him. The boat came closer to the island and shut off its engines. The searchlight shone directly on Amadeus, blinding him to whoever was on the boat. A voice tempered by whiskey and age spoke to him.

"My wife has a twelve-gauge shotgun aimed at your head. Now, son, why don't you tell me who you are and why you're sitting on an island in the middle of Raquette Lake."

"My name is Amadeus Brunmeier, and I know how to destroy the demon gates."

46

The man and woman scrutinized Amadeus and murmured among themselves. Amadeus felt heat rising under his collar before they motioned for him to come aboard. They asked him no more questions as they made their way back.

The two-story lodge was in the old Adirondack style: pine siding, a low-sloping roof, and a wrap-around porch on both floors. Native stone ran around the base of the house. Their upgrades included a couple generators, barbed wire, and metal gates over all the windows. The family was named Conner. Some teenage children were holed up in their rooms.

They sat around the fire. Mrs. Conner brought Amadeus coffee and a first aid kit. Her body was as thin and rigid as her shotgun. He went to the bathroom to clean up. Sitting on the edge of the bathtub, he winced as he pulled the damp gauze back off his leg. Some clotted blood stuck to it; removing it renewed the bleeding. After more iodine, a fresh bandage, and a lot of pain, he felt better about his wound, but not much else. Amadeus returned to the living room.

"Sorry about the shotgun," Mr. Conner said. His silver hair stood in contrast to his dark skin and young face. "Impending demon apocalypses make people a little crazy. You understand. Just the other day, we had some people running up here on four wheelers. They shot at our house but when we shot back, they turned tail and ran. Reckon they were looking for some abandoned place to wait till this thing blows over."

"I don't think it's going to blow over," Mrs. Conner said. "Unless, of course, this young man is right. He sure sounds confident. So, Amadeus Brunmeier, tell us what you've got."

"Let me show you," Amadeus said. The phone started up, but there was mud in the memory card slot and the screen was cracked. Amadeus didn't want to risk damaging the memory card. Laroux's phone didn't have a memory card slot. "Um, do you have a computer here?" Mr. Conner said they did. "Can you turn off the internet connection, Mr. Conner?"

"Call me Charlie," Charlie Conner said. "That's funny. You won't find any internet out here, not these days. Used to be, but somebody cut the cord years ago. Part of the charm, don't you think?" He fetched an old notebook computer from the storage room. "About the only thing we use this for is looking at pictures." Amadeus placed the memory card in the notebook's card reader and the Conners huddled over the computer, their heads close together as they read the text and watched the videos. Mrs. Conner mumbled the words as she read.

Amadeus studied their faces as he watched them watch his videos and read his story. He spent nearly an hour answering their questions. As he answered them, he became aware of places where he could improve his narrative for clarity. Slowly, the tension in the room seemed to melt. Everyone relaxed, and Amadeus smiled. They believed him.

When all their questions had been answered, the urge to sleep fell over him like a fleece blanket. As Charlie talked about something, Amadeus closed his eyes, intending only to rest them for a moment. The next thing he knew he was awake in a strange place in front of a stone fireplace. He sat up with a start, then relaxed as he remembered all that had happened. In the dark of the cabin, he felt safe for the first time in a long time. He liked that feeling. Eventually the ticking grandfather clock lulled him back to sleep.

In the morning, he awoke with the smell of biscuits in the air and the prelude to a plan in his mind. Amadeus sat with the Conners at a sturdy wooden table. Four young teenagers, three girls and a boy, sat at a smaller card table nearby. The oldest girl looked to be about sixteen, and she gave Amadeus a furtive smile. Aside from that, they talked among themselves in hushed tones, occasionally looking over at Amadeus and giggling.

"I need to get to a town with a fast internet connection and then to a train station. The people I'm trying to stop, they're powerful, paranoid technocrats; they're the reason my craft crashed. I want them to think I'm dead, but if they watched that on satellite, I could have brought them here. I'm sorry."

"Maybe they couldn't see because of the dark," Mrs. Conner said.

"He's talking about Tivooki Systems here, pumpkin," Charlie said. "I'm sure they've got thermal imaging and things like that."

"I need to leave. For my safety. And yours."

"That's right, you do. No offense. Boonville is a little over an hour away," Mrs. Conner said. "Charlie could give you a ride out there."

"Does Boonville have a train station?"

"Nope," Charlie said. "But Utica has a bus station and it's only a little farther. From Utica, you can take a bus to Albany. There you can catch a train. Boonville isn't good for much except for drinking beer and playing the lottery. Come to think of it, I have a librarian friend in Utica who I expect would love to help you out; he's on a committee to end the Tivooki monopoly. We can get you there, don't you worry."

After breakfast, Mr. Conner readied a battered blue truck. With Amadeus' help, he loaded a big metal tank in the back. Amadeus asked what it was for. "For diesel fuel, just in case your plan doesn't work and the world rewinds back into the dark ages. At least we'll be able to generate electricity if we need to."

Before Amadeus stepped into the truck, the girl who had

smiled at him during breakfast came off the porch and stood pigeon-toed before him. She handed him a little bracelet made of baling twine and glass beads.

"Um, I made this and I want you to have it. It can, like, ward off evil," she said. Amadeus smiled and fumbled with one hand to attach it. She gave him a mock-exasperated sigh, took it from him, and deftly fastened it to his wrist. "Good luck, for what it's worth."

"Thanks," Amadeus said as he climbed in and shut the door. Charlie placed something heavy in Amadeus' hand. It was a six-shot Colt revolver.

"Just in case her bracelet doesn't work," he said.

47

The news poured out of the truck's radio like effluent from a sewage treatment plant. State and local governments were in lockdown mode. The few military units not on overseas deployments were mobilized. Grocery store shelves had been stripped. In some places, looters overran malls. Pockets of rioting had broken out in most cities. Cell networks were overloaded.

Amadeus tried to shake the feeling that none of this was real, that this was just a radio drama. Or a movie. Or a nightmare. Yet, his throbbing leg told him he was definitely awake.

They passed an uncovered military transport. Rows of soldiers sat in the back, clutching their rifles. Amadeus locked eyes with a man who looked about his age. He wore a look of forced bravery. The transport passed and the mud flaps caught his attention: a jolly roger. The smiling skull and crossed femurs reminded him of pirates, of hackers, of Grassal and ... of file sharing. Specifically, quasi-legal, peer-to-peer BTv2 protocol file sharing. With his site on a single server, even with multiple mirrors, it probably hadn't lasted ten minutes against a skilled and dedicated foe. But spread the file out over hundreds, thousands, then millions of people, and the battle was over. He only needed to seed the file long enough until a few people had complete copies. Once they were seeding, Amadeus expected it would spread like an epidemic. Too bad he hadn't thought of this twenty-four hours ago. He hoped he would get another chance.

When they arrived in Utica, Amadeus wondered if everyone had left. Only a couple cars sat on the street. Bits of paper and trash tumbled along deserted sidewalks. The downtown reminded Amadeus of something he had seen in a zombie movie, or maybe just a random picture of sleepy, small-town America, complete with the art deco signage of the Stanley Theater. On the changeable marquee of the "Now Playing" sign, someone had arranged the letters to say "Man vs. the Subluminals. Arm Yourselves. Protect the Weak. Help your Fellow Humans."

Above the theater, something glinted from a window. He squinted. The barrel of a rifle sat on the window sill. Scanning the other windows, Amadeus counted five more rifles and riflemen spread out over the next two blocks, and these were just the ones he could see.

People, he realized, were taking action. While some cities might be rife with chaos and confusion, at least this little town had banded together. Amadeus wondered why people would start looting electronics. He could understand groceries, medicine, and firearms, but stealing flexscreens and washing machines?

"There's the library," Charlie said, nodding to a low-flung concrete building beside the road. He parked the truck in front. They both got out. "Looks closed." He cupped his hands around his mouth and yelled, "Hello?"

A man wearing a maroon cardigan and a ponytail opened the door.

"Charlie?" he said. "Weren't you staying at Raquette?"

"Got someone here who needs your help," Charlie said. "Amadeus, why don't you explain what you need?" As Amadeus told a shortened version of his story, the librarian became increasingly excited.

"Whatever you need is yours," the librarian said. "You can use an office computer. Full access; no filters or firewalls."

As he had expected, his site was down. A quick look at the traffic logs showed that he'd been hammered with millions of requests from a couple thousand IP addresses: a classic distributed denial-of-service attack.

Amadeus copied his video to a computer for the librarian to watch, then he sat down at another machine. Charlie busied himself with magazines. In Amadeus' email he found a message from Annie:

Amadeus, thank you for sending this to me. I knew you didn't do what they said you did. I've talked to my editor. She says we're going to run with this. Good work.

Smiling with relief, Amadeus downloaded a client-side program, placed an offline version of his website into a file called "gate_crasher.zip," and made a torrent tracker file. He sent the tracker to Sal, asking for his help. Next he uploaded the tracker to his mostly unused social media accounts, then sent a mass message to every university and high school friend he had in his saved contacts. He also posted the tracker to several popular technical sites.

After five minutes, he had twenty seeders, people who had received parts of the file from Amadeus and were now sharing it with others. Five minutes after that, two people had the full contents of the file. If he guessed correctly, this number would increase exponentially as word spread. Unless the internet shut down, which wasn't entirely unimaginable, the world would have access to the plans. He logged onto Grassal's chat room and found a private message, dated yesterday:

Hey brother, I hope you're okay. I'm not sure what happened, but when I woke up two days ago, all communications channels were down and everyone was gone: Jones, Lilly, the Koreans. It's like they just disappeared in the night. The compound was completely empty. I didn't know what else to do, so I left. Remember the girls from the train? I'm staying with them until we can figure out what's going on. You know where they live. These are scary times. Right now we can still post here. I think it's still secure. You should join me if you can. Good luck, and hopefully see you soon.

Amadeus replied, telling Grassal about his site, his plan to distribute it, what had happened to the Pachyderm, and that he would come as fast as he could. Right now, constant motion sounded like a good plan. With that, he checked the seeds again. Up to a hundred. It was working. Wondering what had happened in Colorado, he logged off. The librarian came over and shook his hand.

"That's far out, man," he said. "Nice, and exceedingly clever." Amadeus thanked him then asked the Conners to take him to the bus station.

At the bus station, people sat on suitcases and taped cardboard boxes. A sign said all routes to New York were closed. There was a train station in Albany, though, and that would take him to San Francisco. According to the digital board above the counter, they still had tickets. Charlie waited in line with him, not bothering to make small talk. As they waited, the number of seats dwindled from ten to five to one and, just before Amadeus stepped up to the window, the last one sold. A young man with a shaved head and a long, scruffy beard had bought it.

"Excuse me," Amadeus said, "did you just buy a ticket for Albany?"

"Yeah, I got to get to my girl before all hell breaks loose."

"What would you take for that ticket?" Charlie said. "It's very important this man gets to Albany. Would you take a hundred for it?"

"Sorry chief, not selling it. They've already marked up all the prices, hazard rates, you know how it is," the young man said. "No more tickets until tomorrow."

"Look," Amadeus said. "You can get a ticket tomorrow. If I don't get to Albany today, I'm going to be up shit creek. What about three hundred dollars and a broken phone?" Amadeus pulled out his phone and handed it to the young man. "You can get the screen fixed and re-sell it. It's probably worth another two hundred, at least."

The young man considered it. "How do I know that thing's not stolen?"

"I promise you it's mine. I don't want to give it away, but I have some very important work to do."

"Um." The young man said. Amadeus looked at Charlie. His face was turning red.

"Son, if you don't take the offer," Charlie said, trailing off as he discreetly lifted the front of his shirt to reveal a handgun tucked into his belt, "we might have problems. It's a very good deal for you."

"Fuck it, take the ticket," the young man said. Charlie smiled and handed him three hundred dollars. Amadeus started to give him the phone but the young man refused it.

"I don't know what you two are up to, but that's probably stolen. I don't want a damn thing to do with it."

"Look," Amadeus said, "it's not stolen, and it works fine, it just needs a new screen." He powered the phone on and let the young man hear the phone's cheerful startup music.

"Okay, I'll take it," he said.

"One more thing," Amadeus said, still holding the phone. "When you get home, but no sooner, take the back off and reconnect the RF transmitter and GPS chip. You'll just need to plug in a couple wires, real easy."

"Whatever," the man said as he took the phone.

"Wise decision," Charlie said. The young man stuffed the phone in his pocket and left the station. Given the ticket was worth twenty dollars, even with hazard fees, Amadeus thought they had treated the young man fairly. They walked over to the platform. Rumbling buses waited for their passengers. People hugged as the drivers loaded their luggage aboard.

"They were tracking you with that, weren't they?" Charlie asked, smiling like he knew a secret.

"Before I disconnected the transmitter."

Charlie nodded in appreciation.

"What was your job before all this?" Amadeus asked him.

"High school algebra teacher," Charlie said. "Before last week, I'd never handled a gun in my life."

Mrs. Conner came into the station and stood beside her husband as Amadeus waited for his bus. Amadeus thanked them both for their help and asked them what they'd do next.

"You know what we're going to do, Amadeus," Charlie said. "I'm going to build a couple Gate Crashers, then tell anyone who'll listen how to build them, how to use them. Not everybody uses the internet, you know."

"Maybe it's best if you stay with your family," Amadeus said.

"They can take care of themselves up there. Not many people going up that way, now that the yokels know we bite back. Besides, if I don't, who will?" Even though he'd only known him a short time, Amadeus gave Charlie an awkward hug and thanked him for his help before he boarded his bus to Albany.

He sat with his waterproof bag in his lap. In his bag, he had the bandages Mrs. Conner gave him, a couple bottles of water, and the handgun. Amadeus didn't like carrying it, especially on a bus full of families and children, but he couldn't exactly throw it in the trash. Of course, at the train station, he might have to. He expected security would be heavy and tight. Yet, when his bus stopped at the transfer depot outside the train station, people were spilling out the doors of the station, packed tight, shoulder to shoulder. A man stood on a box and said the trains were running double capacity; all westbound express lines were standing room only. Amadeus waited in the queue. People around him pushed and jostled, frantic and impatient. Behind him, Amadeus heard an older man behind him telling his wife he had heard something about a way to locate the demon gates. Amadeus smiled and wondered if his solution had reached critical mass.

The security checkpoints were nonexistent. Everyone simply walked through. He decided to keep his gun. He guessed—correctly, he would later learn—that no one was prevented from taking weapons with them, registered or not. The government, or at least the station supervisors, had decided their passengers needed less protection from each other than from inter-dimensional demons. After an hour and a half, Amadeus pushed aboard the train and found a place in the hallway to sit. To fit, he had to keep his legs drawn up close to him; his entire body occupied only a square meter. He took a couple pain pills in anticipation of the long, cramped ride to San Francisco.

On either side of him, suitcases pressed into his arms, but he liked the secure feeling he got from it, like being in a childhood fortress built of couch cushions. All around him, people stood or sat pressed against each other, talking about their plans, their work, anything to take their mind off things. Most people planned to go to one small town or another.

From his place on the floor, he could see only denim-clad legs. He needed to sleep, but every time he closed his eyes and began to drift off, he had a vision of the demon he had killed. In this vision, instead of trying to maul him, the demon gazed upon him while Amadeus' own mind was filled with unintelligible, alien sounds, as if the creature was somehow communicating with him. The notion that the demon had any degree of sentience made it that much more terrifying. Each time the vision recurred, he opened his eyes and shook his head, but soon he gave up trying to fight the bone-deep exhaustion. Sleep came, but only after the sounds faded away to nothing louder than the rustling of leaves in the wind.

48

Amadeus awoke with no idea how long he had slept. His wound throbbed with pain and his legs and butt were numb from sitting on the hard floor. The train was stopped. Some passengers departed. Even more boarded. A voice announced they were in St. Louis. A chemical red sky covered the city. Another announcement came over the PA system, but Amadeus couldn't make out the words. Outside, people packed the platform, waiting for the next train. He wanted to move around but realized if he was going to keep his spot, he best stay put. So he did.

The train screamed on through the day and the following night. Just before dawn they arrived at San Francisco Station. Aching and hungry, Amadeus left the train with his little waterproof bag slung over his shoulder. The early morning air was sticky and cool but not cold. He needed to contact Grassal. Amadeus decided to find a library with public computers, but only after breakfast.

Breakfast was pancakes, bacon, eggs, and hash browns ... he hadn't realized just how hungry he was until he gazed upon the menu. He washed it all down with a few cups of coffee and left a generous tip for the long-suffering waitress. On his way out, he asked the waitress where to find a library. She pointed then gave him vague instructions that he couldn't quite follow. If nothing else, he could head in the general direction and ask someone when he got closer.

Unlike Utica, San Francisco was still going about its business. On the street, people seemed in no hurry to go anywhere. Unlike New York, where everyone had worn something semiformal, here most people were dressed in khakis and untucked oxford shirts. A few men wore ties. Something about this place Amadeus liked, but he couldn't say what. This was the place his heroes came from, internet pioneers and technology innovators ... but it was also the same place that produced a man as rich and crazy as Maximilian Ross. Maybe, Amadeus thought, that is the price of living somewhere interesting: a few people are bound to take weirdness to a whole new level.

He found the library with no problem, though on the way one man tried to sell him drugs and another asked him for a cigarette. He declined both. Both men were quite polite in their solicitations. Inside, he signed in to use a computer and waited. Most of the terminals were occupied by young people, but also by a couple scruffy guys with big beards and jackets. No one sat next to the scruffy guys. Amadeus thought that was strange until he came close enough to smell them. Taking a seat, he accessed the chat channel and found a message Grassal had left yesterday. The new message read:

Hope you're in town by now. Nice work on the site. The code's a little dirty; I took the liberty of making some improvements and re-seeding it. Right now I'm staying in the Mission District. At Fisherman's Wharf, there's a giant crab at Pier 39. I'll look for you there at 10am and 4pm for the next few days. Greasemonkey out.

Amadeus checked the time: 9:30am. A map showed the meeting spot was only two kilometers away, and he estimated that if he walked he could be there in time to meet his friend.

He logged off, left the library, and received directions to the
Wharf from a guy lounging on a bench. The air was thick with
morning fog and smelled of baking bread and sewage. After a
cramped night on the train, he enjoyed the freedom of
movement, but his throbbing wound and his cramped legs
forced him to stop for frequent rests. One of these rest stops
placed him in front of a cell phone shop with English, Spanish,
and Chinese printed in cut vinyl. A television screen filled the
window. Amadeus watched.

A video showed two news anchors holding cordless phones
and popcorn bowls. A scrolling caption at the bottom read,
"*Times of America* reports demon gate detection device
developed by murder suspect Brunmeier." Amadeus smiled and
resumed his walk, reaching Fisherman's Wharf at three minutes
to ten.

Most stalls were empty, though a few people still wandered
around. He finally arrived at the giant crab sculpture, its body
covered in vines. Underneath sat a man staring out at the water.
A cane rested beside him. Amadeus squinted. The man
resembled Grassal, but his hair was too long and his build too
lean. Regardless, Amadeus went closer. When he'd covered half
the distance to the crab, the man turned and Amadeus
recognized his friend.

"I thought you were somebody else," Amadeus said. Besides
the longer hair, a patchy beard clung to his face like moss on a
rock. Instead of his usual loose, grey trousers and black shirt,
Grassal now wore denim jeans and a colorful tie-dyed shirt.
They embraced. Grassal picked Amadeus up in a big bear hug
and swung him around as if he were a sack of flour. Amadeus
laughed then ended up gasping for air in Grassal's powerful
grasp. Amadeus had to smack his back to get him to let go. They
stood facing each other, sizing each other up, and began to
laugh like two maniacs hallucinating.

"Your video, that was brilliant, telling your story at the same
time as giving a little tutorial in demon gate mitigation. The

same pundits who called for your head? Now they're calling you a hero."

"Thank god for hypocrisy."

"That's the good news. Here's the rest. The day before everyone disappeared, Lilly told me she overheard her father on speakerphone, yelling at someone, saying they were wasting their time, chasing shadows, that everything was exactly as it seemed, and nothing more. She said the voice sounded like Gravity. I'm not sure what he's been doing, but apparently he's been busy."

"That still doesn't help us," Amadeus said. "What I really need to find out is what happened to Lilly."

"About that ... when I said everyone disappeared, maybe I was jumping to conclusions. When I woke up that day and found everyone gone, it kind of left me spooked, so I bolted. But ... maybe I left too soon."

Amadeus smiled. "When she came to Prague, she said that her father had designed the panic room for her. She hated the idea, of course, said if there was an apocalypse that she'd rather die with everyone else, but ..."

"But if Jones thought some bad shit was going to go down, he might not have given her a choice."

They turned their heads towards nearby shouts. A man wearing several jackets was yelling at some invisible accuser, waving his arms around like a firebrand preacher.

"A few weeks ago," Amadeus said, "that guy and my father were the only people who had actually seen demons and believed they were real."

"Amazing," Grassal said. He gazed off like a sailor scanning the distant sea for coming storms.

"What? How people change opinions faster than you change your underwear?"

"Very funny, but no. Meter maids. Look down there. No matter what, they're still out giving tickets." Grassal started walking towards the parking lot. Amadeus followed close behind. A golf cart was parked beside a familiar-looking Jeep. Grassal headed straight towards it.

"Did you steal Lilly's Jeep?" Amadeus asked.

Grassal smiled. "Steal might be too strong a word. Nobody was using it, so I borrowed it for a few days. I intend to take it back."

Beside the Jeep, a man with long hair was writing something on a pad. Grassal shouted at him. "Hey, we're just leaving. Come on, be a pal, don't ticket me." Something about the man seemed familiar, and when he turned around, Amadeus recognized him: it was the same man who had followed him in Prague, the black-eyed man.

Fear prickled his skin, but that fear was accompanied by an electric mix of something else. Bolstered by his friend's presence at his side, Amadeus charged, ignoring his injuries and aches. The man reached into his pocket, but before he could pull anything out, Amadeus sprang, wrapping his arms around the man. Grassal jumped in and knocked them both to the ground. Someone screamed.

A small crowd gathered. Amadeus scrambled to his feet and began to kick the man's ribs. Grassal pushed a knee into the man's chest and held his head, smashing it against the concrete. The black-eyed man moaned and croaked for help. Amadeus felt hands pulling him backwards. Before Amadeus was off him, he tugged at the black-eyed man's coat, revealing a handgun tucked into a leather holster. Someone yelled that the man had a gun. Nearby, two other men pulled Grassal off.

Amadeus struggled free of the arms that held him. He looked back. Around him stood a group of pissed-off onlookers. "I'm done, I won't touch him," Amadeus said, though he reached into his bag and wrapped his fingers around the handle of his gun, just in case.

"Amadeus, who is this guy?" Grassal said, then took another look at the man. A flash of recognition showed in his eyes. "Wait, is this the piece of shit that killed Ramona?"

The black-eyed man was now on his knees, trying to pull himself back up. Grassal dashed forward and kicked him again, knocking him back down.

"That's no meter maid," Amadeus said to the crowd. The black-eyed man smiled then reached for his gun. Amadeus pulled his out first and leveled it at the black-eyed man. "Don't move. Put your hands up." The man winked at Amadeus but didn't put his hands up. Amadeus pulled back the hammer on the gun. *Click.* "Put your hands up, right now, and tell me who you are." The man showed no fear. He appeared to be on the verge of laughter. At the sight of firearms, the crowd around them had fled, though a few still watched from a distance.

"You won't shoot me. You are only an irritation. Just like your father. And I am the man who neutralizes irritations." Blood ran from the black-eyed man's nose, but he didn't seem to notice.

Amadeus felt the gun shake in his hand as his brain processed what the man said. Did this man just admit to killing his father? He took a couple steps closer to the man, keeping the gun aimed at his head. Amadeus was near enough to see the blue corona of his irises and the sheen of sweat on his forehead.

"Grassal, get his gun," Amadeus said. Grassal removed the gun from the black-eyed man's belt. "Did you kill him? Did you kill Tommy Brunmeier?" Amadeus said.

"Amadeus," Grassal said, "we need to move." The black-eyed man laughed and spit some blood onto the concrete.

"Did you kill him?"

"I neutralized him," the man said. In the distance, Amadeus heard gunshots then a familiar, high-pitched animal shriek. Amadeus allowed his gaze to dart around before returning it to the man on the ground before him.

"Neutralized him. What the fuck does that mean?" He could pull the trigger right now and see this man die as he had seen Ramona die, as he had seen Laroux die.

"Amadeus ..." Grassal said.

"You want to run away," the man said. "No one would blame

you if you did. I know you recognize that glorious sound."

"Did you kill him?"

"Um, Amadeus ...?" Grassal said. A demon's bellow sounded out like the rumble of a thousand trains, shaking the city. Glass windows of the office towers facing the wharf shattered and crashed to the ground. Amadeus and Grassal both turned to look. When they looked back, the black-eyed man was sprinting away. "Chase or run?" Another roar, followed by more glass crashing.

"Run. Definitely run," Amadeus said.

Grassal tossed him the keys. "You can drive. I'm still not so good with a stick shift." Amadeus shrugged and got in the driver's seat, taking off before Grassal had closed his door.

"What about Zella and Lucretia?"

"They're playing in San Diego tonight, so they'll be fine." Grassal adjusted the mirror in an attempt to see the demon.

"Then let's go to Colorado. You've got a Jeep to return."

49

The radio announcer's frantic, smoke-roughened voice reported on the scene in San Francisco, yelling to be heard above the *fwopping* of helicopter rotors. "Folks, a massive demon is rampaging on the One, tearing people and cars apart like they're nothing more than scraps of trash. Makes the L.A. riots look like an Easter egg hunt, the aftermath of the '92 quake a Black Friday sale. Okay, wait, the demon, it's turning, away from the city center. It's ... running away? No, going up an on-ramp. It's on the freeway. I've got a view of it now. It's bigger than the Manhattan Monster or any of the others we've seen. Jesus, Mohammad, Mary and Krishna help us. It's as big as a yacht. And it looks like, from where I'm at, I don't even know ... Cthulhu has risen, people. Stay in your houses. Commuters, if you're headed north on the One, take the first exit ramp you see —traffic is backed up due to road destruction."

"Um," Grassal said, yelling to be heard over the announcer, "we're headed north? Yeah?"

Amadeus nodded.

"This thing is following us."

"We'll be fine," Amadeus said, calm as a doctor. "I've dealt with demons before. How do you think I got this?" Amadeus lifted his loose pant leg to show Grassal the dirty bandage that covered his calf. Amadeus didn't mention the demon that did this to him was no bigger than a small dog ... and dismembered. "It's all good, Grassal. Nothing to worry about." Amadeus drifted through traffic, quick and competent.

"You heard him. The size of a yacht."

"Yachts come in different sizes."

"A big fucking yacht. If Ross had a yacht. That big."

"Grassal," Amadeus said, looking over at him. "Relax. I've got this."

They had just started across the Golden Gate Bridge when a sound like a whale in an echo chamber vibrated the Jeep windows. The roadway ahead of them lurched and heaved. A piano-sized claw reached up from below the bridge and grappled at the orange suspension cables. As it tried to gain purchase, its claws scraped over the cables like a plectrum pulled over guitar strings. The creature's weight wrenched some of the metal railings loose. The demon straddled the bridge from the bottom.

Amadeus slammed the accelerator to the floor. The Jeep kicked them back in their seats as the turbocharger engaged. The road ahead of them, just before the main suspension tower, swayed upwards then exploded. Concrete and steel shrapnel sprayed in every direction. A chunk shattered the Jeep's windshield and landed in the backseat. Grassal yelped. Amadeus flinched but kept the Jeep steady. Cars ahead of them swerved and smashed into each other. Grassal unstrapped and kicked out the windshield, giving them a clear view of the road ahead.

The demon started pulling itself through the hole it had made in the bridge. Its claws scraped long gashes into the left-hand lane. More concrete flew into the air and the demon's head appeared like a waking nightmare. An array of mammalian yellow eyes leered from beneath an exoskeletal shroud. Below its eyes, the demon's face was sloped and shaped like a plow, two plates cleft vertically down the middle. The demon roared and the plates split to reveal a white mouth ringed with tentacles, like the top of an anemone. Placoid scales, like sharkskin viewed under a microscope, covered its body.

Behind the demon, an oncoming semi jackknifed and turned over, slamming into the back of the demon's head. The demon swatted the truck away like it was an annoying insect, sending tractor and trailer spiraling into the bay below. At the same moment, Amadeus had to swerve right to avoid an oncoming motorcycle. He slammed into the driver's side of a red sedan. The sedan reacted by pushing back, forcing them left, towards the slashing, grasping claws of the demon, which was still trying to pull itself through the hole.

"Crazy son of a bitch!" Grassal said.

Amadeus tried to accelerate, but their vehicles were locked together. He held the wheel firm as they approached the hole. The sedan veered right. Amadeus cut right and slammed the accelerator to the floor. The Jeep slipped past the cracked edge of the hole with two meters to spare. Something long and grey flashed past the passenger-side window then struck the red sedan, knocking it against the suspension cables. The sedan ricocheted like a tennis ball, flipped, then began to skid on its roof before it smashed into an SUV. Amadeus veered right to avoid the wreckage. Behind them, the demon had gained its footing and now stood on the bridge.

They reached the other side of the bridge just as the north tower buckled. Cables began to snap and lash through the air. Rending metal whined, piercing their eardrums. In the rearview, Amadeus saw a cable snap, whip the demon, and knock it sideways. The announcer's voice screamed from the speakers as they entered a tunnel.

"Folks, the Golden Gate Bridge is crumbling. That fucker tore it apart. Where's the military? Where? Years of overseas wars and they can't even protect us at home? Forgive my digression. Okay, it's off the bridge, headed north. It's climbing over Waldo Tunnel, headed for Marin County."

Grassal glanced at Amadeus. "That means it's going to ..." At the tunnel's end, they saw the demon straddling the highway, batting at the exiting traffic like a kitten swiping at a string, shredding some vehicles, missing others. Amadeus downshifted, redlining the engine, and slid into the left-hand lane. No one wanted to go downtown today.

"What the hell are you doing?" Grassal said.

"Getting through."

When they flew out of the tunnel, the demon's claw rushed towards them from the side. Amadeus pulled the parking brake and the Jeep spun around, but the claw caught them straight on and scraped across the roof, lifting the Jeep a meter off the ground. The fiberglass top ripped off. The Jeep landed with a *kruchunk*, jarring them against their seat belts.

The tires chirped as they landed. Amadeus straightened the wheel as the demon pulled the hardtop apart and flung away the pieces. Meters behind them, the demon smashed a white van like a beer can, flinging it off the road and starting after them.

Amadeus pushed the Jeep hard, RPMs in the red, driving in the right-hand median, leaving a plume of dust and rocks. The demon gave chase, galloping along behind them, but they were faster, and soon the distance between the Jeep and the demon began to grow. By the time they reached Marin City, the demon was well behind them.

Grassal's face was pale and his large hands were balled into fists that quivered on his lap. Both he and Amadeus squinted against the wind and bugs coming through the non-existent windshield.

"You worry too much," Amadeus said.

"Funny how that goes," Grassal said. "Tell me something. Why doesn't that scare the living shit out of you?"

"Brother," Amadeus said, "what's another demon? Since the day I graduated UConn, I've been orphaned, shot at, and chased by the Cambodian military. I've seen innocent people die before my eyes. I've killed a demon. I've survived a

Pachyderm crash, nearly stepped on a land mine, and slept close to a beautiful woman ..." Amadeus checked the rearview but saw only open highway. "What's a little high-speed escape?"

"Wait a second," Grassal said. "That last bit, did you just say ... you mean to tell me you and Lilly?" Grassal gave Amadeus a sly, Indianapolis-used-car salesmen grin.

"I'm working on it. Definite progress." Amadeus wasn't about to tell Grassal what really happened.

"That explains a lot."

"Like what?" Amadeus said.

"Like why, when I tried to kiss Lilly, she gave me the 'you're a brother to me' speech," Grassal said.

"Really?"

"Really. I knew that was bullshit. It was never about me and her. She did let me kiss her cheek, though." Amadeus scrunched his brow at this, and Grassal slapped his shoulder. "I'll admit it was first-class, but we're as innocent as schoolchildren! No worries."

"Buddy, you showed me how to look up porn in fourth grade. Your definition of innocent troubles me."

Laughing, relieved, with the setting sun at their backs and the demon far behind them, they drove east.

50

As the land changed from high desert to mountains and the sun hung low in the western sky, Grassal told Amadeus about his time at the compound. He said Jones would stay in his bedroom-office for days at a time. Each time he emerged, he seemed a little edgier and a little stranger, like a man who knew he was about to lose everything and couldn't do a damn thing about it.

"One evening, Lilly had me follow her into her room. When we got inside, she turned the music up and whispered something in my ear. She said, 'I think my father is insane.' This was a few days after she got back from Prague. I know it broke her heart to say it. She thought it might be the tumor, pressing on his brain, making him crazy."

"Tumor or not, that fucker tried to kill me," Amadeus said. "There were too many coincidences, I should've seen it. I mean, every time I went somewhere, a demon or the black-eyed man showed up. Jones was feeding the Pachyderm's location data over to whoever has been building demon gates."

"I don't think it was just our location. They knew exactly where to find us in San Francisco. So either they accessed my chat channel, or we've been under satellite surveillance since this all started."

"Whatever, Laroux was right. Jones was using me. When he

saw what I'd done with the Gate Crasher videos, I guess he—or whoever he was working for—decided I was too much of a risk to keep around, so down I went."

"But that last demon, it wasn't just running around destroying shit. It was after us specifically. That would mean ..."

"That these demons can be controlled."

"How would you even do that?"

"I have no idea."

They listened to the sound of rubber on asphalt and the beating of wind. The heat blowing from the vents was nearly useless in a topless vehicle, but it kept Amadeus' fingers from becoming numb. He collected his thoughts and was soon ready to lay out what he thought he knew.

"I have a theory on Jones. Suppose that Maximilian Ross—or someone else—is the mastermind behind everything. Let's just say it's Ross. Now suppose also that he has satellite tracking capability, and was able to follow us all the way to Jones' compound. When we showed up at the compound, Ross contacted Jones and made him some kind of offer. But that doesn't explain why they didn't just send someone in to kill us then. I mean, they tried in Denver."

"For one," Grassal said, "we were in an underground bunker. For two, maybe they knew we had something useful. I mean, if they were able to recover the system logs from your dad's computers, they would've seen a large file transfer at the time of the attack."

"Ah, that makes sense. And if it was Ross, he would know about the biometric security. He'd also know that I'd need to go to New York, Prague, and Siem Reap. Another possibility: maybe Ross was involved, but Jones wanted the plans for himself, and gave Ross just enough to keep me from getting killed early on. One way or another, the only reason I made it as far as I did was because I was being used, and someone wanted to keep me alive. Now? Well, I'm worse than useless to them."

"Brother, that is a badge of honor you should wear with

pride."

"Damn right."

Night had fallen, the air had turned cool, and a million little points of light lit the sky. They drove for nearly twenty hours, stopping for energy drinks, fuel, and to relieve each other of driving.

Finally, their headlights illuminated a sign that read "Leadville, 15km." Amadeus had thought he recognized the silhouettes of the mountains, like familiar people standing behind a movie screen. He felt relieved the drive was almost over. After all this was finished, he hoped to spend some time in one place without driving, flying, or walking anywhere. A cabin, maybe. Or a compound.

The demon, according to the radio, had been engaged by the military somewhere in the Nevada desert, though no reports had come for at least an hour. Amadeus hoped it wouldn't make it this far. But if it did, at least they were in a compound. Even a demon that size couldn't get in through a three-meter layer of granite or a meter-thick steel door. At least he hoped.

"What if Jones is inside?" Grassal asked. Amadeus wanted to say that they would shoot the Judas like he was a rabid dog, but Jones would have information. Besides that, he couldn't do that to Lilly.

"If Jones is in there, we tie him up. A part of me wants to kill him and let that be the end of it, but that wouldn't be the end of it. We need to get some answers. And to wait this thing out."

Amadeus turned off the paved road and drove up the mountain until they reached the stone wall that doubled as a vehicle entrance to the compound. Grassal jumped out and keyed in some numbers on the control pad. Nothing happened. He tried again, then pulled a tablet computer from his pocket.

"I've got to fix this," he said. "It could take a couple minutes. Hopefully Jones didn't catch the backdoor I left on his home automation system."

As Grassal worked on the computer, Amadeus caught a whiff

of something familiar carried on the night breeze, a combination of decay and sulfur and ammonia. Grassal tapped quick, arrhythmic bursts onto the screen of his computer. Clouds obscured a blood-red moon.

"Grassal, I hope you can hurry up with that."

"I'm working as fast as I can, but the backdoor had a bug that caused a segfault. That's fixed, but I still need to rebuild from source."

"Do you smell that? One of those things is nearby."

As if his words were an invocation, the air trembled with a warbling roar. A dark shape loomed in the distance. After a moment's squinting, Amadeus recognized the demon from San Francisco. It had followed them. Only, instead of being the nimble beast that had pursued them hours ago, it now swayed and shook like a flag in a storm. Yet, still it drew closer.

"Grassal, hurry."

"Almost."

Amadeus watched as Grassal's eyes darted from his computer to the keypad and back. The creature's howl pierced the night. Grassal didn't look up. Moments later, a green light flashed. The earth trembled as the thick steel door began to rise.

The demon was nearly upon them when the gap between the ground and the door was high enough to permit a baseball. Amadeus dropped to the ground, let out his breath, and squeezed beneath the door. From inside, Amadeus called for Grassal to follow.

"Not yet."

The door was now waist high, but still Grassal remained outside. The demon drew itself up into the air. Amadeus watched as Grassal flattened himself against the wall. The demon came crashing down and smashed the Jeep under one talon. Grassal entered one last command on the control panel then ran inside.

Together they dashed down the corridor. The demon swiped the Jeep aside and tried to squeeze through, but it was unable to fit its body through the opening. As the heavy door lowered onto the creature's neck, Amadeus understood why Grassal had remained outside.

Now a safe distance down the corridor, they both began to wave their arms and yell. This infuriated the creature, and it continued trying to push itself inside, oblivious to the door closing above it. Soon, the door had the demon pinned to the concrete floor. When it appeared to realize its predicament, the demon roared and tried to back out, but its head was too big, and the door too strong. The demon flailed and thrashed and moaned but couldn't free itself.

The demon snapped at him, but Amadeus had plenty of room, and inched forward to get a closer look. Its yellow eyes were tire-sized and the rectangular pupils throbbed.

"We should kill it," Amadeus said. "We can't just leave it there."

Grassal nodded his agreement, and together they ran down the hallway and into the hangar. There, Amadeus filled a pump sprayer with gasoline while Grassal searched for something in the back. Amadeus grabbed a propane torch and a striker from a workbench. Grassal came out with two shotguns and a box of ammunition.

"Found these in—" Grassal cocked his head and furrowed his brow. "What was that?"

"What was what?"

"I heard someone calling my name."

"You're hearing things."

"Weird. Never mind," Grassal said, then shook his head as if he were disappointed in himself. "Let's do this."

When they returned, the demon had given up trying to free itself. Now it whimpered, as if it knew what they were planning. The stink had grown worse. Amadeus' stomach still hadn't adjusted to the smell, and he fought to keep from retching. Standing at what he judged to be a safe distance, Amadeus pumped the sprayer, aimed, depressed the trigger, and emptied the contents onto the demon.

Amadeus, a voice said. The voice sounded like the wind blowing through the forest behind his home in Stamford. Amadeus looked over at Grassal.

"Did you say my name?" Amadeus asked.

Grassal shook his head. "I thought I heard my name."

"We must be hearing things. Too much stress, not enough rest. Let's get this over with."

"The faster the better," Grassal said. "This thing has no idea why it wants to eat us any more than a vulture knows why it wants to eat roadkill."

Amadeus.

Ignoring the voice that whispered his name, Amadeus lit the torch and tossed it toward the demon. Flames whooshed over the demon's face and the demon shrieked, trying to whip the flames with its long black tentacle-tongues. Again it tried to back out of the door frame, but the door held fast.

"Fire into the eye socket," Amadeus said. "If this creature has a brain, then that's got to be the bull's eye."

Amadeus.

The voice had grown urgent. He looked around, half-expecting to see a stranger with a megaphone standing in the hallway, but no one was there. He returned his attention to the task at hand and aimed his shotgun at the demon's eye. Grassal did the same.

They fired. *Fwlop!* The eye exploded, splattering flaming, gelatinous bits of demon eye into the air. Amadeus felt his skin sizzle as a chunk of burning goo landed on his chest. His mind flashed to the dissolved bodies in New York and for a moment he thought he was melting, but Grassal wiped the goo away with his shirt. All that remained was a searing, throbbing pain that ran from the right side of his chest up to his left cheek, like someone had pulled a glowing red rod from a forge and dragged it across his skin. Amadeus sucked air through his teeth.

"It's not that bad," Grassal said, looking him over. Amadeus leaned against a wall and put a finger to his neck. Even touching it felt like the sting of a hundred wasps, but at least the skin was intact. All this time the creature bucked in the door frame like a defiant horse, though it was apparent the creature was growing weaker. Grassal fired round after round into the demon's eye socket. After two reloads, the creature finally died. Its corpse blocked most of the threshold, but there was room for a grown man to squeeze through if they needed to leave.

Grassal kept his shotgun trained on the creature's corpse. "Even a snake with its head cut off can still bite." Amadeus nodded in agreement. "You good?"

"Never better," Amadeus said. "But let's get inside."

They headed towards the hangar, but just before they were out of sight of the door, Amadeus heard a scuttling sound. He turned to see a demon the size of a mastiff blotting out the light between the dead demon and the doorframe.

We are not what you think.

Grassal raised his shotgun to fire. Amadeus placed a steadying hand on the top of Grassal's shotgun barrel. They exchanged a glance of shared understanding, and Grassal lowered his weapon.

Amadeus squinted, trying to get a better look, but he didn't dare move any closer. They watched as the demon stood on its hind legs, and put its front legs over its head, forming a semicircle. Silhouetted against the early morning light, it looked like an upright kettle bell with legs. The voice again spoke:

Others are coming. They are uncontrollable.

With that, the creature dropped back to all fours, turned, and darted out of the door.

Amadeus stood as still as a mountain as he tried to process what he had just seen. He felt Grassal's hand on his forearm, pulling him back, and Amadeus allowed himself to be led away. Each step they took echoed through the empty halls. Inside, Grassal fired up the main power system while Amadeus double-checked the rooms. He willed himself to forget what he had just seen.

Grassal called out from the data center. "Some of the hard drives are gone."

Amadeus checked the rooms again; no signs of anyone. Only the panic room remained. He tried the round handle of the panic room door. It was locked. Amadeus noticed a new keypad had been installed on beside the door frame. The wall still bore a pencil's leveling marks. Steel shavings littered the floor below.

"Grassal, I think you were right. There's a new lock on this door. Think you can open it? It's like the one outside." Grassal came over and examined the lock, nodded to himself, then spoke.

"It could take a while. But I'll get it. No problem," he said before trotting off to fetch some tools.

Amadeus went to the data center while he waited on Grassal. He tried to pull a news site up on the wall screen, but the connection was down. Laroux's phone, however, still had an internet connection, and Amadeus used it to pull up a news aggregator. The first headline he saw stood out in brave, bold letters: "Gates Crashing Around the World." He clicked through and read some summaries, which included, "U.S. President supports calls to see charges against Brunmeier dropped. *Times of America* reporter Annie Brunmeier, aunt of Amadeus Brunmeier, is receiving credit for breaking this dramatic story while also laying out a convincing defense of her nephew."

Unable to stop himself, he cried out with joy. He felt like a child who wanted to show off a sterling report card. Of course he owed credit to his friends, but this was because of his work, his initiative, his risks; if he hadn't done this, who would've?

"You okay, buddy?" Grassal said, yelling from the hangar. Amadeus told Grassal about what he'd just read. He responded with a happy whoop.

"Don't get too excited. We're not done yet."

Grassal paused for a moment, then locked eyes with

Amadeus.

"This is just getting started, isn't it?"

"I'm afraid so."

He read more reports of scenes from around the world, from Bangkok to Birmingham, New Delhi to New York. Video footage showed crowds of people with cordless phones, parabolic antennae, and other clever modifications on his original design. His favorite was the cigarette-smoking old lady in Seattle with her green Tupperware dish and phone. People also held pieces of the gates, thrusting them over their heads like victorious athletes holding sparkling trophies. From outside, Amadeus heard metal slamming against metal. Amadeus went to check on Grassal. When he found him, Grassal was swinging a sledgehammer against the door.

"You're not seriously trying to beat the door down like a barbarian?"

"Just trying a manual override," Grassal said. He stopped and leaned on the sledgehammer like it was a cane. "I needed a break to work out some aggression."

"I thought you installed a backdoor," Amadeus said, gesturing to the wires that ran from the access control panel to Grassal's tablet.

"I did, but this is isolated from his main home automation system."

"So what now?"

"I extracted and decompiled the access control system's binary file and transferred everything to my tablet, but the actual access code is encrypted. So now I've got a script running that's checking every combination, but there's still a one-second delay between incorrect attempts. If it's four digits, there are only nine thousand, nine-hundred and ninety-nine combinations, but I think the code is five or six digits ... so it's going to be a little longer."

"How much longer?"

"My tablet has four cores, so depending on the length of the combination ... between forty-five minutes and seventy hours. Sooner if I stumble onto the right combination."

"Grassal, I hope you're joking."

"The cold equations of combinatorics are nothing to joke about."

"If that ... thing followed us here, others could, too. This place could be overrun. So we need to make it faster," Amadeus said.

Grassal nodded. "I can't argue with that."

"What about that distributed processing program you wrote?"

"For the cluster we used for playing 'Zombie Attack,' with really good AI?" Grassal said.

"That's the one. I'm not sure if you could use it here, some of the computers are pretty trashed ..."

"I thought about that, but it's non-trivial code and it's stored in an external repository. The internet is down, and my tablet doesn't have data."

Amadeus smiled and pulled Laroux's phone from his pocket, verified he had a connection, and passed it to Grassal.

"First-class, my friend, first-class," Grassal said, tossing the sledgehammer aside.

51

Of the nine computers Amadeus found, six were usable as nodes in Grassal's distributed processing program. One of these was the unfortunate statue his uncle had given him. For each node, Amadeus installed the software and Grassal handled the cluster orchestration. Within twenty minutes, each node of the system was busy doing its share to try every possible combination of digits. Grassal estimated the upper limit was now only about thirty-seven minutes.

Waiting and pacing as he monitored the program output, Grassal told some jokes he had told before. Just after the one about the pirate with a steering wheel on his crotch ("aaargh, it drives me nuts"), Amadeus thought he heard a hint of something both familiar and unknowable. He shushed Grassal with a raised finger and a haunted look.

"You hear that?" Amadeus said.

"It's nothing, probably just the air recyclers."

"No, it's something. Many somethings. Just listen."

Grassal listened. His eyes grew wide.

"How long's left?"

Grassal glanced down at the screen. "Just under ten minutes."

"I'll go check it out."

"Amadeus."

"What?" Amadeus raised his eyebrows.

"Just ... be careful. That's all."

"Sure."

Amadeus left a shotgun for Grassal then ran down the corridor. When he rounded the corner, where the demon should have been, he saw only darkness through the half-opened door. Blood remained, but the demon's body was gone. Cautiously, Amadeus crouched under the door then stepped outside and gave his eyes a moment to adjust to the dark. He wanted to take a look around before he closed the door.

Two hundred meters ahead, on the dark land that lay before him, a violent black sea churned. Floating on this sea was a larger black island. The island was the demon they had killed, and the black sea was a writhing carpet of smallish demons, thousands of them, gnawing and rending each other in order to dine on the big demon. The half-eaten corpse of the big demon floated on top of them like a crowd surfer at a rock concert.

As a group, Amadeus deduced, they had taken the path of least resistance, moving the corpse down the hill. He wondered why none had thought to come inside. Maybe they couldn't resist the cannibalistic temptations of a delicious meal.

Trying to keep as still as possible, he inched over to the control panel and entered the code to close the door. A polite female voice told him to try again. He tried again. Still unsuccessful. The voice warned him he should check with an administrator. Amadeus mumbled a curse and tried one last time. This final attempt caused the voice to say that the alarm system was being activated.

"Shit," Amadeus said.

A klaxon began to wail. Amadeus jammed more buttons and watched as a ripple ran through the demon sea. A few at the edges broke away. Not knowing what else to do, Amadeus smashed the control panel with the butt of his shotgun. Nothing happened. He gave up and slipped back inside. A couple demons were creeping up the hill. He hoped they hadn't seen him. He ran back down the corridor, listening for the clicks of claws on concrete.

The compound was dark and quiet, save for emergency lights and the wailing alarm. Grassal nodded to the computer. "I think your little alarm killed the lights, but we should have the code soon."

"Good. We don't have much time. You do not want to know what's outside."

"Try me."

"If all the gates so far have been one-lane highways, then somebody just opened up a quadruple expressway. It's a goddamn demon sea out there."

Grassal glanced down at his shotgun, then took a deep breath, and put his hand on Amadeus' shoulder. "We're not leaving here, are we, buddy?"

"Don't talk like that. Let's just get the door open and get inside," Amadeus said. "But if we, uh, if we die here, I can't think of a better man to make a last stand with. You've been by my side all my life. I ... just want you to know I appreciate it."

Grassal nodded. "Are you frightened of dying?"

"We've all got to go sometime," Amadeus said.

"That's what I like about you, you've—do you hear that?" Grassal said, freezing like a statue. Amadeus nodded, his eyes shooting to the location of the sound. They stood with their backs to the door. A minute passed, but they heard only silence. When the progress bar read 98%, the scuttling sound started again. The sound came closer, closer ...

Suddenly, a goat-sized demon charged them from the left. They both opened fire, filling the hangar with echoing blasts. Amadeus emptied his shotgun, then used clumsy, shaking fingers to shove shells into the loading flap. Grassal fired slower for accuracy, and with each shot, the demon staggered. It had an arachnid body but instead of a head it had one big eye and a writhing anemone-like mouth on the front of its torso.

Though oozing black blood, the creature refused to die. It

came closer. Grassal called for cover fire. Amadeus took an extra moment to aim for the eye. He fired.

The shot tore open the right side of the demon's mouth. When he was down to one shell, Grassal said, "Ready." Amadeus fired again. The spider demon finally dropped. The computer beeped.

"It's unlocked?" Amadeus asked.

"The queue still has to clear. Eight seconds," Grassal said. Amadeus narrowed his eyes and shot the dead spider demon again.

Grassal furrowed his brow then pointed his gun at Amadeus. "Whoa, hold on now," Amadeus said.

Bang!

Amadeus spun around. Another demon staggered towards them, a chunk torn from its flank by Grassal's shotgun blast. Amadeus aimed as it advanced. Grassal fired again. It fell. Then, from behind it, another emerged. Amadeus looked towards the shadows around the hangar entrance. Hundreds of yellow orbs bobbed and blinked in the darkness like a pestilence of fireflies.

"Grassal ..." Amadeus said. *Beep. Beep.* Over the din, he heard a series of metallic clicks.

"It's open!" Grassal said. He unplugged the statue from the cluster and tossed it to Amadeus, who caught it and pocketed it without knowing why.

As a group, the demons emerged from the shadows and crept towards them. Amadeus threw down the handle for the door and pulled. The door was heavy. The demons moved closer. Amadeus dropped the shotgun and pulled on the door with both hands, finally making an opening wide enough for both of them to squeeze through.

Before they could slip inside, a demon sprang from the darkness. It flew through the air towards Amadeus, talons outstretched, mouth agape. Amadeus stared, his body frozen. Grassal pushed Amadeus through the open door, putting himself between Amadeus and the demon.

Grassal fired. The demon spun and tumbled to the floor. A second later it recovered itself then darted forward with electric speed. Grassal pulled the trigger.

Click.

The demon sprang, biting down onto Grassal's calf. Grassal screamed and flailed. Amadeus grabbed Grassal's shotgun and fed a round into the loading flap. With one hand, he aimed, squeezed the trigger, and shot the demon pointblank in the head. The shot decapitated the demon, but not before it had torn off Grassal's right leg below mid-calf. A few stringy tendons dangled from the wound like red noodles.

Amadeus pulled Grassal inside, then pulled the door shut, but the primary lock wouldn't engage. He tried again. Still nothing. The door had vertical catches at the top and bottom. Each catch was three centimeters in diameter. As soon as he slid the upper catch into place, the door shuddered. Outside, demons scraped and clawed and threw themselves against the door. He slid the lower catch closed and wondered how long the catches would hold against the stress. Knowing Jones, he guessed a very long time.

Grassal howled in pain.

Amadeus stripped off his shirt, wrapped the mangled end of Grassal's leg, then tied it off with his belt. He slid the statue under the belt and gave it three twists, making a primitive tourniquet. The shirt soaked with blood almost immediately. As he worked, he tried to remember the layout of the panic room as Lilly had described it to him. She'd said there was a long hallway that led to an elevator, and you had to take the elevator down to the "living area" and storage room. Grassal's best hope was that Jones had stockpiled medical supplies along with everything else. Even then, with the amount of blood he was losing ...

Something large banged against the door outside, leaving a guitar-sized dent in the metal. Still, the door held.

"Sorry, buddy, we have to walk now. Put your arms around me," Amadeus said. Grassal's screaming had abated, but he gave no acknowledgement. Amadeus laid down the shotgun, put his hands under Grassal's arms, and began to drag him. Amadeus fell backwards then tried again.

"I'll get you down there, don't worry. Remember what you told me, buddy?" Amadeus said, straining to pull Grassal's big body down towards the elevator. "You fall, you get back up again. That's the secret. You remember that? Always get back up. I'll always get back up, and so will you."

Grassal's body stiffened as another scream escaped his mouth, but just as soon as it had started, Grassal's head lolled. Amadeus knew he was losing him to shock.

"One more time," Amadeus said. Straining every muscle in his body, he pulled Grassal towards the elevator. Amadeus' legs burned from exertion, but he finally managed to half-carry, half-drag Grassal into the elevator. Amadeus pushed the down button. They both collapsed onto the metal floor as the elevator took them down, down, down.

At the bottom, the cage opened to a steel door with a handle like a steering wheel. With one hand he turned the wheel, with the other he held the shotgun, ready to face, and if necessary, kill, Holden Jones. He pushed the door open. The elevator filled with light and the smell of ... bananas.

"What the ..." Amadeus said.

Lilly came running towards him, across what looked like a living room. She started to throw her arms around him then gasped when she saw Grassal lying on the floor, moaning.

"Is he here? Your father?" Amadeus said.

"No, he's gone, but he stockpiled plenty of medical supplies. Let's get him inside." Together they dragged him to a nearby couch. Despite the tourniquet, blood leaked from Grassal's wound onto the concrete floor. Amadeus held Grassal's leg in an elevated position. After closing the door, Lilly put a pillow under Grassal's head and covered his torso with a blanket.

"He's in shock," Lilly said. Grassal was pale. His lips had a hint of blue. Lilly handed Amadeus another towel and told him to apply pressure. He did.

While Lilly gathered the supplies from the storage room, Amadeus examined his surroundings. A large flexscreen covered one wall. Books lined another. Nearby was a small kitchen with racks stacked with canned food. Air ducts ran along the ceiling. The entire area was a little bigger than two shipping containers placed side-by-side. Adjacent to the living area was a separate storage room, where Lilly was now, and a tiny bathroom.

"You're going to be okay, brother. Lilly's taking good care of you." Grassal's eyes didn't focus, but his lips were moving as if he was muttering a silent prayer. Amadeus fought to speak through tears. "Stay with us, stay with us."

Lilly returned. Wearing latex gloves, she set to work on Grassal's stump. With deft and quick movements, she applied hemostats, clamping off the arteries. She then made a better tourniquet, doused everything with water and iodine, cut away the ruined flesh, applied a coagulant gel, and finally wrapped the stump in gauze. She then administered antibiotics and a cocktail of painkillers.

"This is bad. If he'd lost any more blood, we'd be in a different situation, but he's stable," she said, running a hand over Grassal's shaggy hair. Grassal was there, but he wasn't there. "We'll keep an eye on it, clean it every day. The antibiotics should prevent infection. If he's lucky, he'll keep his knee." Amadeus sat cross-legged on the floor beside Grassal, holding one of his hands in both of his. An hour passed before Lilly spoke again.

"Now, about you ... I hate to sound ungrateful for the company, it's wonderful to see you, but what the fuck are you doing here?"

"We had some trouble in San Francisco, and Grassal needed

to return your Jeep, so I figured ..."

"He's my Jeep thief? When he wakes up, we're going to have to have a talk about this behavior. But at least he brought it back."

"Um, not quite. That trouble I mentioned? It flung your Jeep down the mountain. Once we got inside, we, well, Grassal, figured out the code for the lock on the upstairs door, but we kind of broke it, too. The lock won't engage anymore."

"As in, 'the lock is broken and I can open the door any time I want?'" As she spoke, her eyes grew wide with excitement.

"Yes."

"That almost makes losing the Jeep worth it. Almost."

"But if you knew what was outside, you'd want to keep that door closed, at least for a little while."

"Demons?"

"Hundreds of them."

"Well, I guess you can stay," Lilly said as a half-smile lit her face. "Oh, if my father knew you were here ... The lock you and Grassal broke? That was his doing. He locked me down here, said it was for my own safety, and that I might be here for a couple years if need be. *Years*, Amadeus. Years. Anyway, thank you."

She gave him a kiss on the cheek then continued.

"There's something wrong with his brain, you know. I think it's the tumor, pressing against the part that controls his moral compass and decision-making. Or maybe he was bought, though I can't imagine what they promised him. At this point, I'm not sure who to hate, so I might as well hate everyone. Except you and Grassal. You're cool."

"Captivity doesn't suit you."

"Damn right it doesn't. I've got nothing to do but read, watch satellite television, and think vengeful thoughts while I workout on that stupid machine." She nodded to a home gym in the corner, covered in a black sheet. To Amadeus, the machine looked like a giant bat. "But I've started writing a book. It's keeping me sane." Amadeus stared into her spruce-green eyes. She sat down and nestled in next to him. "Ami, after what you did, I have to say ... I was wrong about you. I'm really fucking happy that you're here."

"My mother used to call me Ami. No one else."

"Oh, I'm sorry, it just seemed—"

"Natural. It's okay. I ... kind of like it."

"Then come here." She turned towards him. Amadeus wrapped his arms around her. Her body was warm and comforting against his. They held each other close. On the flexscreen, a video showed celebrants in San Francisco parading the smashed fragments of the last known demon gate down a crowded street beneath a waxing moon.

52

For a week after their arrival at the Jones compound, Grassal raved and muttered as he suffered through a high fever. Amadeus and Lilly kept him cool and comfortable. When the fever broke and Grassal was again able to speak, he locked eyes with Amadeus and said, "They're still calling for me. Do you hear them, too?" Amadeus and Lilly exchanged a glance and only nodded their heads. Lilly, who explained that she had taken several nursing classes in high school, said that this was probably a hallucination due to an interaction between the different types of painkillers she had given him. Amadeus did not mention the encounter they had had in the corridor.

In the nights, Amadeus and Lilly made love. The first time was rushed and awkward, but soon each learned how to satisfy the other, and in this they both found comfort. "For the most part, I misjudged you," she had said after the first time. "But I still think you're weird."

For the first week, Amadeus didn't dare open the door to the elevator. When he finally did, the demon smell was still strong. From above, Amadeus could hear the faintest hint of the demons' unnatural howling. Every day for the next week, he opened the door and heard the same thing. After two weeks, Grassal suggested they hang tight; maybe the daily opening of the door gave the demons something to look forward to.

Amadeus and Lilly agreed.

On day twelve, they watched the president of the United States on a satellite feed. He referred to the creatures alternately as "ids"—short for inter-dimensional demons, or "subluminals," a term of unknown origin. Reading from a prepared statement, the president said reports from both military commanders and private citizens confirmed that all demon gates had been destroyed, both at home and abroad. Some subluminals still lurked in rural and even urban areas, but he had issued cleanup contracts to Securaux, a private military corporation that had proved itself quite effective at subluminal tracking and eradication.

Though nearly eight hundred people had died and thousands more were injured before all the gates were destroyed, the damage was minimized by the courageous work of Amadeus Brunmeier, whose present location remained unknown. The president ended by saying that while they had a high-value, unnamed suspect, the organization behind the demon gate deployments remained at large. "I will not rest," the president concluded, "until we capture or kill whoever is responsible for this unprecedented act of terror."

After two weeks, Amadeus accepted that he was going to have a pink scar from his neck and across his cheek to his ear. Yet, with so many dead and dismembered, Amadeus counted himself among the fortunate.

On day thirty, Amadeus and Lilly armed themselves with shotguns and left the panic room. Sunbeams filtered through the skylights in the hangar. Dust particles sparkled in the stale air. The smell of rotting meat and sulfur lingered, likely from the several piles of desiccated demon offal that littered the cathedral-quiet hangar. After a tense sweep of the place, they concluded the stronger demons had eaten the weaker ones before leaving.

Happy to be out of the confines of the safe room, they packed up the few items they wanted to take with them. Lilly found one of Jones' extra wheelchairs for Grassal. Amadeus changed a tire on the hearse while Lilly loaded it up with supplies. Later that evening, Lilly drove them all out of the hangar, past the cracked, sun-bleached bones of the giant demon. Amadeus sat in the back with Grassal, who quipped about leaving the compound in a hearse. Lilly asked where they were going.

"Head east, Lilly. It's time to go home."

Two weeks after he had left the compound, Amadeus stood fingering the blue fabric of the backstage curtains. He felt sick, felt he might vomit on his polished, black shoes. Or worse, the president's polished, black shoes. The president slapped his shoulder and graced him with a reassuring smile.

"Relax, kid. You've already done the hard work. Don't let a little speech twist your titties," the president said. Amadeus nodded and considered this. He held his head up as he strode past a row of Secret Service guys. They gave him silent, respectful nods from behind opaque sunglasses. Around the curtain, standing in the wings, were Grassal, Lilly, Aunt Annie and Uncle Mark. Grassal still used a cane, not yet comfortable walking on his prosthetic. Amadeus hugged them all. Mark whispered an apology for the statue. Amadeus told him that it had come in handy.

Amadeus wanted to talk to each of them, to tell them how much he appreciated them, and to let them know he knew that he wouldn't be here without them, but he had to maintain his focus. His attention, he knew, must remain on the thoughts outlined on the index cards he presently held in his sweaty hand. He imagined tearing a piece of an index card off and stuffing it in his mouth, thought of how satisfying it would feel as he rolled it around atop his tongue ... but he let that thought pass.

A hand caught his shoulder. Amadeus spun around. Before him stood a middle-aged man in a white suit and purple tie. His cracker-blond hair was slicked back. His lips were parted in a smile that did not reach his eyes, which seemed to be penetrating Amadeus in search of a weak point. The man stuck out his hand. Amadeus took it. Something about the man made his stomach queasy.

"Amadeus Brunmeier. Name's Roland A. Jessup. I run Securaux. Great work, just super out there. I'd like to talk with you sometime."

"Now's not a good time, I—"

"You're quite an extraordinary young man with great potential for strength. I think we could really make something out of you."

Amadeus drew himself up to his full height and attempted to push past him, but Jessup blocked the way with his body. An image of frog-faced Davy came to Amadeus' mind. This image was accompanied by a strong urge to punch the man in the mouth. Today, he could probably get away with it.

"Good luck with your speech. I'll be in touch," Jessup said before turning and walking away. Amadeus closed his eyes and tried to shake the encounter from his mind. A few moments passed before the backstage minders locked eyes with Amadeus, motioning that he should be ready to move.

As the Interstellar Sisters sang a triumphant song, the president walked onto the stage, past a confident row of grey senators and stoic generals. Amadeus followed him out, his focus entirely dedicated to crossing the marble without stumbling over his own feet. When Amadeus reached the center of the stage, he knew he would be okay.

In spite of the cool fall air, a bead of sweat trickled down his forehead. He crossed his eyes and watched the bead slide down his nose and drop onto the floor. The song ended. The president began to speak. When Amadeus finally looked out at the crowd, he thought he might faint. Stretching as far as he could see, the crowd before him held flags, banners, and pieces of demon gates. The reflecting pool was orange and auburn thanks to the trees of autumn. Amadeus felt a gentle hand on his shoulder push him forward.

Amadeus started towards the podium. On the way, the president shook his hand like someone pumping a well. Amadeus swallowed hard, kept the vomit at bay, and smiled to the crowd. They roared with applause and adulation. Amadeus placed the index cards on the podium. His face, he realized, bore a huge grin. He tried, unsuccessfully, to suppress it. He waved to the crowd. They cheered louder, vibrating the water in the reflecting pool. Even the trees seemed to bend backwards from the sound. With the statue of Lincoln behind him, Amadeus began.

"Thank you," he said. His voice boomed across the crowd and over the city, out to the suburbs, the mountains, and the sea. Silence fell like a curtain.

"Good afternoon. I cannot tell you how proud I am to stand before you at the feet of this great man. Almost two centuries ago, he made great sacrifices to hold this country together. I only wish I could say my motives were as noble.

"Most of you know my story; it began when my mother died, when my father could not accept that her story had ended. Thus began the chain of events that brought us all here today. He did what he did not because he was some mad scientist, but because he loved his wife, because he couldn't let go. I can only hope to love someone as much one day." He looked over at Lilly. Her face flushed crimson.

"But this is no longer only my story or his story. This is the story of my friends." He gestured to Grassal, Lilly, and Annie. They bowed to great applause. "This is the story of the people who helped me. Some survived, but too many did not. Let us not forget them. And this isn't just the story of people I know, but all of you who remain anonymous to me. You who listened to what I had to say. You who built Gate Crashers. You who took action. If it weren't for you, I—we—wouldn't be standing here today. And though today we can claim a victory, I fear the worst is yet to come. In the future, we must continue to stand together against those who would divide us for their own ends."

He paused and waited for the echoes to subside before he concluded his speech. Every eye was upon him, and he would finish like a lion.

"My friends, this is not my story. This is not my friends' story. This is not your story ... this is our story!" He raised a fist in the air. "Together, we stopped the plans of a powerful enemy. Together, we protected our world from those who would destroy it. And together, we will move forward. To a better world, to a better tomorrow. So, to each and every one of you, I just want to say ... thank you and good luck!"

The Interstellar Sisters started another song. Amadeus waved again, then put his arms around Lilly and Grassal. The applause shook the air like an earthquake. Together, they all left the stage. Behind the blue curtain, Amadeus shook hands with a long line of well-wishers. At the moment their faces began to look the same, he felt a hand on his shoulder. He turned around. Gravity stood before him. He looked ten years younger.

"Where have you been?" Amadeus asked.

"Backstage. Amadeus, that was a fine speech, but there's no time for foppish pleasantries. I need you to come with me."

"But I've got to give some interviews, and there's a press conference ..."

"Do you really want to do all that?" Gravity said.

Amadeus thought for a second then shook his head.

"I didn't think so. Lilly, Grassal, I'll get him back as quick as I can."

"You better hurry," Lilly said, winking at Amadeus. "I've got plans for him."

"Not again," Grassal said, shaking his head.

Gravity loaded Amadeus into the back seat of an SUV. A middle-aged woman in a military dress uniform in the passenger seat turned around to greet him. Amadeus noted the three silver stars sitting on her shoulder.

"Amadeus, I'm General Janette Nguyen. A pleasure to meet you. Claudius here has told me all about you," she said. Amadeus nodded and shook her hand. Gravity opened his door and sat in the driver's seat. Amadeus asked where they were going, but Gravity and the General just smiled at him. They followed the expressway to Langley, Virginia and parked in a garage outside a clean, reflective office building. Inside they walked down a long hallway illuminated by fluorescent lights. Evenly-spaced steel doors lined the walls. At the end of the hallway, two suit-clad men stood outside a door. They nodded to Gravity. Both men twisted keys in separate locks. A buzzer went off. The door opened.

"Go on in," Gravity said. "The melodramatic bastard says he won't talk to anyone but you." Amadeus stepped into the cell. The door clicked closed behind him. In the corner, a man was strapped to a chair. A black shroud covered his head. Amadeus pulled the shroud off. Jones stared back at him. The pupil of his right eye was the size of a marble.

"Amadeus, my boy, so good to see you. I must apologize for crashing the Pachyderm. It was a terrible misunderstanding. But everything worked out in the end." He paused and studied Amadeus as if Amadeus was just a broken machine. "I do hope you'll take good care of Lilly. She thinks you're a smashing fellow."

"What do you want, Jones?" Amadeus stared into Jones' big eye.

"Oh, I just wanted to share a fascinating tidbit I recently learned."

"Go on."

The cell smelled of disinfectant and urine. After a month spent living in an underground bunker, he wanted nothing more than to be outside. During that month, he'd always imagined if he encountered Jones, he would feel anger and rage, but now he felt only pity. He had come to accept everything that had happened to him, to his life, and he was looking forward to the things to come.

"During your little adventure, you set off with certain basic principles that were false. It's understandable, given the way things played out."

"What do you mean?" Amadeus said.

"Oh, it's just a little thing."

"You've played me long enough, Jones. Get to the point."

"Your father is alive ... and working with Maximilian Ross."

Afterword

Thank you for reading *Reaction. The Emergence* series continues with *Redemption,* where we learn what comes next for Amadeus, Grassal, Lilly, and company. Here's a preview: things go horribly, horribly wrong.

If you've enjoyed this work and would like to support me in my future endeavors, there are a few ways you can help. You can leave a quick review on Amazon, rate this work on Goodreads, or share it with a friend.

For more information about my work, visit www.sethmbaker.com. While you're there, please join my mailing list and I'll keep you up to date about new releases.

As always, I appreciate your time and patronage.
Seth M. Baker

Acknowledgements

Thanks to all the people who have helped to make this the best book possible, including beta readers Stacey Buckner, Chris Enix, Anthony Case, John McCalister, and Jake McClendon; Anthony Tietjen for reading this work aloud; Deranged Doctor Design for the fantastic cover design; Stephanie Diaz and Celestian Rince for proofreading this work; and my ever-patient wife, Tiffany, for everything else.

About the author

Seth M. Baker has worked as a software engineer, international English teacher, freelance writer, and pizza delivery driver. He's been making up stories since he was a kid.

He grew up in West Virginia, USA and has traveled extensively. His earliest memory is of a wildfire consuming the hill behind his house.

He lives in a misty Appalachian valley with his wife and sons.